DISCARD

BLOOMINGTON PUBLIC LIBRARY

A11905 988124

P9-EMQ-845

OCT 2002

DISCARD

PICTURES

FROM AN

EXPEDITION

ALSO BY DIANE SMITH

Letters from Yellowstone

PICTURES
FROM AN
EXPEDITION

DIANE SMITH

VIKING

BLOOMINGTON, ILLINOIS
PUBLIC LIBRARY

FIC
Smi

VIKING
Published by the Penguin Group
Penguin Putnam Inc., 375 Hudson Street, New York, New York 10014, U.S.A.
Penguin Books Ltd, 80 Strand, London WC2R 0RL, England
Penguin Books Australia Ltd, 250 Camberwell Road, Camberwell, Victoria 3124,
Australia
Penguin Books Canada Ltd, 10 Alcorn Avenue, Toronto, Ontario,
Canada M4V 3B2
Penguin Books India (P) Ltd, 11 Community Centre, Panchsheel Park,
New Delhi–110 017, India
Penguin Books (N.Z.) Ltd, Cnr Rosedale and Airborne Roads, Albany, Auckland,
New Zealand
Penguin Books (South Africa) (Pty) Ltd, 24 Sturdee Avenue, Rosebank,
Johannesburg 2196, South Africa

Penguin Books Ltd, Registered Offices: Harmondsworth, Middlesex, England

First published in 2002 by Viking Penguin, a member of Penguin Putnam Inc.

10 9 8 7 6 5 4 3 2 1

Copyright © Diane Smith, 2002
All rights reserved

Photograph page iii: Corbis

PUBLISHER'S NOTE: This is a work of fiction. Names, characters, places, and incidents
either are the product of the author's imagination or are used fictitiously, and any
resemblance to actual persons, living or dead, business establishments, events, or
locales is entirely coincidental.

CIP data available

ISBN 0-670-03129-1

This book is printed on acid-free paper. ∞

Printed in the United States of America
Set in Goudy
Designed by Nancy Resnick

Without limiting the rights under copyright reserved above, no part of this publication may be reproduced, stored in or introduced into a retrieval system, or transmit-
ted, in any form or by any means (electronic, mechanical, photocopying, recording
or otherwise), without the prior written permission of both the copyright owner and
the above publisher of this book.

This one is for Barr
and the triceratops skull still missing
from his grandfather's ranch.

We are separated, finally, not by death but life.
We cling to the dead, but the living break away.

—CAROLYN KIZER

PICTURES

FROM AN

EXPEDITION

TO: Collection Committee
FROM: John Wilson
DATE: Sept. 20, 1919
REGARDING: The Starwood Collection

Dear Sirs:

In April of this year, I asked a Miss Eleanor Peterson, of Great Falls, Mont., to help me identify a representative list of paintings, drawings, and other effects, presumed to be associated with her friend and teacher, Augustus Starwood. Most of the work was completed the summer of 1876 in Montana (then the Montana Territories) during a paleontological expedition supported by Yale College, which employed Miss Peterson along with a number of students and others. This work, part of an extensive donation of western artifacts and memorabilia given to the Institution by Baltimore resident Jennifer Bartlett in memory of her uncle, is one of the most complete collections of Mr. Starwood's artwork uncovered to date. Although not considered a major artist in his day, it is our opinion that this particular body of work and personal memorabilia merits consideration given the period of time the collection covers, a particularly turbulent time in our Nation's history.

Miss Peterson appears to have a wealth of personal knowledge about Mr. Starwood and an excellent memory of the summer they spent together in the badlands of Montana. She rejected the standard Institution catalogue forms, a supply of which were provided for her use, preferring instead to write her remembrances on the enclosed unbound pages which she numbered using a system of her own design (thus, the numbers in this particular record do not reflect our own internal records). Although her reflections tend to be wide-ranging and often move beyond the specific items in question, I believe this document, written in Miss Peterson's own hand except where noted, will prove to be a valuable addition to the cataloguing of any or all of Mr. Starwood's work deemed appropriate for the Institution.

I also request that the journal and other effects unsuitable for the Institution, be returned at your earliest convenience, along with the personal correspondence addressed to Yale College, which apparently she never received.

Respectfully submitted,
John Wilson

Eleanor Peterson
Great Falls, Mont.
April 6, 1919

Mr. John Wilson
Smithsonian Institution
Washington

My dear Mr. Wilson:

You asked what I remember of that time.

I remember the way the Montana summer seemed to be over before it had begun, and yet how each day seemed to last forever.

I remember the dirt, the wind, and the ever-threatening weather.

I remember Augustus working on a bluff, his easel shaded by a large canvas umbrella, the river coursing through the landscape down below.

I remember the rush of water over stones and over me, too, when Maggie convinced me to accompany her on her evening swim.

I remember sitting with my back against a tree as the stars slowly revealed themselves one by one in the darkening sky.

And the bones. I will never forget the bones.

The Sioux, Cheyenne, and Crow could tell you more about that time than I ever could. How men wandered across their land, took their teeth out upon demand, and picked up stones with no value. They were not interested in gold, but dug deep into the earth for the buffalo's ancestors. They were harmless, these men, so the tribes let them move about their lands without interference, but the Indians also knew that the men were crazy and should be avoided whenever possible. Had I known then what the Indians knew, I, too, might have kept my distance even though I was faced at the time with a future of little or no prospects, and was presented with what I believed to be an opportunity to enter their profession as a colleague and a peer.

I must assume that the drawings of ammonites you mentioned in your letter are from Augustus Starwood's collection. The one you asked about in particular is an ammonite Augustus labeled a suicide, a designation I thought absurd at the time. Augustus had strange notions about a lot of things, although I must admit many of his opinions proved to be correct in the end. Even his theory about that ammonite. When any creature develops such an unconventional approach to making its way through life, it is destined by the laws of evolution not to survive.

As for other memorabilia, as you referred to it, I still have one of Augustus' silk robes, embroidered with thirteen dragons, but I cannot imagine this would be of particular interest since all of his robes were originally from China. I also have two landscapes he painted at the time, and some of his drawings and sketches. Many of these, I can admit now, were stolen from Augustus, but only to keep them from being destroyed. He did not consider them representative of his work, although in retrospect they marked a major shift in the way he viewed and represented the world.

I also have two portraits he painted while we were in Montana, but with those I am not yet ready to part. I would be willing to bequeath any or all of Augustus' paintings to your institution, if you could guarantee that they would remain with those in your possession, and that you would at some point in the future assemble a show. In spite of Augustus' contempt for spectacles and displays, I believe his work deserves at least one public viewing.

You asked, too, what I remember about the region's natural history, but I fear I was too distracted to be much of a skilled observer and at the time was unable to appreciate the stark, almost desolate beauty of the place. James Huntington, who often visited our camp along the Missouri and later opened his home site to us when the Indians started their move to the north, had an extensive scientific library to which he generously let me refer. But other than some brief notations about the birds and insects inhabiting the area, the work of an amateur I can assure you, there is little which I could recall that would be of much scientific or historical interest. To this day I carry with me a small collection of rocks given to me by Mr. Huntington, who insisted at the time they were mere trifles and not meant as a gift. Although I am not willing to part with them, you are welcome to see them if you think they will help further your work. I also kept a journal, but it was lost with some other personal items that summer, although in retrospect I'm sure my entries at the time would have proven to be perfunctory at best.

I later constructed a timeline of sorts, an illustration of the layers of time fashioned, I suppose, after those developed by the scientists with whom I worked. My amateurish attempt to identify the layers of space and time through which we all traveled to bring us to that fateful summer in Montana on a bluff overlooking the Missouri River, the Sioux, still flush from their victory, camped just to the south. But rather than the millions of geological years that the scientists envision, my timeline is layered in hours and days and months and years. And mine is a chart of living, breathing men and, I dare say, women, not ancient rocks or extinct beasts. Again, this is a personal item but I would be more than willing to share it with you if it will help you better understand Augustus' body of work.

One of the very first things I learned from working with Augustus, who was a scientist at heart, is to open my eyes and question what the subject matter reveals, be it the landscape of a person's face or a wayward ammonite from the ancient past. I am now confident that there is the smallest window, a mere heartbeat really, when man and weather and geology and time all align, and the secrets of the earth are revealed. Fatelines, someone once referred to them, as he explained how science was slowly unveiling the earth's true secrets. I view your request as an opportunity to identify where our own collective fatelines came to pass.

Most sincerely yours,
Eleanor Peterson

1. Photograph, Woman with Bones

To trace my own fateline backward, and identify where my path started its trajectory west, I simply need to recall the day the photograph you've labeled "Woman with Bones, Philadelphia" was taken in the library of the Academy. I have a weathered copy of that photograph in my own personal collection, but there are images from that day that will remain with me always: the empty, cavernous space with its sweet lingering scent of leather and wax; the light falling in hot, dusty patches from the windows high along one wall; the smoothly polished floor marked by dulled pathways where the shelving once stood. I remember, too, how I removed my spectacles, and how the sunlight caught the edge of one of the lenses and refracted into a fleeting rainbow of light.

The photograph does not adequately capture the roomful of bones I was documenting for the Academy, but instead focuses directly on the woman I once was: no longer young, never particularly beautiful, immodestly staring into the camera without concern for what it revealed, much the way Augustus taught me to look directly at him while he worked. It was at the photographer's request that I have pushed back onto my haunches and quieted my hands, but as usual my shirtsleeves are rolled to the elbow and my apron is covered with dust and dark splotches of paint. My hair, already showing signs of gray, flames out around my head in a way that Augustus would have represented as a halo or a wild garland of weeds, but to me simply appears unruly. And, as you have noted in your citation, I am surrounded by very large bones. I was working on the Academy's hadrosaur at the time.

Although they do not appear in the photograph, I would

soon discover that two men were standing in the doorway, silently watching as I scrambled from one end of the expansive space to the other, placing each rib bone in descending order, trying to estimate, from the femur to the metatarsals, where and how to position the bones of the legs. This aspect of my work was always a bit like assembling an enormous puzzle, with each bone creating a picture of the beast, albeit a two-dimensional one, as if the creature had been pressed, like something fragile as a flower, for display under glass.

As I arranged and rearranged the position of the bones, I tried to imagine how the creature might have lived and moved and should therefore be represented. It was amazing to me then, as it still is to me now, that science can discover everything it needs to know from the bones, but only if the men working on them are open to seeing what these relics in fact reveal. It is amazing, too, that it does not matter much if the bones once belonged to a man or a beast, since once the skin and flesh are stripped away, we are all more similar than unique in almost every single way. Darwin's work should not have come as a surprise in that regard.

It was hot that day in the Academy, with the sun beating down on the emptying building, baking the cavernous library space like a kiln. I pushed at my damp hair and wiped my brow with my sleeve, and then reached out to adjust the location of a dorsal vertebra. Only then did I notice the two men intently studying me in much the same way that I was studying the bones.

One man, the younger of the two, I had met before since he often visited the Academy, checking on the status of the fossils and inquiring after my work. This gentleman, who never told me his name although he made it clear he was from Yale College, presented himself one day in my small Academy workspace, and proceeded to handle the large tibia I was documenting, comparing it to the illustrations in my book.

"This is excellent work," he told me at the time. "The Captain will be most pleased." He smoothed his hand over the bone.

He had the look of a scholar, this man from Yale, with thin

black hair combed straight back from his forehead, and pale, translucent skin suggesting not enough time interacting with the living, and too much time working with the skeletons of the dead. He wore a long black woolen coat and a gray silk scarf at his throat, even though the spring days were growing longer, hotter, and, as summer approached, more humid. And he was preternaturally still, slipping in and out of my workshop like a phantasm, his white hands soft and pliable, like the wax used to reconstruct and display the dead. I soon came to expect his visits, although I did not look forward to them.

The other man who entered the library that day was a stranger, older than his friend, with a complexion suggesting years spent at sea. Unlike his long, lean companion, this second man was red-faced, short, and stocky, with a bushy brown beard and mustache and casual yet gentlemanly dress. This second man joined his friend and lifted one of the heavy fibulas, turning the leg bone carved from clay until it shimmered momentarily and then was lost again in the library's oblique light.

"I like it," he exclaimed to his pale companion. The man's voice echoed through the empty library. "Excellent work. Well done. Well done."

The man ran a thick finger over the bone and placed it carefully against the adjoining tibia to ascertain whether or not the bone had a proper fit. With great concentration, he rocked the tibia back and forth in the air.

"A perfect articulation," he boomed again. "Very nice indeed."

I began to thank him but quickly realized he was speaking not to me, but to his companion, the man in black, who managed a thin, weary smile as the other man continued to handle the large, stiff bone. I replaced my spectacles, satisfied that my employment at the Academy was about to reach a successful conclusion since even these gentlemen from Yale College appeared to be pleased with the quality of my work. As I prepared to remove myself from the room, the man with the beard bellowed again.

"Now, this is interesting." He drew his companion's attention to the animal's foot. "It's missing a metatarsal," he declared. "Didn't my *Claosaurus* have a fourth metatarsal? What happened to the fourth metatarsal?" he demanded to know.

His friend raised his eyebrows as if to say he hadn't seen it, but by then the gentleman with the beard had turned his attention to the curve of pubis I had smoothed out and appended to what had once been no more than a broken piece of bone.

"Ah, but will you look at this," he said. "Excellent work. Excellent indeed."

The man was practically shouting at his friend but since he was still not speaking to me, I started to retreat, stopping only long enough to remove my journal. Before I could reach it, however, he scooped it from the floor.

"I need that," the bearded man announced. Roughly he riffled the pages.

"Look," he said, speaking again to his companion as if I were inhabiting an invisible world. "See how she sizes those vertebrae, comparing the cervical to the dorsal to the caudal? Quite lovely. I'm very impressed. This is exactly what I need. My uncle would be most pleased." He flipped through a few more illustrations. "Where did she receive her training?"

The man in black started to explain my brief career as an assistant to Benjamin Waterhouse Hawkins in New York and how, with no formal training, I had learned my craft working as an illustrator for the leading artist in the world of science, but his companion cut him short.

"Yes, yes, that was a shame what happened to that project," the older man declared. "But what can you expect, dabbling with the politics of that city while trying to appease the curiosity of the masses? Have you seen the drawings of the creatures they were planning to construct? Pure flights of fancy, I can assure you. Those beasts are probably still buried out there somewhere in Central Park. Best to stay clear of all of that, would have been my advice. Still," he added thoughtfully, "she has a certain talent, there's no denying it. Feminine intuition, I suppose."

Again, he turned his attention to the bones.

"Forgive me," I said, inching toward the man with the beard, "but may I please have my journal? I am certain it will be of no interest to you."

At these words, the man in black grew paler by the second, his eyes burrowing even deeper into his skull. But the other man, the red-faced one, was not in the least bit deterred.

"Forgive *me*," the man blustered. "It is I who have been rude. Call me the Captain," he said. "Please. Accept my hand. And my apologies."

The Captain reached his free hand across the skeleton, still holding my journal folded tightly to his chest. As he leaned toward me, I could feel myself pulling away, my head turning slightly, my body readying itself for retreat. But then, focusing on the apparent generosity of the man's offered hand, I, too, reached out, my fingers touching his.

"How much do they pay you here?" the Captain demanded to know.

"Excuse me?"

"What is your salary?" he asked. Before I could respond, he added, "Can't be much, since even the Academy knows there is little value in these futile attempts at public displays." He said this with undisguised contempt.

I understood the question but still I hesitated, uncertain about the nature of what he really wanted to know. Apparently the man took my confusion as reticence to negotiate, so he blustered right past my reserve.

"It doesn't matter," the man announced. "Whatever it is, I'll double it. I have too much to worry about right now without adding quibbling about salaries to my list."

At this proclamation, the Captain's slim companion sidled up to him and whispered something about the fact that I had only been hired to help with the Centennial Exhibition and then to document this skeleton in preparation for the Academy's move. Surely he must realize that I was not a regular employee of the Academy, but nothing more than a day laborer.

"Doesn't matter," the Captain boomed. "I want her. I need her. Actually," he continued, pausing to compose his thoughts, "it is Patrick who needs her. Or he may never make it home."

At this bit of news the young gentleman from Yale raised his chin ever so slightly and let out an almost silent "Ahhh" of understanding. Then he pointed that thin, reptilian smile of his in my direction.

"I believe, Misssss . . ." The man in black hesitated. "Forgive me. I do not recall your name. It is Miss, is it not?"

"Peterson," I told him.

"Yes. Peterson, then. I believe you are being offered employment. Extremely well paying employment, I might add. Not the sort of day work you have been doing for the Academy, although it will certainly require the same sort of skills. If, that is, you are interested in working at Yale College." He said this as if I might have missed the point of what was being offered.

As the man in black explained to me the conditions of my employ, and of the travel to the Territories initially involved, the Captain examined the repairs I had made to the animal's mandible. He grunted an approval, and then hoisted the large hadrosaur skull over his head and smiled warmly at the toothy piece of bone.

"'Alas, poor Yorick, I knew him well,'" he said.

And then the Captain's booming laugh echoed through the cavernous library, empty except for the two men, me, and the bones.

2. PORTRAIT, WOMAN AND LACE CURTAIN

I'm fairly certain that the portrait in oil you've listed as "Woman and Lace Curtain" was painted in part that same afternoon, when I told Augustus of the news. You can tell for certain it's from that same period if you compare it to the photograph taken at the Academy, although you should note that in Augustus' hands my filthy work clothes were inevitably transformed into wispy, angelic-like garbs.

"Of course you can't go," was Augustus' immediate reply when I told him of my news. "I am not done with you yet."

To this day I can still see him standing there in his robe, his long white hair glowing in the late afternoon light, as I told him of what had transpired. He kissed my fingertips lightly and told me that if I wanted his advice, I needed to wait for him on the other side of the room, closer to the window.

"Just stand over there, my darling," he said, stopping for a moment to cough up whatever was getting in the way of his breath. "Then I promise to give you all the advice you could ever desire."

It was hot in his rooms, hotter even than in the Academy. Sweat beaded along my forehead and the small of my back. Again I tried to speak, but Augustus waved away my words.

"Not yet," he said, placing a finger to his lips. "I'm thinking. Take that chair. The one next to the window."

Outside, men were sawing and hammering, having moved their attentions from the Centennial Exhibition to prepare for the city's own celebration of the Fourth. Someone called out to a friend on the street, while down the hall a baby cried, fighting off sleep, and children shouted and laughed and raced up and down the stairs. But when Augustus worked he never seemed bothered by the heat or the noise. He stood in the deepening shadows, coughing again and waiting, I suppose, for me to do as I was told.

I pulled the chair away from the open window so that the workmen on the street could not see me, but kept it close enough to enjoy the breeze fluttering the lace. Anticipating Augustus' next request, I unpinned my hair. Watching me closely, Augustus adjusted the angle of the chair to perfect the light and loosened the ties of my dress. Still not speaking, he ran his hands through my hair so that it fell wildly down my back and across the front of my shoulder. He lifted my left arm onto the back of the chair, so that my upper body faced him and the room, while the rest of my body was turned toward the shadows.

"Beautiful," he declared, touching my face, the way he often did during these sessions. Only then did he tell me that if I was ready for his promised advice, it was this: that I must never leave that chair. "I need you," I remember him telling me. "Sitting there in that warm northern light is where you belong. It makes you look young again, Eleanor."

I always enjoyed sitting for Augustus when in Philadelphia. Compared to the stark conditions of my own room at that time, no more than a campsite really, his was a lush and luxuriant shrine, with caged birds and potted plants, unfinished canvases stacked against the walls, brightly colored scarves and cloths draped over tables and chairs, and strange displays of moss-covered wood, multi-colored rocks and shells, and peculiar-looking dried-out bugs, frogs, and fish that Augustus collected along the Schuylkill River before his health began to fail. Confined now to the city because of what he referred to as old age and infirmity, Augustus had arranged his odd collections into miniature dioramas along tabletops and ledges, and had painted vast, mist-covered landscapes and seascapes as backdrops for his Lilliputian world.

Since he could no longer collect artifacts on his rambles, as he referred to them, his passion had shifted to the collection of ammonites, which were delivered to him through the mail. It was these ancient creatures of the sea, displayed on a lace-covered table next to his bed, that I spent hours drawing, trying to capture, at first in often clumsy fashion, the evolutionary function and beauty of their million-years-old shells. Augustus would analyze and critique my illustrations, instructing me how to use the side of my pencil to add depth, or how to use the slightest hatch marks to suggest contour and form, always most generous with his advice and patient, too, given his reservations about my focusing on what he dismissed as the minutiae of his domestic life. If he had his way, he insisted, I would tackle subject matter of more artistic and, thus, lasting appeal. But then the secrets wrapped up in shells and fossils held no fascination for Augustus, who once confessed he preferred flesh over bones.

"I have a new ammonite for you, my darling," Augustus announced from behind his easel. "It has just arrived, direct to my room from the Cretaceous. As your teacher, I thought it only fitting that I should provide you with a few lessons in living. It's a regular little morality play, that ammonite."

"Augustus, please," I countered. "They are offering me a great sum of money."

"You're missing my point," he replied. "If you promise not to move, I will show you."

From the back of the room Augustus retrieved an ammonite still partially encased in a piece of the sandstone in which it had been discovered. He placed the prehistoric creature on a small table, where the opalescence of the shell hinted at its original colors of silver, blue, and pink.

"Now, don't move," he warned, returning to his work, "but I want you to notice how this ammonite started its early years spiraling in neat, concentric swirls, but at some point in its life spiraled outward and then back again, as if in defiance of its heredity. Do you think you can represent that, my darling, you who are determined against my good counsel to be a mere illustrator of bones?"

"But it's all askew," I noted. "As if it lost its way."

"Precisely, my dear."

"Augustus, please don't be difficult," I pleaded. "I need to speak to you about this. It's not just the money. It's an opportunity to have a real profession. Please."

Augustus stared at me from behind his easel.

"A profession?" he said, with clear contempt for the word. He put down his brush, wiped his hands on his robe, and stepped into the patterned light infiltrating the room through the curtain of lace. "Is that what you want, Eleanor? When I first met you I had the distinct impression that you wanted to be an artist. Not a mere technicist toiling away in academia." He looked as if I were now the object of that contempt. "Casting and displaying bones to pacify a public numbed by war, destitute from economic depression, and now hungry for diversion is not art, my darling. I would think there could not possibly be enough money in the world to pay you for that."

He wiped his hands again, poured out a small tumbler of whiskey, took a swallow, and placed the remains on the table next to the ammonite. The liquid glowed like ancient amber trapped within the confines of the glass.

"These men are not making any significant contributions to science, Eleanor, but rather shuffling bones around to prove their latest theory," he said at last. "You have told me yourself that they are living by and large in a world of their own design. One which, I feel duty-bound to point out, will never include the likes of you."

When I started to object, he stepped forward and inched my chair closer to the window.

"Now sit still, Eleanor. And relax, if you don't mind. Couldn't we just for this moment pretend that you are not wasting your life toiling for ingrates who neither see nor appreciate your finer qualities?"

"Augustus, you know I cannot afford to turn away any opportunity, even for a fraction of what they have offered. But that's not what I am asking you now, even though that kind of money would make a big difference in the way that I live. Can you imagine having enough money to do as I please?"

In spite of my earnestness, I could not help myself. That kind of money seemed so far from my grasp that I inadvertently laughed. Augustus, blessed with a small income and an occasional society commission that he condescended to accept, also appeared to be amused, but his laugh sounded more like a snort, which turned into a prolonged cough.

"It is hard to imagine, isn't it?" I asked, trying to engage his usual good humor. "Think of it. Not having to worry all the time. To eat and drink as you please. To travel."

"I hate travel," he reminded me. "It fouls the bowels."

"Well, then I could pay you for the lessons you provide, and you could hire a real model. A different one for each day of the week."

"Forgive me," he said, wearied by my plans, "but it's getting late. If you don't mind I'll keep working while we continue this . . ." he hesitated, and then added, "this discussion."

Augustus studied his canvas for a moment and then lifted my hair so that it would fall back onto my shoulders, its gray flyaway edges reflecting the last of the light.

"So, Eleanor," Augustus said, as he settled back behind his easel, "if you would be willing to work for Yale College for even half the money, or whatever it was you said, what is the nature of your problem?"

"I have to travel to the Territories," I explained. "To Montana. They want me to assist someone who is exploring in that region. It's only for a month or two."

"And?" he queried.

"It seems an unusual request, that's all. To send me off on my own, to work for a man I've never met."

Augustus ignored me, his attention focused on his work. When I did not continue, he looked up impatiently. "Go on," he said.

"Remember that man from Yale I once told you about? The one who dresses in black and looks like death walking into my workshop? This afternoon he went out of his way to assure me that the fieldwork in question would be much the same as the work I'm doing now for the Academy. Documenting and illustrating and the like. But it does seem odd somehow."

Augustus stared at me now as if he did not quite believe what he was seeing.

"Odd?" he asked. "I would think you would be more concerned about the savages and heathens who live in that part of the country than some rich gray-bearded fool from Yale College who prefers to prolong his childhood by digging in the dirt rather than pursuing a real profession. You have always expressed disdain for those kinds of men."

"It's not that. Surely even I can tolerate a month or two living away from the city." Then it was I who hesitated. "The other day I overheard one of the scientists complaining about these two men," I explained. "He said the Academy would have more to show for its work on the hadrosaur if Yale had not sent funds directly to the workmen who were uncovering pieces of the beast in the New Jersey marl. He suggested that the men from Yale were nothing more than common criminals in the way they had stepped in and taken over another's discovery."

Augustus spread more paint onto his palette, mixing two colors into a third with his thumb.

"So what exactly is the problem, Eleanor? I would love to stand here and make small talk all evening, but I'm losing the light."

"It's that I was instructed to tell no one of my destination. Or of my plans. Even the man who offered to hire me would not give me his real name. It seems strange, that's all."

For the first time that evening I think I had his full attention, although he avoided my gaze.

"And so how did you respond to them?" he asked, mixing yet another color.

"I said I needed time to think about it. And asked for permission to discuss it first with my family."

"But you don't have a family," he reminded me.

"I know that. But they don't." I looked at him directly. "That's why I'm talking to you."

Augustus daubed at his paints as he often did when our talk turned to my work at the Academy. At first I assumed that our discussion about this offered employment would follow a similar path, but Augustus ignored me for such a long period of time, focusing instead on the canvas, that I began to fear he had forgotten the question altogether. Just as I was about to drift off into concerns of my own, Augustus drew my attention back to the ammonite.

"I want you to pay close attention to that shell, Eleanor. You realize what that is, do you not? What your scientist friends might consider an anomaly of nature. For it's a suicide if ever there were one."

Now he was simply being rude.

"I'm serious, Eleanor. Look at that outward spiral. It's a death contortion, pure and simple. What you see before you is a creature that deliberately set out to destroy itself. Born with God-given talents of symmetry, that creature made a conscious decision to throw those talents to the wind and head out in its own direction. You see the price it paid."

I reminded Augustus that he didn't believe in God, to which he replied, "You know that, but that suicidal ammonite doesn't."

With this declaration we were both silenced, leaving me sitting in the fading light while Augustus retreated to the shadows. A wan breeze wisped the curtains across my back. It was Augustus who finally broke the uncomfortable quiet that had settled like the dark upon the room.

"I think I have seen enough for the evening," he said. "You are free to go."

Reluctantly I refastened my dress and wished him a good evening, knowing full well I would take the offered employment with or without his blessing or advice. He was my neighbor and friend, but I did not owe him any more than he in turn was willing to give.

☙

I still have the letter I discovered tucked under my door that night. I reproduce it here for your records.

May 25, 1876

My dear Miss Peterson,

I hope this letter finds you well and that you are free to leave the Academy and depart for the Territories no later than the first week of June.

My instructions for you are simple. If you agree to enter into my employ, you must travel to Ogden, Utah, where you should transfer to a train bound for Franklin, Idaho. In Franklin, take the Concord coach to Helena, where you can hire transport to Fort Benton in the Montana Territory. I can assure you that these instructions should not present you with any difficulty, as travel in this part of the country is now relatively routine. I would not hesitate to send my own daughter on such a mission, if I had the good fortune to be blessed with one.

When you arrive at the Benton Hotel, ask for further instructions and your supplies. I will notify the manager at the hotel, with whom I have established an account, once I receive word that you are indeed headed in that direction. I will also contact my associate in the field to inform him of your impending arrival.

I have given serious thought to your understandable request to discuss this journey privately with your family. To ensure that they do not object, I urge you to engage a relative to accompany you, an elderly companion perhaps who can enjoy the mountain scenery and keep you company during your short stay in the West. However, I must again insist that you inform no one else about your destination, particularly your former employers at the Academy, many of whom have a tendency to gossip about such things.

I trust these arrangements will be to your satisfaction and will allay any fears that you or your family might have. I look forward to a long and productive collaboration with you at Yale College in the fall.

I remain,

most truly yours,
the Capt.

P.S. Enclosed you will find a draft for the sum of three hundred dollars. I believe these funds should be more than adequate to comfortably accommodate travel and expenses for two.

3. Hand-Drawn Map, Mont. Territory

I cannot remember exactly what I said to convince Augustus to accompany me west for the summer, but I clearly recall that his decision gave him what can only be called a new purpose in life. He purchased maps, and then complained when he discovered I did not know the exact mileage between Pennsylvania and Montana. He purchased new boots, and then complained that they hurt his feet. He carried his potted plants, one by one, down the three flights of stairs to the hotel lobby, and then complained that the hotelier was certain to allow the plants to wither and die. He was more agitated than I had ever seen him. I believe he was looking forward to the trip.

On the day we were scheduled to leave, Augustus appeared at my door an hour early, dressed in a pale blue linen duster, which swept the floor in spite of his height, and a large-brimmed straw hat tied under his chin with a strip of reddish leather. He carried a large valise with his painting supplies, including rolls of canvas, and a spyglass to keep an eye out for Indians, while in his other hand was an ornate wire cage containing his birds, Ferdinand and Miranda. His easel and a large striped umbrella made of heavy canvas and whalebone strips were both furled, secured with cord, and tucked under his arm. He waited on the landing, calling me Cousin Eleanor, and wondering aloud what could possibly be taking me so long to get ready to go.

Augustus relished the use of the word "Cousin" that summer, as if he were a minister traveling with his ward, or a member of a religious sect in search of the promised land. Cousins. In retrospect it seems absurd, but how else to explain our friendship? The

Captain had limited his offer to a member of my family but no one could have possibly mistaken us for brother and sister. Certainly not husband and wife. For a moment I considered father and daughter, but rejected it knowing Augustus' vanity would be sorely wounded.

We settled into our train compartment, with plenty of time to spare, I was quick to point out. After closing the window, Augustus removed his hat and duster and placed them with great ceremony on the leather-covered seat. The birds, in their cumbersome cage, he deposited next to that, reserving the third place in the arrangement for himself.

I, too, started to make myself comfortable, since the narrow confines of the compartment would be our home until we reached Utah. As I started to settle in, my attention was drawn to the crowd swelling along the platform. Some hurried to leave, and others rushed forward to call out their good-byes, while the gentleman from Yale College pushed through the crush, his black suit bobbing up and down amid the colorful human sea. I tried to point the man out to Augustus but he was busy unpacking his *Collected Works of Shakespeare*, which would prove to be his constant companion that summer.

As the man in black made his way through the crowd of hats and bonnets and parasols and umbrellas, the train rumbled and emitted a burst of steam. With some difficulty, I reopened the window and called out to him. His pale, stern face brightened at the sound of my voice. He rushed forward, waving a heavy leather-bound book high over his head. The train jerked slightly, and then again. The man in black hurled himself in our direction.

"Cousin Eleanor, please, tell him to hurry," Augustus admonished, "and then close that window. The fumes will ruin my lunch. And look. All that commotion is upsetting Miranda." He slipped a scarf over the cage to quiet the squawking bird.

I waved again, reaching out to retrieve the book the man from Yale was attempting to deliver. The train lurched. He lifted the book into my hands, and then pushed through the crowd as the train slowly crept from the station.

"This is your master journal," he shouted up at me. "Everything you do this summer should be entered here," he said, "with duplicate entries and notes sent to the Captain every week no matter what your situation. Is that clear?"

I assured him that it was, and thanked him.

"You will also find a more detailed map of your destination," he continued, now breaking into a trot to keep up with the departing train. "You must under no circumstances discuss the map with anyone. And you must reach the site immediately if your contract with Yale is to be binding. Do not dawdle. Do not stop for sightseeing in Yellowstone Park. There will be plenty of time for that on your return trip home. Is that also clear?"

Again I assured him that I understood, although I fear I might have laughed slightly at the tone of his demands.

"And whatever you do," he shouted, now even more serious given my indiscretion, "take care of the journal. Keep it with you at all times, and show no one your work. Absolutely no one, no matter what they tell you, do you understand?"

I waved my agreement as the train withdrew, leaving the young man standing there, alone on the edge of the platform. With one last wave of assurance in the man's direction, I started to return to my place in the compartment.

"Oh, do close that window, Cousin Eleanor, before I absolutely die," Augustus said before I could return to my seat. Augustus removed the scarf from his now quieted birds, unwrapped one of his sandwiches, coughed, opened his book, coughed again, and then flapped the book shut.

"What is all this mystery about anyway?" Augustus took the journal and stared at its blank pages. "There's nothing here, Cousin. The book is a blank. I would say they have a very misguided sense of self-importance, wouldn't you?"

I started to explain how science and men's reputations were now advanced in the technical press, and how my documentation would be used for any published reports. But none of this interested Augustus. He discovered the map tucked inside the front cover, closed the empty journal, and unfolded the map on his lap instead.

"I suppose you're not supposed to discuss this with me, either?" he asked.

On the map, a small, cramped script marked the town of Fort Benton. The Missouri River was indicated by a wavy black line drawn across the paper's width, and three triangles were penciled in, representing the camp. But since the map lacked scale, it was difficult to determine where the camp was located. Or where Fort Benton was in relation to the rest of the world.

I reminded Augustus that the Captain had promised more complete directions once we arrived at the Benton Hotel.

"Well, I should certainly hope so," Augustus exclaimed. "How can they expect us to find anything with a map like this? We're traveling to the end of the earth without a compass, if this map is any indication."

It was then that Augustus noticed that most of the territory to the east and south of the river had been marked with the simple phrase, "*mauvaises terres*." Augustus raised his eyebrows. "Cousin, this sounds like my kind of place," he said.

Reaching again for his Shakespeare, Augustus hesitated.

"And for heaven's sake, Cousin, open that window," he demanded. "How do you expect me to breathe if I can't get any air?"

4. Study (Peterson), Leaf Impression

You asked what I remember of our travels. I remember spending long hours on the train's platform watching great white clouds mound up along the horizon, letting loose torrents of rain, thunder, lightning, and wind, only to disappear, leaving the earth moist and shimmering in the hot summer sun. I remember how large herds of animals similarly appeared, skittering in the wake of our passage. And I remember birds, great giant flocks of them, swirling overhead in noisy bursts, creating a storm of their own before they, too, vanished from view. Having never been outside the tight confines of the city, these new vistas were like a revelation.

Augustus took no interest in the wildlife or the landscape, preferring to sleep for hours on end with the window of our compartment covered with a scarf, or to disappear for even more hours into the familiar landscapes of Shakespeare's plays. When I questioned him about his apparent lack of interest in these new lands, he commented that he could never hide in such a country. "If I had wanted to cast my fate upon the sea, like a solitary pea upon a pond, I would have taken up sailing and purchased a boat."

By the time we disembarked in Utah along with several travelers headed for the new national park, Augustus had become even more sullen and withdrawn. He stood on the platform and took in the view. At one end, a man plunked on a guitar and two boys chased a three-legged dog down the tracks. At the other end, men on horseback hollered and whistled as they coaxed along a small herd of cattle, stirring up dust and strange western smells. Beyond the station, as far as the eye could see, stark gray mountains rose like sentries, guarding the promised land.

"Cousin, this is not what I had in mind," he announced. Augustus draped a scarf over his birdcage and wiped his face with a handkerchief. "Look at those mountains," he said. "I feel like I might swoon. Good God, how will I ever survive?"

At this comment, Augustus was approached by a small man with a big voice and a bad leg.

"Survive, my friend? Why, you will flourish in the presence of such splendor. 'Twas, after all, the Grand Architect Himself who pushed these craggy mountains into the sky. They are here to watch over us, and all of His creation. And that includes even you, my dear sir, and your fine companion."

Augustus smiled without emotion at the small man standing next to him, and then sat down on a wooden bench, turning to face in the opposite direction.

"We have nothing to fear in the shadow of the hand of God," the man continued. He flexed his arms and breathed deeply of the hot, dusty air. He pounded his fists against his chest. "We are blessed, my friends," the man persisted. "Blessed indeed."

Augustus stood up as if readying to leave, but he started coughing so hard he had to bend over to catch his breath. He returned to the bench, covered his face with his handkerchief, and pretended to sleep. When the man looked as though he might join him on the bench, Augustus pulled his hat down over the cloth on his face.

"Eleanor," Augustus whispered from beneath his elaborate covering. "Do something."

"Forgive me for interrupting," I said, walking up to the man, "but I was wondering if you might tell me when the next train to Idaho is expected. As you can see, my cousin is feeling poorly, and we are anxious to reach our destination so that he might be able to rest."

"Should be here any minute," the man announced. "Any

minute. In fact, I'm afraid my benefactor has been delayed and we will be forced to take a later train. But the creatures we are hunting have been waiting for us all these years. I'm sure they'll still be there in the morning."

I walked along the platform as if seeking out the missing train. "You're a hunter, then?" I inquired of the man hobbling beside me. "Buffalo?"

"Only buffalo I ever shot turned out on closer inspection to be nothing but a common cow." The man had a loud, loose laugh. "No, I'm a collector," he corrected. "Documenting God's record writ in stone. Just in from the field and about to head off again, if my colleague ever gets here. Let me show you."

He lowered himself onto his knees and opened his bag. I feared he was about to reveal a supply of Bibles for sale but the carpetbag was packed instead with odd-shaped parcels wrapped in brown paper and string.

"I know this must seem unlikely," he said, pulling one of the packages from the bag and unwrapping it, "but this was once part of a giant creature of the sea." He handed me a well-preserved vertebra, with a smooth rounded end. "Mosasaur was its name," he explained. "Lived on ammonites and others of its kind. Found a large piece of this fellow's skull, too, with many of its teeth still intact, but that piece was over three feet long and wouldn't fit into my bag. There were some boys from Yale College who would have loved to get their hands on this lovely specimen, I can tell you, but I found him first," he added. "And they can't deny it."

"This is from Utah?" I asked, feeling a disorientation similar to that which appeared to be haunting Augustus.

"Kansas," he replied. "This is not commonly known, of course, but Kansas was once buried beneath an ancient sea. I have fishes, too, if you're interested. And sharks. They lived in Kansas as well."

Augustus called out my name, but I could not take my eyes off the small man on his knees digging through his bag. He handed me a shark-like tooth as if to prove that what he said about oceans was true.

"I see that you are fascinated by fossils," the man continued. "Let me give you one of my calling cards before you and your cousin depart."

He rummaged again and retrieved a thin sheet of sandstone in which an almost perfectly round leaf was imprinted.

"A *Protophyllum*," he announced. "Professor Lesquereux named this specimen from the Dakota Formation after me."

"Eleanor," Augustus called out again. "Our train."

When I tried to return the fossil named in his honor, the man raised his hand to refuse it.

"Please," he said, "you would do me a great honor if you would accept this with my compliments. Think of me and all of God's wonders when you gaze upon it."

I started to thank him but realized I did not know his name.

"Forgive me," he said, "but I don't feel I am at liberty to say. It's not you, please understand, but these days a man can't be too careful. They've taken to bribing the telegraph men so even our most basic communications are no longer secure."

He rewrapped the vertebra and snapped shut the bag.

"When I was a young man," he said, all the bravado now gone from his voice, "I sent my very first specimens, the absolute cream of my collection, to the Smithsonian. I did not ask for payment. The letter from Secretary Baird acknowledging my contribution was worth more to me than gold. Of course, there was no money in fossils then. No rush to publish before the next man. No searching for fame based on these fragile relics from the past. We all shared our discoveries freely and explored for the pure exhilaration of being in the field. But times change," he added. "Now it's not like a science at all. I have colleagues who act as if it is a war."

He picked up his heavy bag as if resigned to the new way of the world.

"The Indians referred to Professor Hayden as He Who Picks Up Stones Running," he said, "but I don't know how anyone could run if they had to carry around bags like this."

With that announcement, he carried his cumbersome bag down the platform, listing to one side and then to the other, the bag on his right offsetting the limp on his left.

"So what has God writ in stone?" Augustus asked as I rejoined him. "I hope it is not more commandments for things I cannot do."

"Leaves," I replied, showing him the fossil. "The history of the planet written in bones and leaves."

5. DRAWING, DEAD MAN'S CHARIOT

When Augustus and I reached Idaho, we boarded a Concord stage, which Augustus referred to without the slightest hint of irony as the dead man's chariot. There was a driver, who was drunk most of the time, and four other passengers, two women, a boy, and a nun on her way to work in a hospital in Helena. One of the women had not heard from her husband in months and, having received no news from his regiment, feared that he might be dead. Another was traveling with her son to Fort Benton to reclaim the land she and her husband had once worked. She, too, had not heard from her husband in several months, but informed me when the other woman could not hear her that she could only *hope* that he was dead.

The six of us shouldered and elbowed our way across a desolate landscape in a perpetual cloud of alkaloid dust, stopping only long enough for meals of cold coffee, bread, and bacon, for which we were charged a dollar apiece. But if the stagecoach ride was arduous for me and my fellow passengers, all of whom were close to delirium from lack of sleep, it took an even greater toll on Augustus, who withdrew so far into himself that I was beginning to fear he might not survive.

When it seemed as though our confinement in the coach might never end, we were then forced to disembark and walk the steep inclines of the Continental Divide since, by this time, the horses were as weary as their passengers. Sullen and weary to the bone, Augustus placed his birdcage upon the floor of the coach and stumbled out into the bright summer light. I waited for the anguish or even anger to be hurled in my direction or, worse, a flat refusal to travel one mile more. But instead Augustus did an almost inexplicable thing. He closed his eyes, dug his hands into the pockets of his duster, flexed his shoulders, and breathed deeply of the hot, dusty air.

As the other passengers obediently followed the coach up the mountain, I waited to determine whether or not Augustus was feeling up to the challenge, assuring him that the driver could not refuse him passage if he was indeed ill. Augustus smiled but said nothing, and walked down to the narrow creek that paralleled the wagon road. I followed him to the upper embankment, fearing that now that he was freed from the confines of the coach, he might simply refuse to move.

Through the trees, I could see Augustus dip his handkerchief into the rushing water and wipe the dirt from his face. He dipped it again and ran the cloth over the top of his head and dusty hair. He cupped his hands and scooped the icy water into his mouth, letting it spill down his chin and chest. He took another deep breath and looked up at the mountains and trees that surrounded him in all directions. Each of these activities was punctuated with dramatic releases of breath, as if at some point in his life he had forgotten how to breathe, and was now relearning this very basic technique.

"Augustus, are you all right?" I called down to him. It would only be a matter of minutes before the coach and its trail of passengers would disappear from view.

He looked up from the creek, the dappled light wavering across his face. With much ceremony, he bent down for another drink, remoistened his handkerchief, and took another deep breath. Only then did he return the straw hat to his head and scramble back up the embankment. The coach was now at least a half mile up the mountain, nearing a bend in the road.

"Augustus, are you sure that you're all right?" I asked again. "We really need to go."

Again, he flashed that winsome smile in my direction, taking another deep breath and releasing it slowly into the air. "I've never felt better in my life," he declared.

Then, after drawing my attention to the beauty of the trees, the sky, the very ground upon which we stood, he strode past me like a man reborn, as if that fragile frame which he inhabited only came to life after breathing in the thin mountain air. He bounded past me and proceeded straight up the rutted road, the wind flapping the folds of his linen duster like the wings of a giant cerulean bird. This was just one of Augustus' many mysteries which would reveal themselves to me, like the earth itself revealed its many secrets that summer in Montana.

6. Drawing, Traveling North

By the time we reached Helena, storefronts and doorways had been decked out in red, white, and blue bunting in preparation for the Centennial, and banners and flags flapped wildly along the boardwalks. The main street of town, or the gulch as they called it, was crowded with men and horses and wagons filled with people and every variety of goods. Although the population numbered only three or four thousand at the time, Helena was surprisingly bustling given the depression debilitating the rest of the country. Placer works were still in operation, but the mining camp was being transformed to meet the needs of farmers and ranchers taking root in that part of the world. The small capital city, with its cosmopolitan air, was a welcome relief after the long and tedious journey by stage.

We decided against staying at the St. Louis Hotel with its pretensions of the East, and instead booked rooms at the Last Chance Hotel, a name that Augustus found most appealing. While Augustus ordered a bath for himself and a bowl of fresh water for his birds, I ventured back into the lobby to hire transport for the remainder of our trip.

"There's Jake, down the street at the livery," the man at the front desk told me. "Runs a stage back and forth to Benton, but he only travels when he's in the mood, and only when there are enough men along should he encounter any savages."

I suggested that it might be preferable if Augustus approached him on our behalf, but the man shrugged, unimpressed by the prospect of Augustus walking into the stables with his long white hair, his hat, and his linen duster.

"Jake's not the easiest man, and that's a fact," was all the man would say. "But you might be able to convince him. For a price. But then again, he might not want the responsibility. You never can tell about Jake."

Outside, a rainstorm had swept through the valley, wetting the roads and settling the dust. I can still recall the sweet smell of the air, like freshly mowed hay, and how the sun was low on the horizon, casting long cool shadows through town. The mountains glowed green in the distance but were still white along their crests with what appeared to be freshly fallen snow.

The livery was located on the edge of the gulch where the boardwalk abruptly ended. I stepped down onto the dirt, still damp from the rain, and cracked open the top half of the barn door. The hot, moist smell of confined animals washed over me like a wave. Inside, horses shuffled in their stalls, the only apparent sign of life, as I called into the dark and dusky interior. Getting no response, I swung open the bottom half of the door, casting an oblique patch of yellow across the floor. As my eyes adjusted to the dark, I thought I could sense, if not outright see, someone currying a horse. I called out a greeting and, receiving no reply, ventured into the barn. Thinking I could hear someone or something up above me, I called out again.

As I stepped forward, a large forkful of hay tumbled onto the floor, sending up a sweet-smelling cloud of dust so thick that for a moment I could not breathe. The horses stomped their feet in their stalls. I thought I could detect the shape of a man standing overhead.

"I came about your stage to Fort Benton," I called out.

Without a word, the man walked over to a ladder, which reached from the floor near my feet into the darkness above, and pulled it into the loft. After stowing the ladder, he turned to go.

"I can afford to pay whatever you want for the trip," I called after him. "Or I could purchase some horses and return them at the end of the summer. You can name your price."

I could hear him moving above me in the loft, closing a door or cabinet, but still he said nothing. A horse whinnied. Without thinking, I reached out and stroked its head, placing my face next to its nose and mouth. The animal's breath was moist and warm against my cheek.

"I bet you'd like to get out for some sun and fresh air, wouldn't you, boy?" I whispered to the beast.

"Don't even think of it," a voice barked from the next stall. "He'd just as soon shoot you as see you walk out of here with one of his horses."

"I wasn't thinking of taking the horse—" I started to explain, but the voice cut me off.

"Don't be wasting your time in here. Jake won't be of any help to you. Too much bad news about Indians."

The person speaking hefted a saddle across one of the stall gates, ducked under a railing, and headed for the livery door.

"I'd offer you my hand, but it's pretty dirty right now," the person said, softer now. "Come out here where we can talk."

I followed the figure, dressed in leather overalls and a hat a couple sizes too big. Once in the sunlight, I realized that she was one of the women from the coach. The one with the child.

"I can help," she informed me in the same clipped fashion she used inside the livery and when I first met her on the coach. "I have a good team of horses. And a wagon. You can hire them both, if you'll hire me, too. And the boy. We leave for Benton in the morning. I could use the company. And the money."

I must admit, I was taken aback by her offer, but the woman was not in the least bit deterred. "It's a good wagon," she argued. "And you can ride comfortable enough in the back. I've got saddles, too, if you prefer to ride. Won't charge you any more than you would have paid old Jake in there, and I can get you to your destination. Said you were headed past Benton, as I recall. Down the Missouri, if I remember right."

When still I did not reply, she added, "Jake won't take you. I can guarantee you that. And if you travel with me, I won't make your father get out and walk."

"Cousin," I informed her, but she ignored me.

"Won't be an easy trip," she said. "Will take us a week even if I push the horses hard. But we can make a little bed for the old man in the back of the wagon if he starts to feel poorly. The name's Hall," she said, as if it were settled. "Mrs. Hall, but you can call me Maggie. In fact I'd prefer it, if you don't mind. It's the only name that sounds like it's mine. I'll pick you up at the hotel in the morning when I'm ready to go."

I returned to the hotel to find Augustus sitting out front with his sketchpad, transfixed by the life of that small mountain town. Having captured the three horsemen on paper that you have as part of your collection, his attention had shifted to a Chinaman, sitting on his haunches, smoking a long-stemmed pipe. As I approached, Augustus quipped something like Montana must be where the dispossessed move when they have no place else to go. When I assumed he had all but forgotten I was standing there watching him work, he added, "Cousin, I'm going to fit in here just fine."

7. Drawing, Gypsy Girl

We traveled all the way to Fort Benton in the back of Maggie's wagon, fighting off icy mornings, hot, dusty afternoons, and the constant swarming of bugs. Her boy, who was christened James but referred to as Jeb, coated his face and hands with grease to protect himself from their bites, but the smell of bacon only served to attract more flies. At times his face was covered with them. Augustus designed his own defense, a sheet of netting he draped over his hat and tied around his neck, giving the impression of a beekeeper or an eccentric old lady on her way to church. I tried to construct a similar covering for myself, but immediately felt stifled, as if I were wrapped in a shroud.

At first I resigned myself to their persistent assault on my face and hands, but one afternoon a fly crawled under my hair and bit me so hard on the nape of the neck that I feared I had been shot. It was then that I took to wearing one of Augustus' silk scarves tied around my head and hair, with the long tail and fringe draping down my back. Augustus, who had been in an unusually ebullient mood since crossing back over the divide, seemed particularly delighted, joking and laughing and referring to me as his Gypsy cousin as he bounced in the back of the wagon along what, in Montana, passed for a road. The charcoal and pencil drawing you have titled "Gypsy Girl" is, I believe, from our travels during that period.

When on the road, Maggie stared straight ahead as if wearing blinders, and had little to say to either one of us, in spite of Augustus' good-natured attempts to engage or entertain her. At midday, when she stopped to rest her passengers and the horses, she still avoided us, cleaning and tightening and checking for the earliest sign of a problem or anyone not doing what needed to be done. She treated her boy with an even-handed fairness that did them both justice, but it was clear from the outset that he, too, was expected to pull his own weight and to contribute in place of the man who had deserted them.

And yet whenever Augustus offered his assistance in making or breaking camp, she told him that if he wanted to help he should stay out of her way. So night after night, as Maggie and Jeb unpacked supplies, laid out the buffalo hides that served as our bedrolls, and tied up tarpaulins to keep out the rain and the early morning dew, Augustus sat under his netting and sketched. After dinner, he recited speeches from *The Taming of the Shrew*, including the parts of Katharina, lines which he would deliver with an affected high-pitched voice, sending Jeb into fits of giggles.

When he exhausted the soliloquies from that play, Augustus promised to tackle Prospero, a part he now felt qualified to perform because he, too, had been cast from a tortuous sea onto an island of great wonders, a foreign country inhabited by magical creatures who knew how to hunt down the bounty of the land and turn powdery flour into the staff of life. What more could a king ask for? he demanded to know, using his most stentorian tone of voice, after downing the last of the skillet bread and wiping crumbs from his chest. He even promised to introduce young Jeb to the character of Caliban, "the original monster from the deep and the foulest-mouthed creature who ever roamed the stage," he informed the wide-eyed youngster, but only if he could convince his mother to take on the role of his sweet Miranda.

"Now, you stop that nonsense and be agreeable," Maggie warned, "or I'll leave you right where you are, with no one but the Indians and the wolves to listen to your tall tales."

"But my dear Mrs. Hall," Augustus countered from beneath

his swath of netting, "I have journeyed west for just that reason. To live amongst the wolves and the Indians and the other wild creatures of the night."

As if on cue, an owl called from the trees down by the creek. It hooted again and flew low overhead, so close that we could hear the whoosh of its wings as it moved through the darkness. Then came the sounds of an animal barking, and then a yipping from beyond the trees, and then a howling from yet another location. They were savage, hungry cries that seemed to surround us, like the stars that encircled us from horizon to horizon. For the first time since leaving Philadelphia, I began to fear I might have been swept into a territory that was not my own.

Maggie put more wood on the fire, sending sparks out in defiance of the night, and instructed Jeb to fetch the horses from down by the creek and picket them next to the wagon.

"Nothing to worry about," she said, looking at me for the first time that evening. "Just a bunch of old coyotes and wolves enamored of the moon. Don't want them to spook our animals, though."

Augustus emerged from beneath his netting and stood before the fire. The flames snapped brightly, and shimmered off the gold embroidered dragons on his robe. He held a lantern in one hand and his book in the other.

"'If thou more murmur'st,'" Augustus bellowed into the dark, "'I will rend an oak, and peg thee in his knotty entrails till thou hast howl'd away twelve winters.'"

Jeb, having returned with the horses, now sat on his knees looking up at the man towering over him. I could sense that he wanted to ask about Caliban and other monsters from the deep, but Augustus' severe demeanor warned against any further sound or speech.

Again the creatures howled and yipped and threatened as if circling our camp. Augustus turned from the fire and held the lantern out before him like a beacon, the light slicing through night. When still the animal cries continued, Augustus raised the lantern, turned his head toward heaven, and howled like a man possessed.

The night was silenced, as Augustus stood his ground.

Maggie, disgusted by this display of apparent madness, stood and retrieved the lantern from Augustus' hand. "We'll have no more of that nonsense," she announced before trailing off to the wagon in a small circle of light.

This comment, like many of Maggie's admonitions, resulted in yet another one of Augustus' new contented chuckles, quite agreeable to all who came in contact with it. Even Maggie was starting to soften in the presence of it, and she was a hard woman to please unless one was willing to stay out of her way and be, as she insisted, agreeable.

8. DRAWING, INDIAN AND BEAR

You should know that the man depicted in this drawing was in
reality a white man who simply preferred to dress that way. He
traveled everywhere with that bear, which was tame, or as tame
as you can assume a wild beast to be. The white man called himself Little Bear, a name he said had been bestowed on him by the
Cheyenne, but Augustus insisted that the man's real name was
Harry or Ed, and threatened to change his own name to White
Man Who Runs Walking.

When we first met Little Bear, Augustus accused him of talking nothing but nonsense, but I think his real irritation with the
would-be Indian came later, when Little Bear refused to sit for a
portrait, claiming that a medicine man once warned him that the
process of capturing his likeness on paper or canvas would somehow capture his soul. That other Indians regularly sat for Augustus, and for photographers who visited their camp, did not in any
way alleviate Little Bear's fears. In many ways, it seemed to make
him even more anxious.

With one exception, the drawings and one small watercolor
Augustus hastily made of Little Bear during that summer never
seemed to capture the man's soul at all. As I remember him, Little Bear was much better natured and interesting-looking, if not
outright handsome, than Augustus ever cared to represent him.
He braided his hair Indian fashion, which he said represented the
weaving together of his mind, body, and spirit. And, like I said,
he affected Indian dress, preferring fringed leggings and beaded
leather shirts and feathered headgear, a costume which had the
potential to lead to some confusion and, in our case, quickly did.

When we first encountered the two of them in Fort Benton, the bear paced up and down the boardwalk outside the hotel, grunting and begging for food, while Little Bear attempted to sell Indian moccasins and beadwork to passersby. Both the bear and the man approached as our wagon pulled into town but Maggie shooed them away with her hat.

The bear, it turned out, was easier to intimidate than his master, who entered the spacious hotel lobby and waited while we arranged for rooms and inquired after messages from Yale College. The clerk did not, contrary to the Captain's assurances, have any directions or instructions for us. In fact, the hotelier claimed to have never heard of me, Augustus, or our scheduled arrival. Nor did he know of anyone who referred to himself as the Captain, although when pressed, the man did admit that he had heard stories of an encampment on the Missouri, out past the trading post east of town.

"They don't want visitors, though. It's a closed camp from the sounds of it, with no one allowed anywhere near the place. I'm not sure what's going on out there, but Little Bear can probably tell you more about that than I can," the clerk said. "That's his part of the territory, not mine."

The Captain's camp was a full two days' ride to the east, but in spite of my insistence that we leave Fort Benton immediately, it took us three days to get ready to go. First, we had to bargain for Little Bear's services, and then he needed to make suitable arrangements with Maggie to care for his bear, since Augustus flatly refused to allow the animal to travel with us when we left town. He wanted to be taken seriously when we entered the Captain's encampment, he said, and not be mistaken for some traveling curiosity. Then, for the same reason, Augustus insisted on the purchase of proper field clothes for me, explaining that men in those conditions might not know what to do with a woman in their midst. I needed to look and act like a lady when we arrived, he informed me, although he was perfectly content with his own exotic traveling costume and any first impression that he might make.

And we did, I must tell you, make an impression. After hiring Maggie's son to accompany us and help us establish a small camp of our own, we followed Little Bear along the river and then down a narrow canyon, until we climbed back onto a high plateau. Only the cook and teamster were in camp when we arrived. Seeing Little Bear dressed in full Indian regalia, they started shouting to one another as if they were under attack. Little Bear, having encountered these sorts of welcomes before, pulled his horse off to one side.

"They'll be easier on women," he said in his flat, monosyllabic way.

Augustus spurred his horse into the lead, his duster waving wildly around him and his mount. Never having been on a horse before, I held on and did the best that I could to keep up from behind. In their initial flurry, the two camp attendants had pulled out rifles and upended a table to prepare themselves for the assault. They crouched behind it, revealing only the tops of their hats. A large black dog trotted out to greet us, barking and wagging its tail. One of the men started hollering at it, too, and then the second man reappeared from behind the table. He pointed his gun in our direction.

"Oh, for heaven's sake," Augustus shouted back at them. "Unless you plan on shooting the dog, put those guns down."

Augustus dismounted, gave the dog a perfunctory pat, and then stopped to dramatically dust himself off. "It's filthy out here," he announced.

The men stood with guns in the ready, holding their position behind the table. The first man looked like he had never eaten a healthful meal in his life. Even his head was undersized, leaving his hat to balance upon his ears. The other man appeared to be overenamored of food and drink, resulting in flushed cheeks, arms the size of hams, and short and stubby hands.

"We're looking for a gentleman by the name of Patrick Lear," Augustus informed them. "You don't happen to know him, do you?"

The two men stared first at Augustus and then at the others in his party, confused as to which of us was the most disconcerting: the woman, the boy, the would-be Indian, or the man dressed in flapping blue linen and a wide-brimmed hat. When still they did not respond, Augustus left his horse pulling at a solitary tuft of grass and walked up to the table. Eyeing the coffee simmering by the edge of the fire, he breezed past them and picked up the pot, using the edge of his duster to shield his hand from the heat.

"How about a cup of coffee?" He held the simmering pot in their direction, as if offering a toast.

"I don't know about this," the first man said. He took the pot away from Augustus. "You'll have to talk to the doctor and he won't be back until dark. Meantime, I'm not sure what to tell you." He seemed more confused than outright unfriendly.

"Well, my good man, you could tell us where to find cups. Then you might inform us of the location of your privy, if you have bothered to establish such a thing. Finally, it might be useful to know where our assistants should pitch our tent and establish the rest of our meager camp before it gets dark, as it no doubt will. All of that would be most helpful." Again, Augustus smiled in their direction.

At this the second man spoke up.

"This here is a closed camp. I'm not sure what you want or where you're headed, but you can't stay here. No one can."

"Dr. Lear should be expecting us," I explained, joining the men at the upturned table. "We're here at the Captain's request. We, too, are in his employ," I added, as if that might be enough to change the men's minds.

The two men looked at one another, preparing I'm quite certain to expel us forcibly if need be, but just then the dog barked again and went scurrying off to greet another visitor walking toward camp, a red blanket folded like a flag across one arm.

"You must be the party Patrick told me about," the man called out as he reached the camp clearing. "James Huntington," he said, offering his free hand to Augustus. "Good to see you," he said, offering his hand next to me.

Noting the overturned table, Mr. Huntington hesitated only for a moment before setting it right and placing the folded blanket upon one end. The first man, who I would later learn was the camp cook, pushed the blanket onto the ground, muttering something about nits.

"Bill," Mr. Huntington said, retrieving the blanket and dusting it off. "You've made coffee for our guests. Good man. I could use a cup myself."

Mr. Huntington was, by his own definition, a hunter and gatherer, an explorer who traveled the world collecting stories, artifacts, and experiences that he claimed brought meaning and order to his life. Having seen an envoy of Indian chiefs en route to Washington, he had spent the last two years traveling through the West, uncovering histories and cultures more exotic than he had ever witnessed abroad. Indians, surprised to meet a white man who was both generous and interested in the stories of their tribes, welcomed him into their camps and onto their reservations.

He was amused, therefore, when he learned that the cook and teamster had assumed Little Bear was an Indian. Yes, Little Bear's skin was brown from the sun and he wore his hair in braids, but those leggings, Mr. Huntington exclaimed, pointing to Little Bear, who was unpacking the wagon with Jeb, were of Blackfoot origin. His shoes were clearly from the Cheyenne and the cloth shirt was from the Crow or possibly the Sioux. Our patchwork Indian, was how Mr. Huntington referred to Little Bear, without the slightest hint of condescension. Augustus took to the man at once.

9. LANDSCAPE, RIVER WITH THREE ENCAMPMENTS

Meriwether Lewis described that stretch of the Missouri River where we first camped that summer as an endless scene of visionary enchantment, with multi-colored sandstone walls carved by wind and river and rain into strange and fanciful shapes, pelicans and geese soaring overhead, and grizzly bears roaming along the steep ravines. Had Captain Lewis taken the time to venture inland, however, his reports might have been more in sympathy with how fellow explorer, Sergeant Gass, described the scene. According to this explorer, the land was barren and desolate, without encouraging prospects. This is most certainly how it appeared to me.

To my untrained eye, both the Missouri and the land through which it coursed were indeed bleak. Unlike the fresh-flowing mountain river that carved away canyons outside of Helena, the water here was gray, flat, and turbid, and the landscape was devoid of any discernible sign of life except for occasional patches of cottonwood, scrubby pine trees, yellow-blooming cactus, and bursts of grass. The cottonwoods and pine trees provided little in the way of shelter or fuel, although the birds seemed to enjoy them, and the cactus, in spite of its unexpected beauty when in flower, made travel as difficult and sometimes as dangerous as the snakes which slithered out to warm themselves in the heat of the day.

"River with Three Encampments" must have been completed not too long after we arrived, since at that time a Crow Indian hunting camp was situated just to the north and west of us. In the painting, you can see the hundred or so Indian lodges across the river, along with Patrick Lear's campsite with its three wall tents, two wagons, and about a dozen horses picketed next to a stand of cottonwood trees. Our lone tent was pitched off to one side, next to two paltry chokecherry bushes. Augustus even added the large boulder he used as a backrest and the simple wooden table and chair that served as my workspace that summer.

As you have noted, this particular landscape was painted in short, bright lines of color, uncharacteristic of Augustus' previous work, as if he had awakened overnight to a new vision of the world. When I asked him why he had chosen to paint our camp-site in such quick, bright brushstrokes, he explained that too much attention to detail would obscure the true nature of the subject. Or worse, capture it permanently, artificially setting it in stone.

What Augustus' landscape with all its sunshine and light has failed to depict, however, was how ill-equipped the Captain's camp was for the conduct of science or art, much less for the basic necessities of living. There were no facilities for bathing or other forms of basic hygiene, no privacy of which to speak, and certainly no accommodations for a woman traveling on her own. The field crew went about their personal business as if I did not exist, and even Patrick Lear was unable or unwilling to acknowl-edge my sex.

When I pictured my promised employment with the museum at Yale College, I was naïve enough in spite of my years to envi-sion it as something like the best of the times I spent in Philadel-phia. As the man in black had suggested, I had been nothing more than a hired hand while at the Academy. Still, I had an op-portunity to learn from educated men, men outside of the arts who regularly reviewed and critiqued my work. Like the Captain, these men were gentlemen from families of wealth if not prestige. They treated me with a courtesy befitting their rank, and were grateful in an offhanded way for what I did, since I was helping them document and bring to life their discoveries before they were put on public display. And even though I often worked in the back of poorly ventilated rooms, I was never too far removed from the excitement of their discoveries. Shipments of bones and other fossils arrived regularly from the field, and men would talk into the night, smoking, sipping whiskey and tea, and discussing where the new finds might fit into a von Baerian view of the world. In the morning, they would often still be sitting there, arguing about Darwin, Lamarckian inheritance, and God, rewriting science and history as they talked.

While I was never much concerned with the minutiae of their discussions, I had great hopes that by being witness to them I might better understand how the bones of a creature could form the framework for an animal's survival, and that by capturing the basic architecture of these beasts I, too, might in some small way contribute to a new history of the world. I was even hopeful, in a way that I would never have admitted at the time, that once at Yale College my contributions might be recognized and the overall conditions of my employment might improve.

As Augustus would tell me later that summer, I had much to learn while in Montana.

10. Study, Man Inhabiting Two Worlds

Patrick Lear and the three students from Yale College returned to camp just before sunset and, after handing their horses over to the teamster, the beleaguered students wandered down to the river for a bath. Looking around his campsite at the unfamiliar faces eager to greet him, Dr. Lear turned without a word toward the safety of his tent.

The leader of the Captain's expedition was an imposing figure, a man with a refined intelligence, who clearly was used to being in command. Unlike Mr. Huntington, who was casual with his status and comfortable with his body and clothes, Dr. Lear dressed with excessive care, in almost military fashion. Even his field clothes were immaculately cleaned and pressed. He stood almost six feet tall with dark wavy hair turning to gray, and his clean-shaven face was pockmarked and weathered, marred on one cheek by a scar from his ear to his chin. I would later learn that this wound was not suffered during the war but received later in a barroom brawl. Whatever was used to do the cutting, be it bayonet, knife, or broken bottle, the attack must have been severe because whenever Dr. Lear was nervous or thoughtful, he would chew on the inside of his cheek where the flesh must have been cut all the way through. This nervous habit had the strange effect of making one side of his face appear to collapse almost to his skull, resulting in two very different-looking men depending on which side you happened to be viewing.

"I'm here to introduce my cousin, Eleanor Peterson," Augustus announced, stepping forward to intercept the man before he could retreat. "I want to be certain that she is expected."

"Yes," the man said, standing as stiff and unresponsive as the words he spoke. "I have been advised of her arrival."

"Excellent," Augustus replied. "What good fortune, Cousin. We have indeed stumbled upon the right encampment."

Ever since we had entered what appeared to be a hostile out-post, Augustus had been unusually jocular, trying to charm his way past any resistance to our presence there. He smiled and joked with the cook, ducked his head and laughed at his own in-competence when one of the horses tried to nuzzle his ear, and generally cast himself as the harmless old fool.

"Then I'm certain," Augustus continued, "you can keep my cousin gainfully employed, because I must warn you she is a bun-dle of nerves if she cannot keep her hands busy."

"I have been given explicit instructions from the Captain as to the lady's role," Patrick Lear replied, not at all won over by Augustus' ingratiating manners. "I, in turn, feel it is my duty to inform you both that there is little or nothing to document. I am, however, prepared to follow the Captain's orders as they have been presented to me. Now you must excuse me."

Without another word, Patrick Lear retreated to his white wall tent, leaving us in the company of Mr. Huntington and the three students, who wandered back into camp, their damp shirts clinging to their arms and chests grown lean and muscu-lar from the rigors of the field. Only the oldest of the three had any beard to speak of on his chin, which he stroked from time to time as if surprised that such a straggly shrub had taken root there.

While Little Bear and Jeb pitched the tent that Augustus and I would share, and the cook handed out bowls of bacon and beans and chunks of bread, Augustus sketched and chatted, at-tempting to learn more about Dr. Lear and the true nature of the Captain's work. I could sense that even though he did not think anything was amiss, he wasn't entirely convinced that everything was as it should be.

"Been working out here long?" Augustus asked.

One student, the youngest of the three, looked to the oldest, who we would later learn was the younger man's brother.

"Not long," the older student replied.

"Where exactly are you working?" Augustus tried again.

"Right now we're out past that bluff." The student indicated the vast landscape stretching beyond the river.

Still Augustus wasn't satisfied. "Is it far?" he pressed.

"Yes, it's a ways," the younger student offered. "We just walk along with our noses to the ground, some of us keeping an eye on the streambeds and ravines, while someone else scans the upper reaches of the canyons. We stop when we think we've found something washed loose from above, and then we climb up the cliffs to see what's up there. Before we left home, I'd heard of entire mountains composed of fossils, but I sure haven't seen any. It's not all that interesting. Not what we were led to believe, anyway."

At this, James Huntington interjected. "Not interesting?" he exclaimed. "How can you say that?"

Mr. Huntington had a way of focusing on an individual to the exclusion of all others present, as if he and the one to whom he was speaking were the only two living beings on earth. He turned this full-bodied attention on Augustus.

"What Patrick is working on here is the exact geological boundary between prehistoric sea-bound creatures, those large saurians of the past, and land-based animals which would eventually evolve into the mammals we know today. There are scientists like Professor Agassiz who say that the exploration of the natural world should be pursued to reveal God's grand intent and they dismiss Darwin's theory as some sort of atheistic plot. But the Captain has already discovered birds with teeth and the remains of the original five-toed horse. Patrick could discover even more of those, like the archaeopteryx, that appear to be pieces of the missing links."

Mr. Huntington stood up, excited by the very idea of such a discovery, and then looked embarrassed by his own enthusiasm.

Augustus raised his eyebrows as if silently wondering who had let James Huntington out of his cage. One of the students laughed out loud but in his reverie Mr. Huntington did not appear to notice.

"With all due respect, James, we are asked to risk our necks to uncover a handful of teeth and fragments of bone of questionable origin," the older student responded, "while men of science sit in comfort arguing about the physical basis of life. Even you must realize that such arguments, if we become too closely aligned with them, only serve to alienate us from our families and our peers."

James Huntington shrugged, as if the student's voice were nothing more than a distraction. Or perhaps it was his way of signaling to the young man that the personal must be kept separate from both the particular and the abstract.

It was then that the third student, a young man with reddish hair and a promise of a beard, interjected. "Mr. Darwin has said it is the individual, not the species, that should define our understanding of life on earth." The young man mouthed the words carefully, as if venturing into unknown territory. But whatever reservations he might have had, he continued to press forward with earnestness. "My own hope for this summer is that I might uncover one more individual that will contribute to the debate."

"Now, that is what I would call a real act of faith," the older student scoffed. "The only thing we're going to uncover out here is another dead buffalo. Or maybe a few dead Indians."

Mr. Huntington did not appear to be listening to either one of the young men, for he continued to focus on Augustus.

"When I read some of the works coming out of England, I am the first to admit that I lose my bearings," he said. "It's as if Mr. Darwin has pulled the very earth out from under my feet. And now Mr. Huxley has announced that when he looks at a dinosaur he sees nothing more than an oversized bird, with a large bird-like heart and lungs. The entire notion creates a sense of discomfort that at times I cannot overcome."

The redheaded student was not deterred by the general lack of recognition of him or his ideas. He pressed forward much the same way Mr. Huntington had.

"That's not entirely true," the student corrected. "Professor Huxley has declared that birds and reptiles share a common ancestry, although that doesn't help explain why some of them disappeared."

"Ever hear of the flood, Jack?" the older student asked.

"To be honest, I choose to ignore all of that," Mr. Huntington said. "I much prefer to focus on the discovery and collection of the particular and let others worry about the logical consequences of what has been unearthed. Mr. Darwin himself has admitted the fossil record is weak, and besides, I would much rather climb cliffs, or trail along with my nose to the ground, as this young man has so aptly described it, than be isolated in some back room, limited to the life of the mind."

Throughout the discussion, Augustus had kept his own counsel, his attention directed to his sketchpad as he worked on the study of Mr. Huntington you have listed here. But with this last announcement, Augustus looked up at the man pacing before him. He studied him intently, albeit briefly, before turning to me.

"My dear cousin," Augustus said, "it would appear that you are in for a disappointment. There may not be much in the way of science being conducted here, after all. Art, perhaps," he added, indicating his sketchpad, "but not science."

"I suppose I should explain," Mr. Huntington countered. "I'm the first to admit I'm no scientist. Nothing more than a failed scholar, if you must know the truth, because I'm interested in too many aspects of the world's mysteries to accomplish any one thing well. I've only been granted permission to visit the camp because I have the good fortune to be building a house nearby and I'm one of Patrick's oldest friends. But you must know this is a very fossiliferous region with great potential," he added. "Professor Hayden discovered the nation's first dinosaur teeth along this very stretch of river, and where there are teeth, there are bound to be more formidable remains."

"Well, if there are, we sure aren't finding them," the older student replied. "I think the truth is we've all been sent out here to keep us out of the way." Now he, too, stood, looking bored by the general tenor of the conversation. Still Mr. Huntington ignored him.

"I don't have to keep to the strict prospecting schedule that is imposed on Patrick and the boys, so I'd be happy to show you around if you like," Mr. Huntington continued. "Tomorrow morning, if you're ready for more travel. We could saddle the horses, although I prefer to make my way on foot. There are some beautiful geologic formations and loose rock along the way. Whenever I'm out there, I always discover something new, and I hate to miss any of it because I'm sitting on the back of a horse."

"I can assure you that I, too, would prefer to walk," Augustus replied. "I have seen enough of the back of a horse to last a lifetime. How about you, my dear cousin? Are you interested in searching this otherworldly landscape for crocodile-like monsters from the deep?"

I'm the first to admit that walking through sagebrush and cactus, under a scorching western sun, in a dusty and persistent wind, was the last activity on earth I would have chosen. Still, I said I would be willing unless there was other work to be done. At Mr. Huntington's questioning look I explained that I was there to be of assistance to Dr. Lear. "To document the bones he is uncovering," I added. "Assuming, that is, he has found any bones."

"Oh, ma'am, there are bones everywhere, if *that's* why you're here," the younger student blurted. "I've never seen so many bones."

"Not those bones, stupid," his brother countered.

Before we could continue, Dr. Lear reemerged from his tent. "Peterson is going to be much too busy to be doing any sightseeing as of yet," he informed his friend, using the abrupt, sexless name he always employed when referring to me. "Our so-called Captain expects documentation of everything we discover and has sent me an illustrator to do the work. So it's my job to be sure that she does as she's been instructed. I suggest, therefore," he continued, now directing his attention to me, "that you get to work on this first thing in the morning. He wants to see what we're uncovering here, so he should be informed about these." He handed me a box filled with bones.

James Huntington shrugged. "Perhaps I can take Mr. Starwood out in the meantime. That is, if you are still interested."

"I'm interested in everything," Augustus answered Mr. Huntington, but he was smiling at Dr. Lear.

"Good," was Mr. Huntington's quick reply. "You might also enjoy meeting some Indians while you're here as well. There's a hunting camp nearby. We can try to do both in the next day or two, assuming the weather holds."

With that announcement, both men retired, Mr. Huntington with a bedroll that he carried down to the river and Dr. Lear to his tent. Augustus and I retreated to our own small cavalry tent where two cots with buffalo hide blankets had been placed, separated by a campstool and a lantern. Augustus trimmed the wick and lit it, sending soft shadows flickering around the walls. He then covered his birds, which were already dozing in their cage.

"Well," Augustus sighed, swatting at a moth which circled the light, "since this is going to be our home for a while, my dear cousin, I suggest we enlist your friend Little Bear to procure some canvas for the floor. And a blanket to hang between our cots so that we might enjoy the illusion of privacy, if not the thing itself. I must warn you that I have been known to snore and make other strange noises in the night. Are you sure you can survive living in these conditions, and being forced into such close proximity to an old man?"

"Only if you can tolerate such close proximity to an old woman," I replied.

"Yes, I suppose old is a matter of opinion," he said. "What's in the box? Bits of monsters from the deep?"

I handed him a piece of bone, which was porous and light, unlike their fossilized relations. It had a form similar to a cervical or dorsal vertebra from a cow but it was more likely a buffalo since we'd seen them scattered all along the wagon road from Fort Benton. I placed several odd-shaped bones and bits of bone on my cot and pointed out a deep indentation along the backside of what had once been a mandible.

"Looks like someone has used a rock or other blunt instrument to break apart the skull," I said, "although you can see how it once went together." I held three pieces together to demonstrate what had once been a single piece.

Augustus fingered the smooth, sun-bleached bone. "My dear, this Lear fellow must be a fool to give you skeletons of living animals to document," he said.

"I think he knows exactly what he's doing," I replied, and then told him what the man at the station in Utah said about this being a war.

"If this is war, my darling, whose side are you on?"

"I'm not taking sides," I informed him. "We are working for the same man and our goals are one and the same. But Augustus, please don't push Patrick Lear too hard. I don't know exactly what he expects of me, or why he thinks I am here, but I need this opportunity and I don't want to give him any reason to send me back. These are not good times, and it's getting more and more difficult for me to make my own way."

"I'd be careful if I were you, Eleanor. This is not Philadelphia. If you want my opinion, I think that Captain friend of yours has sent you out here to make sure his troops don't desert."

"Perhaps," I replied. "But as far as I'm concerned, he sent me out here so that I might secure employment at Yale."

11. Drawing (Peterson), Dinosaur in the Grass

After our initial confrontation, Patrick Lear appeared to accept my presence as he did the others in his party. Like the young men who were supporting their own participation in this western adventure, as one student referred to it, I was expected to work hard without complaint and do as I was told. So while Augustus spent the first couple of days in the company of James Huntington, returning to camp late in the afternoon, the pockets of his duster stuffed with tiny prehistoric shells, bits of broken fossils, and even some prehistoric teeth, I established a work area where Dr. Lear deposited his own discoveries. These were buffalo bones mostly, and some smaller vertebrae, probably from deer, but the one I remember in particular being asked to document—in all seriousness I must add, because the man was always very serious when he would present me with his discoveries—was that of a bird, most likely a goose, since there were hundreds of them along the river. Dr. Lear delivered the skeleton with an intact skullcap but no beak or jaw, and deposited the remains in a jumble on my worktable without comment.

All that following morning, I assembled and reassembled the pieces, trying to figure out the bird's basic form. By the afternoon I was able to sketch the pieces in place as if it were assembled and fully articulated. To a second drawing, I added muscular structure and then, over that, stretched a lizard-like skin. The bird's wing bones were used to signify arms held close to the body and I did the best that I could to add a jaw and a believable toothy mouth. To the background I added a suggestion of grass through which my imaginary beast walked as it lunched on the leaves of a nearby tree. With its small head, long neck, round, fat body, and feet hidden in imaginary grass, it could have been a terrestrial version of an early plesiosaur, which was described as having the head of a lizard, the teeth of a crocodile, the neck of a serpent, the ribs of a chameleon, and the paddles of a whale. It certainly looked to my eyes as realistic if not more so than the casts and other reconstructions of Benjamin Waterhouse Hawkins, whose early work in London had a peculiar mammalian look, as if they were nothing more than a herd of scaly rhinos roaming the grounds of the Crystal Palace prior to the great flood.

I tore the drawing of the bird-like beast, or beast-like bird, from the Captain's master journal (page 6, as you've noted), and attached it to the wall behind Augustus' cot. Only then did I commence a series of more exact illustrations of the bones as I had been instructed.

As I recall these events for your records, I can't help but question why I would subject myself to such a pointless endeavor, documenting the individual bones of local animals as if they were extinct. But in my own defense, I was there at the invitation of a man I knew little if anything about and I assumed knew little if anything about me. In many ways, I felt the need to prove myself to both Patrick Lear and to the Captain, and maybe even a bit to myself. And there was something familiar, if not enlightening, about the representation of bones that, even though in the miniature, seemed to fall somewhere between the ancient creatures of the earth and those which roamed the land today. It was like an escape, a dream world where I could lose myself for hours in a well-mapped territory and ignore the small slights and the hardships of living in the field. Besides, as Augustus was fond of pointing out to me, bones are bones. Illustrating a vertebra from the Dinosauria was not all that different than documenting one from an abundant species of bird. If Professor Huxley was to be believed, it could very well be one and the same.

In any event, I spent that first week in camp documenting the bones of extant mammals and birds and did my best to suppress my frustration, be agreeable, and stay out of Dr. Lear's way. Augustus, once he tired of prehistoric beachcombing, as he referred to it, was filling his days with real adventure.

12. SELF-PORTRAIT, A. STARWOOD WITH AMMONITE NECKLACE

As I noted, a Crow Indian hunting camp had been established across the river from ours. The fact that there were a hundred or so lodges, with two or three times as many armed Indians living in close proximity, was perhaps why the cook and teamster had been nervous the afternoon we first arrived. Both men claimed to have seen the worst possible behaviors from Indians, and they did not trust a one of them, even those who, like the Crow, were allied with our military. We would be better off, they advised, if all of us, particularly Mr. Huntington, kept our distance.

The two men's concerns had no effect on Augustus, who could not even imagine a world in which he would travel all the way to Montana and not see Indians. After he had had his fill of geological rambles, he started visiting the Crow encampment where Mr. Huntington, ever the collector, was purchasing religious and other artifacts and interviewing older Indians about their beliefs, convinced that native language and culture would be the first and most lasting casualties of the Indian wars.

At first Augustus trailed along with his sketchpad but eventually he set up an easel to paint, and produced several portraits not listed as part of the donated collection. I can only hope that you eventually have the good fortune to secure at least one of these paintings since the subject matter is of historical and ethnological interest and, for Augustus, marked a dramatic transition of sorts. For the first time, as you observed in the landscape you asked about, Augustus started to lighten his palette and rediscover the natural world. He even viewed himself and his role as an artist differently, as if he were on a mission to capture a people and a place at that specific moment in time.

Freed from the confines of his rooms in Philadelphia, Augustus worked outside in a wind so strong and unpredictable that it would lift his canvas as if it were a sail. He designed a system to secure the canvas to the easel, but then he had to battle the grit and dust, which swirled around him and fouled his paints. But unlike even the smallest of complaints from his Philadelphia subjects, which would send Augustus into fits of despair, even chasing his canvas and easel as they flew toward the river could not distract him from this renewed interest in his work.

For the first time in his portraits, the scenery was transformed from an ill-defined landscape, a mere backdrop against which the figure was placed, into an integral part of the world Augustus was trying to capture in paint. In all of the portraits he completed while in Montana, it was as if the subject and the background could not exist without the other, and both in his hands took on a life of their own.

You can see this for yourself in the painting you have labeled "A. Starwood with Ammonite Necklace." Or "Mr. Two Feathers," as Augustus called it, referring to the eagle feathers in his hat. I can still picture the way Augustus sits front and center in that portrait, staring directly at the viewer of the work just as the viewer is staring at him. The bright red and gold of his Chinese robe have been toned down with the darker palette he preferred in Philadelphia, but the ammonite necklace, with its porcupine quills, blue beads, and prehistoric seashell coated with what Augustus called sacred red dirt, appears to come to life as if it were indeed the powerful talisman Augustus claimed it to be. The horizon on this painting is also sunnier and more inviting, with less of the atmospheric mist characteristic of his earlier work. But it's important to note, too, that the air was remarkably dry in the West, especially when compared to the heavy weather of the East. It seemed like we could see forever that summer in Montana.

Two Feathers was also the name the Indians used to refer to Augustus. Seeing such a tall man with long white hair, dressed in a sweeping blue duster or long red robes embroidered with golden dragons, and sporting two eagle feathers in his hat, must have made the Indians assume he was an elder of great power. Augustus later lost both feathers in one of the summer's many winds, a loss which seemed to genuinely upset him. When he found another feather to replace the two, I started referring to him as Mr. One Feather, a name that did not sit well with him. Augustus had the strangest notions about all sorts of things, including what he considered his personal powers.

During those early days in camp, Augustus and James Huntington formed an interesting alliance, as if they were collectors and explorers from the same private club, traveling together to a remote civilization, which in many ways I suppose that temporary Indian encampment was for them both. It represented a way of life that would end for all Indians, hostile and nonhostile alike, after that summer. Mr. Huntington was right in that regard.

The two men would set forth in the mornings, fording the river where it took a wide, shallow bend, and spend most of the day and sometimes the early hours of the evening with the Indians. While Mr. Huntington interviewed both the men and women in English and Crow, Augustus sketched members of the tribe at work and at play. While in Philadelphia, Augustus had despised children, claiming they made too much noise and carried filth and disease, but he was fascinated by their Indian counterparts, many of whom he would sketch for hours on end and present with their likenesses. The boys were wild and undisciplined, tearing through their camp, counting imaginary coup on Augustus, and shooting at rabbits and birds, preparing to be the hunters and young braves they would one day become. To Augustus these boys were an integral part of nature, as he said he had once been in his youth.

He was also transfixed by the women, who, Augustus insisted, had a strength and demeanor unique to the female of the species, and could do the work of any ten white men he knew. When they weren't insulting their husbands, comparing them to creatures and acts not known in the natural world, they were cooking, cleaning, stringing seashells and elk teeth which were of great currency in the tribe, and decorating the red collars and housings for their horses' heads and tails. Those women and children were busy as bees, not crows, Augustus commented one evening.

"Technically," Mr. Huntington explained to Augustus as they returned to camp, "the word Absaalooke, Absarokah, or Apsarrookai, depending upon whom you ask, means children of the large-beaked bird. Or even more obscure, anything that flies. I'm not sure who first decided that Absaalooke signified the word for crow, but if you look around this landscape, even though there are swarms of crows, the dominant large-beaked bird is the raven, a much wiser and more dignified bird in my opinion."

"Crows, ravens, rooks?" Augustus wanted to know. "I thought they were all the same. They all have big beaks if you ask me."

"I believe they are all assigned to the same scientific family, but the crow is smaller and, thus, technically of a different species. I think even magpies and those little scrub jays you see around here from time to time belong to the same family."

Here Mr. Huntington hesitated and removed his hat. He combed his hand through his long yellow hair as if trying to remember something he had once read.

"I could show you, if you care to visit my library sometime," he continued. "Or maybe on my next visit to camp I'll bring a book or two along. I always travel with a circulating library. Or, I guess I should say, I circulate and carry a library with me. I fear I'm a bit like Sisyphus in that regard."

As they talked, the cook deposited without comment two plates of stew and cups of coffee on a log near the fire, a good distance from the camp table. Mr. Huntington walked over to claim one and Augustus joined him, the two men continuing their conversation sitting side by side on the log. Since arriving in camp, Augustus had taken to eating only enough to keep himself alive, since he did not think much of camp cooking. Mr. Huntington, who was not a large man, shoveled two or three bowls of the deer meat, potatoes and onions into his mouth before he was through. I've never seen a man eat so much, or with such obvious enjoyment, as Mr. Huntington did that summer.

"Most tribes, remember, have stories about ravens," Mr. Huntington continued between mouthfuls of stew and gulps of coffee. "They rank right up there with coyotes as tricksters, for example, while other cultures consider ravens the creators of life."

When Mr. Huntington finished his third helping, and Augustus had eaten two or three bites, the two placed their plates on the table and walked over to our little encampment next to the chokecherries, to continue their discussion. When they abandoned the area near the fire, the cook washed and then dramatically rewashed the log where they had been sitting and only then was I invited to eat with him and the teamster, since Dr. Lear and the crew were still not back from the field. I accepted the offered food but did not join them, as I had grown interested in Mr. Huntington's stories, which had moved from birds and his documentation of Indian languages and myths to a collecting trip Mr. Huntington had made to Northern Africa.

"I walked for miles as if in a dream," he was saying when I joined the two men next to our small fire. "It seemed as though everywhere you stepped golden goblets and strange animal figurines were being uncovered by the shifting sand. I encountered so many artifacts on just that one trip that I would have lost my mind or even my life trying to decide how much of these riches I should bring back with me to civilization, assuming we think of our homeland as civilized. Best to keep on walking, I decided. But it was, without a doubt, one of the most amazing places I have ever been. Nothing but wind and sand and golden remembrances of the past."

"Sort of like this place?" Augustus asked, and for once I believe he wasn't joking.

Mr. Huntington certainly took him seriously. He stopped to consider the question. It was impossible not to admire the man, so intense and yet so gracious was his behavior toward us all.

"Yes, I suppose it was," Mr. Huntington said at last. "I loved that sense of discovery in much the same way. It's like piecing together an enormous puzzle, with each individual artifact adding to our overall understanding of the world."

Now it was Augustus who needed a few moments to reflect. He stood to put another log on the fire and poked at the flames with a stick.

"You describe the world as an artist might, Huntington. I like that about you. But instead of bones or figurines, I apply layers of paint to construct my pictures."

"Exactly!" James Huntington exclaimed. "Art and science are not at odds, Starwood, but are one and the same. In defense of my own eccentricities, the more pieces you are able to collect, the more true to life the final picture becomes."

Mr. Huntington's entire demeanor radiated an intense pleasure at the thought of such a collection. He laughed out loud.

"You must forgive me," he said. "These are my passions. I did not mean to impose them on you."

And with that announcement, he stood and took his leave.

13. PORTRAIT, BOY IN FELT HAT

The young boy in the portrait you have described is Maggie's son, Jeb. At the end of our third week, he and Little Bear rode back into camp with a wagon equipped with a primitive cage, the bear peering from between its wooden railings. Maggie, hopeful that the boy might secure some work running errands back and forth to town, had sent him to Patrick Lear's camp with the mail that had been accumulating at the post office for Dr. Lear and the students. There was also a letter from the Captain requesting my notes, and supplies that Augustus had ordered at the Fort Benton store. Dr. Lear had no interest in seeing either one of them, so he gave Jeb a dollar and was about to send him on his way, when I asked if the boy could stay long enough for me to copy my notes and documentation, and send them on to the Captain.

Dr. Lear looked as if he did not understand.

"He's asked after them," I explained.

"Asked after what?" he demanded to know.

"My documentation. The bones you've given to me to illustrate."

Dr. Lear sucked on the inside of his cheek and looked out past the river.

"It's getting late," he said at last. "I don't want that boy, that so-called Indian, or that bear anywhere near here after dark. This is a closed camp. And those orders come direct from the Captain himself."

Again he chewed on the inside of his cheek, his jawbone moving back and forth underneath his skin. "You've got one hour, Peterson," he said, "and then I want them both out of here."

Jeb smiled sheepishly as if we were fellow conspirators. Little Bear, on the other hand, ignored the man's directive and proceeded to dump a bag of colorful beads, mirrors, combs, and other toiletries, and a large ceramic jug containing some near-lethal form of alcohol, into a satchel. Stripping down to nothing more than a breechcloth, moccasins, and a few feathers in his hair, he walked off to ford the river, followed by his bear, which stopped to roll around in the water like a dog while Little Bear clambered up the embankment on the opposite shore.

In my letter to the Captain, I explained that since my arrival I had been given three boxes of bones, all of which I had recorded in his journal. Other than a few prehistoric seashells, some broken bits of fossilized remains, and two teeth found by my cousin, most of the bones recovered by Dr. Lear appeared to be of a more recent origin. In response to his query, I assured him that I had seen a map of the region, which Dr. Lear had gridded and was documenting as he explored. If there were fossils to be found, I was confident his field crew would find them.

As I finished my note, Dr. Lear appeared again at my worktable and deposited five fossilized bone fragments, a handful of teeth of indeterminate origin, and what appeared to be a fossilized piece of wood. He also presented me with three leaf impressions in stone.

"While you're at it, you should probably tell him about these," he said. He muttered something about the Captain, and then retreated to his own camp, trailed by his dog.

One fossil, the largest of the group, was about the size of my hand, but weighed more than a pound. On one side, it had the golden umber color with flecks of purple characteristic of fossilized bone, but opposite it had the grainy texture of wood. The others had a similar speckled golden coloration, but the porous quality signifying bone. Two of the pieces fit neatly together with a smoothly worn break, which could not have been of recent origin. From the shape and curve of it, I assumed the two pieces to be cross sections of a tibia or other long bone, but I couldn't be sure. The others were small bits of bone, one the size of my palm but broken into a wedge, and the other the size of a small rock, again of indeterminate origin.

Rather than rewrite my letter and delay Jeb even further, I noted at the end that the only exceptions to what I had written were the bone fragments, teeth, and an assumed piece of fossilized wood given to me that afternoon. I sketched the bits of bones in my letter, trying to provide some sense of proportion so that he could see for himself that these particular discoveries would be of little value when attempting to determine the age or identification of the beasts. I quickly illustrated the leaves.

By now the sun was even lower on the horizon, burnishing the far banks of the river with the same golden glow as the fossils I held in my hand. Jeb, who had been amusing himself building a fortress of rocks, rushed out to greet the students, who were making their way back to camp. After tending to their horses, a chore the students allowed Jeb to assume on their behalf, the three young men pulled their filthy clothes from their backs and jumped into the river, as they did most evenings upon their return, providing me with anatomical studies of my own should I ever feel the desire. Patrick Lear walked down to join them and removed his boots. He rolled the legs of his trousers high enough to wade onto the shallow sandbank. Seeing Jeb sitting next to the horses, he shouted something at the boy, sending Jeb scrambling back up the embankment.

"The doctor said it's too late for me to be traveling home now," Jeb said. "Can I bunk here with you and Mr. Augustus? I was told I was not allowed anywhere near the doctor's camp."

I assured Jeb he would be a most welcomed addition, and when Augustus returned with Mr. Huntington I was certain he, too, would welcome Jeb's company. Augustus might even agree to a little Shakespeare after dinner if he wasn't too tired.

Jeb pointed at the two pieces of bone sitting side by side. "Looks like a bone," he said. He weighed the cross section in his hand. "We have rocks like this out by where we live," the boy

PICTURES FROM AN EXPEDITION · 69

continued. "I once found a whole creature from the deep, which I put together behind our house until Ma made me move it because it was getting in her way. Looked sort of like that Caliban Mr. Augustus is always talking about."

"You have bones like this?" I asked.

"They're bigger, but they look like bones. And they fit together like bones. But they're heavy, like rocks. I found one that looked like a skull, too. A big one. It had been squashed sort of flat, but you could tell it was a skull because it had teeth. Ma told me it was a buffalo, but it didn't look like no buffalo I ever saw. It was bigger. And real ugly. I used to dig those rocks out and play with them. But that was when I was little."

I suggested that he bring me one to look at and then he could explain how it fit with the others that he had.

"Oh, I can bring a whole wagon of those rocks if you want me to."

I assured him that one or two small ones would be fine and then I said something that to this day I cannot explain. I cautioned the boy not to say anything about the bones or rocks or whatever they were to anyone else in the camp. Not even to Augustus. I'm not sure why I added his name to the list, except that Augustus was forever making thoughtless, offhanded remarks and Dr. Lear appeared to be so volatile and unpredictable, there was no telling what might happen if he heard of what the boy had said.

"But they're just rocks," Jeb said. "Aren't they?"

I explained that men often travel great distances to find fossils like the ones on my table. Sometimes they pay good money for them, just to add them to their collections, but others steal them, too, after someone like Dr. Lear has done all the work in uncovering them.

"They steal rocks?" This stretched his childish credulity.

"The world has changed," I explained. "Most men of science are honorable, but there are those who are capable of all sorts of inexplicable things."

14. DRAWING, FAT MAN AND MULE

Just as the sun was setting behind the far western bluff, Augustus and Little Bear returned to camp. Augustus carried his easel and a rolled-up canvas, and Little Bear packed blankets, beadwork, and clothing, which he had stuffed into his bag. Little Bear's bear, wet from lolling around in the water again on his way back through the river, was restrained by a chain. They avoided Patrick Lear and his party and instead walked along the embankment until reaching the area of our own encampment next to the shrubs. Seeing Mr. Augustus, as he called him, Jeb ran out to greet the men's return.

As the two men, Jeb, and the bear walked up from the river, a man rode into Dr. Lear's camp on the back of a mule. The rider, tall, fat, and lopsided in his saddle, climbed off and tied the animal to one of the trees. The mule shuddered, as if relieved of a burden almost too great to bear.

Augustus, leaning against the boulder next to our own small fire, asked Little Bear if he had any more liquor.

"This is the good stuff," Little Bear explained, pulling a small jug from the back of the wagon. He took a sip and then handed it to Augustus. "Never touch that other bottle. It'll kill you."

Augustus grunted in agreement and took a large draft from the jug.

"Whaaa," he cried, coughing to the point of tears. "If that other liquor is worse than this swill, I'd hate to be an Indian tonight."

Little Bear took another taste. For a moment, he looked as if he might offer the jug to me, but instead returned it to his satchel. Unlike the others, who seemed to accept my presence, albeit reluctantly, Little Bear was awkward and sometimes even inept, as if struggling to discover the appropriate convention to converse with a woman so far from the rest of the world.

"Looks like there will be one more for dinner," Augustus said, pointing out Patrick Lear and the fat man standing in his camp. Their exact words could not be determined, but from the impression made by their bodies, Dr. Lear was not welcoming yet another stranger, no matter how late in the day. He pointed the man in our direction.

"I suppose, Cousin, you should make the arrangements for dinner, since our dear friend the cook will not want to see me or Little Bear next to his food, given where we've been today. Can you do us the honors?"

When Jeb and I returned with bread, utensils, and an iron pot filled with stew, the new arrival, a journalist named David McChesney, was sitting on one of the upended tree stumps, telling Augustus of his quest. He was looking for a Smithsonian expedition, he explained. Men out collecting artifacts of civilizations long dead. He pronounced the word *arty-facts*. Someone in town had told them about Dr. Lear.

"So I travel all the way out to this godforsaken hole, fighting off rattlesnakes and grizzly bears all along the way, and then your leader over there tells me you're not collecting anything but rocks. Afraid there's no story in rocks," he said. "I need a story before I can go home and I sure as hell don't want to be out there chasing Indians. I'm sick of Indians. They get too much press in the papers back home as it is. If you ask me, Indians are old news. And boring besides."

Jeb handed the journalist a plate of stew. As the man looked up to receive it, Little Bear emerged from behind the tent in full Indian regalia, his idea of dressing for dinner. The visitor stood up, shouted something obscene, and spilled the stew down the front of his vest.

"The food isn't that bad," Augustus said without moving. He

took the next plate Jeb offered. The journalist, still on his feet, let out another string of expletives and fumbled around in his pocket. Jeb moved out of the man's line of fire.

"It's not good, I agree with you on that," Augustus persevered. "But it's not that bad, either. Keep a soul alive, if he knows what's good for him."

Little Bear nodded to the new arrival and then he, too, took a plate of stew from Jeb before sitting cross-legged on the ground.

"Little Bear, meet Mr. McChesney. Mac, meet Mr. Little Bear," Augustus said.

"I don't mix well with Indians," Mr. McChesney started to say, but Augustus dismissed him with a wave of his hand. He swatted at a couple of mosquitoes buzzing around his chin.

"Don't you worry about Indians," Augustus said. "The only Indians around here are the few hundred camped across the river, and they're packing up and getting ready to go on the warpath according to what our friend Little Bear says."

Again, the man swore something about savages, but both Augustus and Little Bear ignored him as they poked and prodded their overcooked stew. The journalist pulled a small metal flask from his pocket and swallowed the remainder in one long gulp. Then he lit a black cheroot and blew smoke in the direction of the fire.

"You be careful around them Indians," the man warned Augustus, as if Little Bear were invisible or simply did not exist. "They take scalps, crush heads, cut off your privates and keep them as souvenirs. And that's just the work of the women." Again the writer sucked on his cigar and exhaled a cloud of foul-smelling smoke. Only then did he give any attention to the thick brown gravy trailing down the front of his clothes. "I don't suppose you have a shirt I could borrow while I wash out mine?" he asked Augustus.

Augustus looked at Little Bear, who pulled a large woman's beaded shirt from his satchel.

"God, I'm sick of Indians," the man muttered, as he trailed off to the river.

"Mr. Augustus, could you read us some more Shakespeare tonight?" Jeb asked once the journalist was gone. "Remember how you said you would teach me about Caliban?"

"Ahhhh, Caliban," Augustus roared. "The monster from the deep." Jeb shuddered, as if Augustus were himself a monster coming to life to grant the boy's request.

"But you see, my dear boy, for me to introduce you to Caliban, I need your mother. Don't you remember? She needs to be my sweet Miranda. You must tell her to prepare for her part and then I will read to you about Caliban in all his wicked glory."

The boy tried not to look too disappointed. Augustus, however, was not finished.

"So tonight," he continued, "in honor of our guest, Mac, I was thinking a little *Mac-Beth* might be in order. What sayest thou, Cousin?" he now said to me. "Could you murder such a visitor whilst he sleeps?"

At this Little Bear let out a whoop of laughter before returning to his stoical Indian demeanor.

"Augustus," I warned him. "That isn't funny. You'll scare that poor man to death. Or worse, he could take you seriously and murder *us* in our sleep."

"All right," he sighed. "But a little *Macbeth* nonetheless? What sayest thou, then? Would you condescend to play my sweet murderous wife, just on this one occasion?"

Before I could respond, a string of the foulest language I'd ever heard was shouted through the darkness, followed by the sounds of a man running up the embankment, falling and cursing as he went. The journalist, now wearing Little Bear's beaded shirt and no trousers, hurried back to the circle around the fire. He started to spew out more of his foul language, but Augustus interrupted.

"Could it be," Augustus asked in his sweetest voice, "that you have, by any chance, encountered a bear?"

The journalist was silenced. His shirt, underclothing, and vest, still wet from their wash in the river, were draped over one arm, leaving a pool of water at his feet. He stared first at Augustus, then at Little Bear and Jeb, and finally at me. I think I raised my eyebrows a bit in his direction, trying to look interested in his response.

"What is this anyway?" the journalist demanded to know. "A circus?"

"No, no, no, it's nothing like that," Augustus reassured him. "We are mere players and this," he said with a flourish, "is our stage. Bear with us," he said, stopping long enough to let the pun sink in, "and we shall be happy to entertain you."

Still the man did not move, as if the simple act of figuring out what or whom he saw sitting by the fire took a good deal of thought and concentration. Apparently this was more thinking and concentrating than this journalist was accustomed.

"So," he said, pausing long enough to wring the excess water from his still-dripping clothes. "What's this going to cost me? I only have a few dollars and some whiskey back on the horse. Nothing else of any value. I don't even have any hair." He pulled back his hat to reveal the top of his head, where, true to his word, only a few wisps sprouted.

"We don't take scalps," Augustus assured him. "But it could very well be that a touch of your whiskey, if it's good, would lubricate our voices. And if we finish off all of yours, I'm sure Little Bear would be willing to replace it with some of his own. Might even invite our neighbors over there and have us a real party. Why, it's our nation's hundredth birthday tonight, as I recall. Might be too early for *A Midsummer Night's Dream* but such an event requires something magical and mysterious nonetheless. I was thinking that tonight . . ." Augustus' voice trailed off as he considered the possibilities. An owl circled once, screeched, and then disappeared.

"What sayest thou, Cousin? A little *Macbeth*?"

15. Drawing, Diving for Fish

I awoke at sunrise to the sounds of the students shouting and splashing at one another down by the river. One of the students passed me on the embankment, a large metal bucket in hand.

"Wait'll you see these fish," he called out. "There must a million of them."

His friends greeted the arrival of the bucket with more hurrahs as they scooped and grabbed and flailed themselves at the fish and at each other to no avail. Even from where I was standing I could see the cause of their early morning reverie: thousands of large yellow fish appeared to be trying to swim ashore, their golden backs and flopping tails shimmering in the light. As the students attempted to scoop up one of the floundering golden monsters, each of which was almost as big as their bucket, Mr. Huntington forded the shallow bend downstream.

"Good morning," Mr. Huntington called, waving his hat as he walked up the hill. The others in camp emerged one by one from their tents.

"Spawning carp," Mr. Huntington explained, pointing to the thick confusion of fish down below. "All up and down the river. They were making so much noise flopping around on the sand that they woke me up. I don't think I've ever seen so many amorous fish in my life." He laughed and then paused to look back across the river where the rising sun was casting verdant shadows across the plateau. "What a beautiful morning," he said. "By the way, Little Bear was right. The Indians are gone."

From where we were standing, we should have been able to see the outlines of the Indian tepees on the horizon. Now there was nothing except for the rise and fall of the multi-leveled gullies glowing buff and deep green against the milky white of the early morning sky.

"Which way did the savages go?"

Mr. Huntington turned to face the journalist, who was still dressed in his boots and the long beaded shirtwaist from the night before. Like his mule, the man's knees appeared to be awkwardly bearing the bulky weight of him.

"Hard to say," Mr. Huntington replied. "It's as if the entire tribe has disappeared. There's not a sign of them anywhere other than the remains any encampment that size is bound to leave behind." And then, with the slightest nod of his head in my direction, he added, "It's possible, I suppose, they're headed out on the warpath. Little Bear said there was a big battle somewhere along Rosebud Creek only a few days ago. And that the Indians won."

"General Crook," the man spat. "Different Indians. I was supposed to be with them. But like I said, I'm sick of Indians."

"You don't look too well and that's a fact," Mr. Huntington said. "A little too much of Little Bear's magic potion last night?"

"I guess you could say that."

The big man rubbed at his beard and lifted his hat long enough to run his sweaty hand across the bare surface of his head.

"I've got to find those men from the Smithsonian and then get myself out of here," he said, walking down to the river. It wasn't until the journalist, oblivious to the antics of the young men downstream, stumbled into the water to wash his face that he caught sight of the fish lurching and flopping around his bare legs.

"Oh, my God," he cried, followed by his usual litany of foul language. He looked as if he might be sick as he scrambled back onto the shore. "I've got to get out of here," he said, wiping furiously at his legs as if he, too, had been spawned upon. "Where's that boy?"

Jeb, who could sleep through any commotion, was still curled up under the wagon where he, the journalist, and Little Bear had spent the night.

"Boy," the journalist hollered, kicking at Jeb. "Get out of there and get my horse."

"Leave the boy alone," Mr. Huntington demanded in yet another one of his unexpected gestures. "I'll get the mule. You get your gear."

While James Huntington saddled the man's mule and the journalist fumbled around with his bag, Augustus emerged from the confines of our tent. Barefoot and still wearing his night-shirt, he scratched and stretched and took a leisurely look around camp.

"Thought I smelled coffee," he said, picking his tender-footed way over in my direction.

The journalist muttered something about filthy Indians and threw the beaded shirt onto the ground. He kicked at it with the toe of his boot.

"Told you we should have murdered the man in his sleep," Augustus said, and then he, too, headed for the river.

"Look at the fish," he exclaimed as he waded into the water. He stroked the slick golden back of one. Striding through the rush of fish until reaching a deeper current, he turned and shouted, "Tell Little Bear to get that animal of his down here. It'll have a feast." Then Augustus eased his body into the river and, merging with a few satiated fish, he floated from view.

16. Watercolor, When the Furies Should Have Descended

Later that morning, as Jeb and Little Bear readied for their return to town, and after Patrick Lear and the boys had left camp for the day, three Indians appeared on the opposite embankment. All three were stripped to the waist and had paint on their faces and feathers in their long black hair. The wind beat at the men's hair and the dark manes and tails of their ponies, giving the impression of fantastical creatures about to fly off at great speed along the ridge. One Indian carried a long staff decorated with a string of feathers, which whipped in the wind.

"Sioux," James Huntington said. "I wonder what they want with us."

Little Bear, his own horse bridled, blanketed, and ready to go, swung onto the animal's back and rode out to greet them. By the time he forded the river and climbed the embankment on the opposite shore, however, the Indians were gone.

When Little Bear returned to camp, he was too agitated to sit his horse, but stood next to it as if awaiting orders. Jeb was also waiting and ready, standing next to the wagon, where the bear, having eaten more than its fill of fish, was dozing on the floor of its open cage.

"I don't think now's a good time to be taking off on your own," Mr. Huntington said to the boy. "Let's wait until after we eat and then I'll make the trip back to town with you. We might even take along another one of the men to accompany us. Doesn't hurt to be careful."

"What about Augustus?" I asked.

"I doubt if they'll be interested in an old man out for his

morning swim," he replied. "But I am concerned about Patrick and the boys. If those braves are interested in anything, it will be the horses. Patrick could lose some if he's not paying attention. You don't know where they are working, do you?"

I had to admit that I knew little about where and how Dr. Lear did his collecting, but I told him of the map where he tracked each day's outings. Mr. Huntington walked over to the adjoining campsite and entered Dr. Lear's tent. As soon as he disappeared from view, the cook exchanged a few words with the teamster, who was saddling a horse. I could not hear what they were saying, but they both appeared to be upset.

Mr. Huntington emerged from Patrick Lear's tent and looked back along the ridge. Nothing. Mr. Huntington said something to Little Bear, who walked up leading the newly saddled horse. Again, the two of them scanned the horizon. Four geese made their way just above the surface of the water, but otherwise it was quiet except for the rush of the Missouri River. Even the persistent wind had died. The two men walked their horses down to the sandy bank and, pushing their way through the last of the flopping fish, forded the river. Once on the opposite side, they rode up the steep embankment.

As soon as they disappeared over the ridge, I walked down to the river to see if I could locate Augustus. He liked these private times in the morning, and was almost guaranteed to resent my intrusion, but I thought it best to at least inform him about what we had seen. I assumed Mr. Huntington was correct when he said that not even an Indian would harm a crazy old man floating around in the water, but there was always the remote possibility that they would act before knowing who or what Augustus was. I followed the sandy bank past where Mr. Huntington had forded the river earlier, but did not see him. I scanned the adjacent shoreline, where Augustus liked to sun himself on the rocks, but still there was no sign.

"Augustus," I called out, but only a sandhill crane replied, its eerie cry piercing the sound of the water slapping lazily against the rocks.

I thought I sensed something moving, but the only thing I could see was a hawk circling the plateau that stretched above and beyond me on the opposite shore. Again the crane called out, but what it was concerned about—me, the hawk, or something else altogether—I could not determine. Four mountain sheep clambered up the embankment and then froze like statues on the rocks.

At the time I was not concerned about my safety, although in retrospect I probably should have been. Still, I decided it would be best if I returned so that I wouldn't be yet one more straggler away from camp. Rather than walk back along the river, I scrambled over the loose rock and up the sandstone embankment to where the land leveled out and then rose again in a series of water- and wind-carved bluffs. Grass was greening in patches, surrounded by large open areas of sagebrush, cactus, and strangely carved rocks and protruding ledges where it appeared the land underneath had given way. One massive boulder directly above me was a composite of a thousand little bits, all cracked and held miraculously but only temporarily in place, waiting for a rush of wind or torrent of rain to wash it away. Beyond that, a thick line of black was slashed across the mountain, a geological fateline marking yet another era of time.

The sun was well overhead and the sky was milky with clouds. I fanned away a swarm of flies buzzing around my face. And then I saw them: two men and a wagon working their way through a gully, which might once have been a thriving stream. One of the men was beating the horses to keep them moving, while the other pushed from behind, shouldering the wagon up and over the rocks and ledges in its way.

"How much farther do we have to go?" the man behind the wagon called out.

"We're almost there," the one working the horses replied.

"I think the river's just over that bluff," the first man called. "Maybe we should give the horses a break."

"Maybe we should give *me* a break," the other one quipped. Again he lashed out at the animals, causing them to lunge across the barren ground.

"Leave those horses alone," a voice above them called out.

The two men stopped as if the devil himself had descended and demanded their souls. The horses, willing to take advantage of any respite no matter what the source, stopped dead and refused to move one inch more. The two men turned, holding down the rim of their hats to shield their eyes from the sun.

Augustus stood over them on one of the rocky outcroppings, the wind flapping the edges of his nightshirt around his legs. The silk robe with yellow dragons that he had donned after his swim flew out behind him like unearthly wings, his long hair a cloud of white against the deepening blue of the sky. As their eyes adjusted to the light, the men noticed me, too, standing on the opposite outcropping, looking no doubt as crazed as Augustus, one of his furies, as he later represented me, ready to take flight in the wind.

"Where the hell are we?" one of the men cried.

"Hell would be a good place for you, the way you are treating those animals," Augustus boomed. "Leave the horses alone. They won't get you anywhere if they're dead and they'll be dead soon enough if you keep beating on them like that."

It was then that Augustus noticed that he was not alone.

"And where have you been, Cousin?" he called out. "Don't you know better than to wander out here in the middle of nowhere? There are hostile Indians about."

17. Study, Men from the Smithsonian

"I can't tell you how good it is to be back amidst civilization," the older of the two men said, taking an offered cup of coffee. "It's times like these that we can all benefit from a little feminine company."

Augustus laughed at what he assumed to be a joke, since he had insisted on several occasions that I was allowing the field conditions in the Territories to wipe away any trace of femininity I had left. But the man, Cyrus Brody, was not privy to Augustus' strange humors and politely continued to explain that the two men were ethnologists from the Smithsonian. They were in the West to collect Indian artifacts, at least as long as their funding held out.

The younger of the two men scoffed. "We like to think we're concerned with science and the preservation of indigenous cultures, of which I personally have had my fill," he said, "but when it comes right down to it we are concerned with nothing more than money. And holding on to our scalps."

Cyrus Brody reached out to ruffle the younger man's hair, which had the underlying color of chestnuts but was now streaked red from the sun.

"He says that, but William, here, has turned out to have quite the talent. His photographs will probably save this expedition and allow us to stay in the Territories until the snow flies."

"Just my luck that I'll be stuck out here for the remainder of the summer and have only myself to blame," William replied.

At Augustus' expressed interest, Mr. Brody stood to retrieve William's photographs, just as Little Bear and James Huntington returned to camp. Both the men and their horses were sweating from the heat of the day. As they approached, the bear awoke from its fish-induced slumber and greeted its owner with a mournful-sounding roar.

Mr. Huntington carried a small pile of driftwood. "It never ceases to amaze me how water works such wonders on wood," he said, caressing the soft, smooth surface of one piece, before depositing the wood next to my worktable. "They look like bones," he added.

The man's voice was distant, as if inhabiting a world of his own making, or seeing the world in another time or another place. He shook his head as if to clear his vision, and turned his attention to our new guests.

"James Huntington," he said, offering his hand to Cyrus Brody. "You must be the chaps from the Smithsonian. I'm sure Patrick will welcome you as well when he returns. He's safe, by the way," he assured us. "They found a few things, a couple more teeth and piece of jawbone which they're documenting on their map, and then they'll head back in this direction."

"Mr. Brody was about to show us photographs they have been taking of Indian tribes in the region," I said.

At the word "photograph," Little Bear, who had also joined the group, turned and walked back to the river. He took his bear with him, apparently fearing that whatever bad medicine was contained in the box of photographs might leak out and affect one or the other or both of them.

"Ah, photographers. Excellent," Mr. Huntington exclaimed. "It's good to know someone is documenting all of this before it's gone."

"Actually, we're using photography," Mr. Brody corrected, "thanks to our ace shot here, as a way to complement our other collections."

"And raise money," William reminded him.

"Well, yes, there is that, too. Miss Peterson explained that you are also interested in Indian cultures. I'm sure you will see how we have manipulated these." The man paused to consider for a moment, and then added, "Well, 'manipulated' is perhaps too strong of a word. Let's just say we have enhanced our images when it is to our advantage."

"Like they did in the war?"

Mr. Brody looked up from the large green trunk strapped to the back of the covered wagon, the box of photos in his hand. "Yes, I suppose that's right," he replied. "Like they did in the war."

Augustus, who had wandered away from the group, saw the two of them returning with the large tin and rejoined us.

"Good," he said. "I like pretty pictures."

"Some of these are far from pretty," Cyrus Brody warned.

He opened the box and extracted a stack of crisp photographs bundled together with a ribbon. "We're sending this collection back with our other remains and memorabilia so that we can keep interest up in the Indian wars. Otherwise people tend to forget, or lose interest, and without government support we would have to go home."

Augustus looked at the covered wagon sitting next to our tent. "Remains? You're not transporting dead soldiers, are you?"

"Soldiers? Good God, no," the man replied with disgust. "The cavalry takes care of their dead. Send men back to the battlefields to bury them. Or at least most of them. Sometimes they wrap the officers in salt and send the bodies back East, but we don't have to handle them." He shuddered. "Fortunately, it is rare indeed that we even see them, since the battlefields have been cleaned up by the time we get there."

"Don't forget that time with Reynolds," young William countered.

"Yes, but that was an unusual situation," the older man explained. "We'd been bunking with the cavalry, so we were right there when the battle was over. And the cavalry was forced to retreat. But even then, only four men had been killed. And most of them were immigrants."

"But they were my age," William protested. "And their bodies so defaced."

Mr. Brody grimaced. "It's funny," he said. "I saw much worse slaughter during the war, when waves upon waves of men were sent to their death. But we believed in something then. Seeing it out here, I agree with William that it is hard to stomach."

"It's gruesome," William confirmed.

"We all have to make sacrifices, I suppose," the older man replied, downing the remains of his coffee. "As I'm sure you're aware"—he was talking now to Mr. Huntington—"this is a critical time for those of us interested in native peoples and their cultures. By the end of this season any Indians left standing will either be killed or herded onto reservations. Either way, their lives, at least as they now live them, will be over, and there will be no way to record whatever dignity they once had. I see this summer as our one and only opportunity to capture what's left before it's gone."

Untying the bundle, Cyrus Brody held out the first photograph. There was a beautiful young woman in a long beaded dress and an Indian brave painted from head to toe as if ready to go to war. He carried a rifle menacingly in his hands as if warning off the photographer or any other person who might get too near.

"This couple had just been married when we photographed them," Mr. Brody explained.

"Looks like Indian marriages aren't particularly happy," Augustus said, "if they have to enter into them fully armed."

Mr. Brody laughed. "We asked the man to hold the gun like that," he said. "As I'm sure you'll understand, some of these photographs are meant to ensure our continued funding. If we only sent back images of happy Indian couples and laughing children playing with dogs, I can assure you we would not last out here for very long. William is getting pretty good at adding the right, how should I say, threatening atmosphere?"

When no one commented, he pulled another photograph from the stack. "Now, this one is authentic enough," he said. "This is a Cheyenne village we encountered earlier this spring. Down on the Yellowstone."

In this photograph, snow blanketed the ground and smoke

could be seen drifting in wisps from the tepees. In the fore-ground, two dogs, so thin their ribs showed through, looked up at the camera but otherwise not a living thing was in sight. One of the tepees had been patched to cover ragged holes along its perimeter.

"Dogs," the man explained at my questioning look. "In many of these tribes, there isn't enough food to go around, particularly that late in the winter. So the dogs start chewing on the hides."

"I take it you're not planning to send this photograph to Washington," James Huntington said.

"Not yet," Mr. Brody replied. "We don't need to elicit any sympathy for their plight. At least not right now."

"Show them the one of the cavalryman, then," William said. "That ought to get rid of any ideas of sympathy."

Mr. Brody hesitated. "That's not something I'm comfortable showing," he said. "Not with women and children here."

"Oh?" Augustus queried. "If you're worried about my cousin, you should know she butchers and dissects chickens and reassem-bles the skeletons of the dead. Nothing will shock her feminine sensibilities, I can assure you."

"We all believe in science here," Mr. Huntington explained. "If there is something that should be viewed, I'm sure we are all interested in seeing it." He looked directly at me. "You don't ob-ject, do you, Miss Peterson?"

"I am hardly a scientist," I corrected. Augustus grinned broadly, as if amused at the odd situations in which I continued to find myself. "But I don't object," I told the man. "I don't want to be the one to prevent the others from seeing it."

Mr. Brody pulled another photograph from the stack. "This one, I can assure you, has not been staged. We found this body after the Reynolds campaign."

Augustus sighed when the photograph was set on the table. "'What dreams may come when we have shuffled off this mortal coil must give us pause,'" he said. Then he, too, walked down to the river.

Even now, I shudder at the thought of that photograph. I re-member my breath catching in my throat, causing me to clench my jaw and make fists with my hands to steal away any sign of emotion, doing the best that I could to ward off a threatening wave of nausea. And then, along with the others, I took a good hard look at what was revealed on the table before us: a young man, not any older than William, lying on his back in the dirt, naked, scalped, and mutilated, his arms and legs slashed open along their lengths like slabs of meat. As if to add the ultimate humiliation, five arrows had been shot through the man's chest and private area.

I looked at Jeb, whose eyes were wide as saucers, transfixed by the horrors of what he saw. Then I looked at James Huntington, who was looking at me. I could feel my eyes filling with tears but could do nothing to prevent them.

"Yes, these are very effective, I'm sure," Mr. Huntington said, picking up the photograph and handing it back to Mr. Brody. "I would hope, for the historic record, however, that you also pho-tograph the bodies of Indians after these battles. As I understand it, our men have given better than they get at least ninety-five percent of the time."

"I can't argue with that," was Mr. Brody's emotionless reply. "But you must admit that no one cares one way or the other about scalped or mutilated Indians." He returned the photo-graphs to their tin, just as Patrick Lear rode into camp.

"Now what?" Dr. Lear demanded to know, seeing yet an-other party of strangers in his camp. He reined in his horse next to where I was standing. "Peterson, I need to talk to you," he announced. His horse was hot and smelled of sweat. "Did you hear me?"

"Yes," I think I replied.

"Then pull yourself together," he barked. He tossed a bundle onto my worktable. It landed with a heavy thud. He looked war-ily at the strangers watching him. "You have work to do," he said.

18. WATERCOLOR, THE CONVERSATION WITH SWALLOWS

The watercolor of the man and woman leaning toward one another in conversation was probably painted by Augustus after I retreated to the river. Mr. Huntington followed me there and carefully made his way down the embankment, carrying two cups and a flask of whiskey.

"I apologize for the photographs," he said, joining me. "I had no idea they would be that gruesome or upset you so."

"It wasn't the photographs," I assured him. Gratefully I accepted one of the offered cups. "I've seen worse."

Mr. Huntington sat down on a large rock and stared out over the water. Hundreds of swallows dipped and weaved over the surface and yet, in spite of this flurry of activity, the air was preternaturally still.

"I love it out here," he sighed, as much to himself as to me. "Whenever I feel nervous or overwhelmed and the world of men makes little sense, I like to sit by the river and watch it slide by. I love the soft smell of it, and the rushing repetition of the water."

"It makes my body feel better," I agreed.

"Makes my brain feel better," he countered. "It's as if all of our personal problems are nothing to the rest of the natural world. Of course, this doesn't hurt, either," he added, indicating the whiskey.

We sat there for the longest time, the two of us sipping our drinks and watching the flat, gray-blue surface of the river, forever changing and yet forever the same, disturbed only by the occasional shimmer of a fish as it rose in search of insects before disappearing again, leaving fields of concentric circles in its wake. The silence was like a blanket that warmed us both.

"Augustus says you are building a house," I said at last.

"Well, let's say I am *trying* to build a house. I don't know if this has ever happened to you or not, but sometimes the world of the mind is so much more fully imagined or real." He paused, trying to come up with exactly the right word. He swirled the whiskey around in his cup. "I guess it's fair to say that there are times when the world of the senses never seems as vivid or true as the world of the imagination."

"And your house?" I queried, not sure how that fit within his explanation.

"Think how disappointing it can be when mere logs and stone and mortar try to compete with this." He tapped the side of his head. "It's hard sometimes." When I nodded my agreement, he added, "That was the knowing nod of a woman who has once tried to build a house herself."

"No." Before even stopping to think, I added, "But I once tried to build a life. It never works out the way you picture it in the beginning."

This time he was the one who nodded in agreement.

On the opposite shore, a deer and two fawns emerged silently from the brush. The animals waded through the river and dipped their heads to drink. They splashed the water over their backs, surrounding themselves with beads of light. The doe led them through the shallows but, seeing us, froze and then retreated back from whence it came.

Mr. Huntington reached out and picked up a small stone.

"The war had strange effects on people, Miss Peterson," he said. "Scientists study those deer or even something as inanimate as this rock, but no one seems at all interested in studying our own species in a similar way. Doesn't that seem odd to you? That we can explain why two elk lock horns and persist, often until one or the other of them dies, but we are powerless to explain why our own species does much the same thing for what we can only assume are very different reasons?"

Six pelicans floated into view, their fat white bodies and the bright orange slashes of their bills contrasting against the gray river. The birds huddled together, turning this way and then that, as they watched the surface of the water for signs of life. Just as they, too, appeared to become placid with the repetitive motion of the water, one of the birds dipped its head and reemerged with a fish flopping against the confines of its long neck. The pelican flapped its wings as if to right itself and then resettled, resuming its silent vigil.

Mr. Huntington examined the stone in his hand. "It looks like a heart," he said, handing it to me.

"I know," I said. I rolled the small stone over and over again in my hand.

"I saw things, like in that photograph, that I never wish to see again in my life." He picked up a rock and tossed it into the water. The pelicans turned in unison to confront the splash but otherwise were not distracted. "It made it very difficult to come home. Most of the men I was with, if they survived at all, went back to their desks or their other day jobs and tried to resume their lives as if nothing had happened. I couldn't do it." He shook his head. "I just couldn't do it."

"I know," I repeated, still focused on the heart-shaped stone.

"That's why I have stayed such good friends with Patrick. I understand how difficult he must seem to you at times, but Patrick was born into a large Catholic family, with too many children and what many considered to be foreign beliefs. O'Leary is the family's true surname. In the academic circle in which he has been trying to work, his family has been an embarrassment of sorts. And then, for an individual with his background and upbringing to forge his own way, to embrace Darwin and his teachings . . ." He hesitated. "It cannot be easy, as I'm sure you can understand."

Again I nodded, although I'm not sure I truly understood anything about Dr. Lear's situation. Or Mr. Huntington's, for that matter.

"We met when we were in college," he continued. "I was forever with my nose in a book, oblivious to most of what was going on, but Patrick was in the thick of it, arguing the smallest point of contention with professors as well as with his peers. He made a lot of enemies, as you can imagine, but it was clear from our first meeting that he was the brightest person in our class. While I looked forward to a life of reading and traveling and collecting, as I believed, in my naïveté, to be befitting a young man of my rank, Patrick was preparing for his doctorate so that he might be accepted and make his mark on the world. He appeared to be interested in everything, and unwilling to be confined to any one person or place. Even I could see that he was destined for something much greater than mere money or privilege could ensure. Then came the war," he added. "It put all of our plans for greatness on hold."

With this announcement, Mr. Huntington's remembrances came to an abrupt halt. He splashed a little more whiskey into our cups.

"I hope you don't object to my sharing this with you, but it might help to know, too, that there was a woman. She was with child, or so she wrote to him, right after Patrick left for the front. He believed God was punishing him for his beliefs and all that he was trying to be, and he became like a man obsessed. He said he was prepared to do the honorable thing, but in the meantime he seemed to be driven by his sinfulness. He took chances no one in his position should ever have to take, sending his regiment into battle only if he himself was in the lead. He was fearless, crazed even, but his men grew to trust him without question and followed him wherever he wanted them to go."

I wanted to ask about the woman and child, but could not find the appropriate words. Sensing my question, Mr. Huntington continued.

"There was no child. I don't believe she intended to deceive him, at least not at first, since I understand that women can be as fearful of their condition as can men. Whatever happened, she later told Patrick that she had lost the child before it was born. There was no need for God to punish Patrick for this or any other imagined sin. He did a good enough job punishing himself instead."

A large bird flew along the river and without warning dove into the river, emerging with a fish thrashing in its beak.

"An osprey," Mr. Huntington said, as the the bird flew off with its catch.

I was grateful for the interruption, the story about Dr. Lear becoming too personal to share. But Mr. Huntington was not deterred.

"I find the natural world satisfying and rich, and enough to make life worth living. Even after the worst of battles, when corpses were strewn at random across a farmer's field or stacked up to provide a barrier to protect the living, birds flew overhead, oblivious to the carnage man had just inflicted upon man. But for whatever reason, Patrick is not willing to relinquish his beliefs. He has told me repeatedly that science cannot teach us how to behave, and that we need to take moral responsibility for our lives." Mr. Huntington shrugged as if not knowing what to believe. "The Bible was open on his bed when I looked through his tent. It's as if he's still searching, hoping to uncover a revelation of sorts, in much the same way he searches here."

He studied my face, as if awaiting a response. When I did not speak, he added, "I hope you do not think me too forward, Miss Peterson, but I would very much like to know what you are seeking on your journey here."

How could I even begin to tell him why I had traveled to Montana? The only thing I could say for certain was that I was not interested in anything as impractical or otherworldly as a revelation.

"I have been offered an appointment at Yale College," I tried to explain. "But I need to do this first."

"Like a test?" he asked.

"I suppose you could call it that. It's most assuredly testing my commitment." I hesitated, trying to uncover the right word. "I was about to say commitment to my art, but Augustus would take exception to my use of that word. I suppose 'craft' is a better description."

"I take it you don't enjoy this." With a sweep of his hand, Mr. Huntington indicated the land, the water, the sky.

"I'd enjoy it more if I had meaningful work. The days out here last too long when you have nothing to keep your mind and body employed."

"Then you can imagine how Patrick feels. We both know there are fossils out here, and that we're looking right at them, but this a big country to be exploring with such a small, ill-equipped crew. My fear is that even if he does find something of significance it will not get him what he wants. Or, more to the point, what he needs."

Given what Mr. Huntington had revealed, I could not help but ask what he thought Patrick Lear was in truth hoping to discover.

"He says it's bones," Mr. Huntington replied, "but I'm not so certain. He probably doesn't know yet himself. Which makes it very difficult to recognize it even when you've found it."

Mr. Huntington pitched another rock into the river and stood to take his leave. "What did you lose in the war, Miss Peterson?" he asked, looking down on me. "A husband?"

In retrospect I find it difficult to explain, but at the time I was not at all surprised by the question. Maybe I imagined him also looking at hundreds of photographs after the war. Hoping. Praying.

"We never had a chance," I explained, my tongue loosened by the drink. "In the beginning, there never seemed to be enough time, and then one day it was simply too late."

"If it's any consolation, it was too late for many of us. We went into battle believing in grand and good things, things our families and hearts told us were true, things for which we were willing to give our lives. But the war stole our souls in much the same way that slavery stole the souls of those for whom we were fighting. It was if a hole had been torn in the very fabric of our beliefs, as if even in human interactions everything Mr. Darwin has written is true, although that is one question of evolution that I, for one, refuse to believe. As I'm sure you've noticed in your own life, even those of us who survived are not the fittest men you will ever meet."

James Huntington looked out over the water again, but appeared to be seeing something else altogether. I handed him my empty cup.

"I'd like you to visit my library sometime," he said, his mood lightening. "I can show you the house, too, if you're interested, although there's not much yet to see, since they're still quarrying stone. But my library's standing, and it's exactly as I envisioned it. Plenty of wall space for books, a good wood-burning stove that even I can't make smoke, a solid desk delivered from my parents' home, and a large window looking out across the river. What more could a man ask for?"

A fleeting smile crossed Mr. Huntington's face and then he fled, as the deer had done, back up the embankment.

19. Self-Portrait, Not a Drop to Drink

The portrait Augustus drew of himself pouring water over his head was done the day we learned of General Custer and his men. I walked up from the river not long after Mr. Huntington to find the journalist standing back at Dr. Lear's camp table with the men from the Smithsonian, Patrick Lear, James Huntington, and the three students. The cook, the teamster, and all but two of the horses were gone, and Augustus, Little Bear, and Jeb were off on a far bluff in search of them. Maggie Hall, still dressed in men's work clothing and wearing a hat that was too big, rode across the clearing to greet me.

"Hope I haven't upset anything," she said, "but I was worried about Jeb."

I assured her she hadn't upset a thing, apologized for keeping him, and started to explain about the Indians.

"I know," she interjected. "That's why I was worried. There's a whole band of them out here somewhere. Sitting Bull's just slaughtered an entire regiment of men. Some general named Custer and all of his kin."

At first I did not believe her, thinking it some sort of heartless hoax. Even with my limited knowledge of the Indian wars, I knew that George Armstrong Custer could never be defeated. Although he was known throughout the East as being steadfast and uncompromising when insisting on fair treatment for the tribes, he was infamous as well for his commitment to killing as many as necessary to ensure that the Indians did as they were told.

"There's talk about it everywhere," Maggie confirmed. "Fear there's going to be warring Indians roaming all over this part of the country. Decided I better fetch Jeb. Didn't want him wandering out here on his own. Thought you and your party should know, too, but looks like they already do."

As Patrick Lear and James Huntington spread a map of the Territories out before them, the journalist waved at the area south and east of us as where the tragedy had occurred.

"Tried to get on a boat headed downriver," the journalist was saying, "but they wouldn't let me board. Even told them I was on official military duty, but still the crew refused to bring the boat ashore. It was the passengers who gave me the word. They shouted the news as the boat steamed by. Decided I was better off back here than out there, hoping to make Benton on my own."

Mr. Huntington looked at Patrick Lear. His friend sucked at the inside of his wounded cheek and looked around the camp. It was getting late, and the barren earth radiated heat the way the distant rocks radiated the last light of the afternoon. Dr. Lear said nothing, but rubbed the sweat from the back of his neck and pushed at his hair, which looked grayer in the dying light.

"If I were you, I'd get the hell out of here and head back to civilization," the journalist said. "Even if you don't value your own scalp, you've got women and children to look after out here."

Dr. Lear, at first lost in his own thoughts, shot a hard look at the journalist. "I would remind you, sir, that there are women and children present. I do not appreciate, nor do I intend to allow my camp to accommodate, such language appropriate at best for a barroom."

When the journalist did not respond, Dr. Lear pursed his lips and looked heavenward as if for a sign. He rubbed again at his face and neck as if trying to ward off a wave of rage, or melancholia. "What do you think, James?" Dr. Lear inquired of his friend. "Is there a danger?"

Before speaking, Mr. Huntington examined the far ridge where the three Indians had appeared that morning.

"To be honest, no," he answered. "And even if there are

tribes moving in this direction, they won't reach us for a few days and they'll be traveling with women, children, and old men themselves. Might want to post a guard on the horses, but I can't imagine that they would bother us if they can help it."

Dr. Lear nodded his agreement as he, too, examined the opposite embankment. His comportment was stiff and distant as his eyes strained as if to see into the future, or to remember something from the past.

"Still," Mr. Huntington added, "I think it only fair to warn you that if anything does happen, you will be blamed. These people are your responsibility while they're here."

"Then I guess we should go," Dr. Lear replied. "It's not as if we have any reason to stay. We don't even have a cook." Seeing Little Bear, Augustus, and Jeb returning to camp, all three still on foot, with Little Bear leading only one horse, he added, "And it looks as though we've lost most of our horses."

When the small party approached the camp, Jeb ran past the men to greet his mother. "Ma," the young boy called out. "You should see what Mr. Augustus found. A real monster from the deep."

Dr. Lear and Mr. Huntington looked to Augustus, who was walking slower than the others, the heat of the day taking its toll.

"I could use some water," Augustus said, as he joined the circle of men. He was not wearing his hat, and the skin glowed red through the fine white hair on his scalp and chin. Walking past the journalist, he added, "Mac, I thought you were gone."

The journalist started to explain about Custer and his men but Augustus waved him away. "You're wasting my time," he said.

Dr. Lear scooped water from the bucket and handed it to Augustus, who poured the cupful over his head. Augustus scooped a second cupful and took a swallow. He spilled out the rest. "Warm," he said.

"Jeb," Mr. Huntington called to the boy. "Can you fill this up with fresh?"

Jeb hurried down to the river and returned with a full bucket, the water sloshing from its sides. We all waited as Augustus swished some water around in his mouth, spat, and pushed his long wet hair out of his face.

"A man could die of thirst out here," he said, spilling yet another cup of cloudy water over his head.

"Could be just another rock," he explained at last. "We were up on the side of that ridge, chasing that worthless cook and teamster friend of his—who now has the rest of our horses, by the way—when I noticed something sticking out of the ground."

Patrick Lear eyed him suspiciously but Augustus didn't seem to care. Little Bear led his horse and bear off to the river while the students amused themselves by swatting at flies. It was so quiet the only discernible sound was the swish, swish, swish of Maggie's horse as its tail fanned the air.

"Jeb, take him down to the river, too," Maggie instructed her son. "It's too hot up here for a horse."

The boy protested but he did as he was told, racing down the embankment with the sluggish horse in tow.

"Looked to my untrained eye like some sort of an appendage," Augustus explained. "Like a giant horn poking through the earth, calling to us from the distant past."

"Buffalo," Dr. Lear said. "They're everywhere."

Augustus shrugged, and pulled a stump into the shade of the tarpaulin tied between the two trees. Leaning back, he stretched his long legs out in front of him. His boots were dirty and already beginning to show signs of wear.

"Patrick," James Huntington said. "Don't you think we should at least see what's up there?" He wore that same earnest, concerned look he'd focused on me earlier. "Just so you know one way or the other? So we all do?"

Patrick Lear pulled at his collar. It was hot. Too hot to be wasting his time chasing monsters from the deep, he seemed to be saying. Augustus splashed more water over his face from the bucket.

"Can you take us back up there?" Dr. Lear asked Augustus.

"Absolutely not. I'm not a member of this party and I'm not moving, unless it's down to the river for a swim. But you can't miss it. Jeb or Little Bear can show you where it is."

Jeb, having left his mother's horse with Little Bear down at the river, stepped from one foot to the other, hoping for just this opportunity to speak.

"I can take you," the boy enthused. "It's not far. And I know how to find it. Mr. Augustus left his hat."

"You put your hat on it?" Nothing in life ever ceased to amaze Mr. Huntington. Not even Augustus.

"As a reference," Augustus explained. He dribbled yet another cup of water over his head and raked his hand through his hair. "The boy can find it. Like I said, you can't miss it."

Again Dr. Lear searched the eastern ridge. "It's getting late," he said. "Let's get packed up and ready to go. We can pick up whatever it is before we leave in the morning. Are you coming with us?" he asked Mr. Huntington.

"You forget, Patrick, I have made a commitment to build a house out here," his friend replied. "And besides, I have grown to love this country. But let me know what you decide."

20. Drawing, The Initial Excavation

The final drawing on your list, "The Initial Excavation," was done the morning after Augustus discovered the beast, for a beast it would prove to be. After indulging in a long early morning swim, Augustus agreed to lead the group back to the site to determine what, if anything, was buried there.

His hat was hard to miss, sitting on the side of the mountain just as he said it would be. Untying it and replacing it on his head, Augustus revealed with a dramatic flourish what appeared to be a strangely formed rock jutting out from the earth. Dr. Lear bent over and washed the surface of the projectile with some water from his canteen. He rubbed the surface clean with his hand. It didn't look like a rock, but it didn't look like fossilized bone, either. Dr. Lear kicked at the appendage with the toe of his boot, clearing away some of the dirt. Still, it was difficult to determine the projectile's origin, so he continued kicking until a small gash was cut into the earth, deep enough to break the projectile free. Again, he washed it and examined it closely, running his finger over its surface. Then he instructed the students to dig around the spot where the piece had been removed. "We should know if there's anything else here before we go," was all that he would say.

The three students swung into the soft earth with pickaxes and shovels. As they worked, Patrick Lear paced up and down and worked the muscles of his mouth. Within minutes, the students hit something large and hard, in marked contrast to the friable dirt in which they had been digging.

"There's nothing here but a giant rock," the oldest of the students announced. "Nothing worth fighting Indians for." The young man put his shovel down as if signaling it was time to go. The other two put down their tools as well, since a portion of the obstruction was now exposed. "We're not going to get anywhere with that rock in the way," another one said.

Dr. Lear brushed the dirt off the rock's surface and wetted it with water from his canteen. He wiped the hard but porous surface clean, revealing a soft golden umber with flecks of what looked like purple and brown. Dr. Lear sighed and rubbed the back of his neck. This was no rock, and he knew it.

"I've seen enough," he said. "We might want to remember where we found this, though, so be sure to mark it."

The students cascaded a pile of loose rock and sagebrush, as if marking a grave.

"Just a bit of horn, probably from a buffalo," Dr. Lear assured Cyrus Brody when we returned to camp. "Nothing to get excited about."

"That's good," Mr. Brody replied. "Because you had visitors again. Up on that ridge. I've seen hostile Indians in the past and I can assure you these looked none too friendly."

John Wilson
Smithsonian Institution
Washington

Dear Mr. Wilson:

Your letter with the list of additional Starwood portraits and drawings, Smithsonian collection photographs, and miscellaneous artifacts arrived today. I was pleased to see Augustus' Indian portraits added to your list. As you noted in your letter, they are significantly different from the other portraits he painted at the time and without a signature it is understandable that you might not think them painted by him. You should know that Augustus often failed to sign his work if he did not think a piece was completed. He even once signed and then painted over his name, assuming he would work on the portrait later, although he never did. He also refused to sign any work with which he was not satisfied, not even commissions, which led to some interesting altercations with his patrons in Philadelphia.

As for the photographic plates and prints you listed, from your catalogue descriptions these appear to be the ones taken by William, the young man from the Smithsonian. As I mentioned to you before, he and Cyrus Brody were using photography to enhance their documentation of Indian cultures, all of which I believe were meant for your collection. While in our camp, William took several photographs in spite of the fact that at one point Patrick Lear threatened to break his camera. I'll do the best that I can to provide you with the background of those photos as well.

I was pleased, too, that you asked about the other individuals in our party. Artists lead what are assumed to be more interesting lives, but Dr. Lear and Mr. Huntington were both remarkable men in their way, albeit mercurial as the Montana weather. Maggie, who joined us after the cook and teamster fled, is equally worthy of remembering, as is Little Bear, in spite of what Augustus used to say about the man. I will tell you what little I know about them, including the two men from the Smithsonian, although they were not with us long enough for me to get to know them well. Their mission was similar to ours, since the photographs they took that summer were nothing more than fossilized light. And they, too, we would soon discover, were collectors of bones.

Most sincerely yours,
Eleanor Peterson

1. Photograph, Missouri River Campsite

The informal photograph you described of our camp and its inhabitants was taken by one of the visitors from the Smithsonian while we waited to learn whether or not we would stay. James Huntington, who had returned as promised to learn of his friend's decision and was most likely informed about the nature of our find, advised that Lewis and Clark had put their critical decision about where to spend the winter to all those in their party, allowing even an Indian woman and a black man to vote. Patrick Lear looked at his own party, which now included a loud-mouthed journalist, two men from the Smithsonian, an old man, two women, three students, a child, and a bear. In all likelihood he did not think of himself as a Lewis or a Clark, so instead acknowledged Mr. Huntington's advice with a nod before walking off with his dog.

"Well, I for one am not afraid of Indians," Augustus proclaimed as we waited on Dr. Lear. "In fact, I predict that if we don't bother them, they will leave us alone. I would be willing to bet my scalp on it."

"I don't think Indians are the problem right now," Mr. Huntington said. "Patrick has other considerations on his mind."

"You mean that worthless bit of buffalo horn?" the oldest student asked. "I can tell you right now I'm not sticking around to dig up some old buffalo."

"That could very well be one of his concerns," Mr. Huntington replied.

"If I were you," the journalist advised, "I wouldn't risk the lives of these women and children at the hands of savages." The journalist lit another one of his foul-smelling cigars and exhaled a stream of smoke into the wind. "Wouldn't trust them with my dog," the man said, coughing and waving his hand in front of his face. "In fact, they eat dogs. Disgusting animals. Disgusting."

"Given our situation, I don't think we have to worry about that." Mr. Huntington said this to the journalist, but the comment appeared to be intended for me. "Still, I think each of us should decide what we have invested in this summer, and what we have to gain. I've made a commitment to this part of the country and intend to stay, but then I happen to believe that we have little to fear given our situation. Each of you may have differing obligations and beliefs," he said, "and different apprehensions and concerns. My advice is to weigh those investments, obligations, and other concerns and make your decision accordingly."

"Investments?" the oldest of the students exclaimed. "We have nothing invested in this venture. There's nothing to be gained, except for maybe a few broken bones from climbing those ridiculous gorges. And even if we do discover something of significance, which from what we've seen so far appears to be unlikely, it'll just be stowed away in some drawer at Yale College. There's nothing in that for us. As far as I'm concerned, this has been an enormous waste of my time. I'm going home and taking out one of my parents' boats before the summer's over and while I still have wind in my sails."

"Yeah, and hair on our heads," his brother added.

"I believe that's a reasonable choice," Mr. Huntington said. "Speaking of hair, what about you, Mr. McChesney? What are your plans? If what you say is true, there is a big story out on that battlefield right now."

"To hell with those Indians," the journalist snorted from beneath a cloud of smoke. "I'm headed home, story or no story. I don't even care if it costs me my job. It's sure as hell better than losing my life. All I ask is that someone gets me to Benton so I don't have to travel out there on my own." He looked around the group for assurances that he could indeed count on an escort, but no one volunteered. "God, I hate Indians," the man said.

"I must admit, I'm getting tired of this as well," Cyrus Brody said, breaking the awkward silence. "Must be this persistent heat. But William and I are in it for the duration. If Patrick doesn't object and he does decide to stay, we'd like to camp here with you for another night or two, at least until we can decide how best to replace the horses your men ran off with, and learn where it might be safe for us to travel. It'll probably be easiest to link up with another regiment of the cavalry, although I, for one, wouldn't mind meeting up with a handful of renegade Sioux or Cheyenne if I thought I would live to tell about it."

"And Miss Peterson?" Mr. Huntington turned his full attention to me. "I wouldn't worry about what Mr. McChesney thinks, but I'm sure you have concerns of your own. You once told me you didn't even like it here."

I can admit to you now that by that time I had grown to hate Montana. It wasn't the Indians. It was me. My clothes were filthy. My hair was thick with dirt and grease. I was plagued by mosquito and fly bites. And in spite of futile attempts to keep myself clean, by the end of each day my body was covered with a thin layer of grit that rubbed my skin, making it difficult if not impossible to sleep. As I contemplated my response, I could taste the dirt on my lips.

"I am willing to wait for now," I said, "but would appreciate being able to consider my options later."

"That's fair enough," Mr. Huntington replied.

Augustus picked at a loose thread on one of his embroidered dragons, but I could tell that he was relieved. He had recently announced that he was feeling better than he had felt in years and couldn't understand why it had taken him so long to discover Montana. The camping cure, was how Mr. Huntington referred to it, and it was working. But it wasn't only Augustus' health that had improved. As you have noted in your letter, his work was changing dramatically, opening in new directions which surprised even Augustus. He was viewing the world and the people in it in a new way. Leaving at that moment might have brought that new revelatory phase of his work to an end.

Patrick Lear's dog bounded up to James Huntington and then turned to greet the rest of us one by one. When the dog approached the journalist, Dr. Lear called him back to his side.

"Patrick," Mr. Huntington greeted his friend. "We were just talking about our plans."

"Why aren't you breaking camp?" Dr. Lear asked. "It's getting late." He looked drained, as if at the river he had shed whatever he had been packing around with him, like Mr. Huntington carried around all those boxes of books.

"I think some of us would like to stay," Mr. Huntington replied. "At least for a few more days."

"For what?" Dr. Lear demanded of his friend. "There's nothing worth staying for here. Under the circumstances, I think we'd all be better off if we headed home."

Augustus took a deep breath of the hot, dry air. The wind slapped the edges of his silk robe. "Well, I, for one, am going to miss this," he said, taking one last look around him.

"I think you all will," James Huntington agreed. "Patrick, are you sure? I can sympathize with your concerns, but given what you told me . . ." He hesitated.

Patrick Lear sighed and chewed on the inside of his cheek. "James, I feel like I'm under attack from all sides out here." The journalist sucked on his cigar and blew smoke in the man's direction. "I think we should discuss this privately," Dr. Lear added.

"What about the others?" James Huntington protested. "Don't you think they should have a say?"

Again, Patrick Lear looked at the party of men, women, and children awaiting his response. When still he said nothing, Little Bear retreated, leading his bear back to its cage. Maggie and Jeb walked off to ready the horses that remained and the two men from the Smithsonian withdrew to discuss their own plans. A flock of birds, chattering in the cottonwoods, grew silent and abruptly took flight, a wave of black against the sky.

"I'll give it a day," Dr. Lear answered his friend. "That will give us time to do a little digging and to talk this thing through. But I want a guard posted tonight just in case."

2. Indian Tepee with Mural

In your collection, you have listed an Indian tepee, decorated with a boat, a bear, a herd of buffalo, some Indians, and a star rising on the horizon beneath a yellow sliver of a moon. When Augustus and Mr. Huntington had visited the Crow hunting camp, Augustus was impressed by the form and structure of the Indians' tepees, attracted to the simple beauty of them. But I believe he also enjoyed sitting in their cool, circular confines. After the Indians pulled up camp so unexpectedly, he regretted not purchasing one from the tribe. Augustus asked Little Bear to help him locate a tepee for his use.

"It's too hot and crowded in that tent of mine," he explained. "An old man needs his sleep to end the heartache and the thousand natural shocks that flesh is heir to. Besides," he added, "I'm too old to end my life baking like a potato."

It was unclear what Augustus planned to do with a tepee once he returned to Philadelphia. Even though it appeared we would be leaving sooner rather than later, Augustus announced that he was still anxious to purchase one, insisting that if Indians could travel on horseback with tepees in tow, so could he. He would furl the hides and poles like he had his umbrella, tuck the bundle under his arm, and board an eastbound train. Or at least that is what he said.

As Patrick Lear and James Huntington discussed their options, Augustus informed the rest of us that he and Little Bear would be leaving for the day. They would be back in time for dinner, he announced, assuming there would be anyone left in camp who knew how to cook.

David McChesney informed Augustus that he would be joining them, but Augustus informed Mr. McChesney that he was wrong, saying the journalist would slow him down and get in his way.

"Me? Slow you down?" The journalist scoffed. When he realized Augustus was in earnest, he offered his horse and saddle if he could travel along with them to the trading post, and if Little Bear would guarantee to get him there in one piece.

"What about your story?" Augustus asked. "Those are the men from the Smithsonian you came here looking for." Augustus indicated the two men resecuring the green trunk to the back of their wagon.

"Like I said, get me to the post alive, and the horse and saddle are yours. I don't give a damn about the Smithsonian."

It was then that Cyrus Brody also approached Augustus. "Would you mind if we joined you as well?" he inquired. "Without horses, we're not going to get far. If this gentleman is in earnest, perhaps we could hitch up his horse with one of yours, transport the wagon, and then even if we can't purchase new mounts, we can at minimum arrange for shipment of our collection back East."

Before Augustus could respond, Maggie stepped forward with a request of her own. "Jeb and I should be getting back, too. If we travel with you as far as the post, we can make the rest of the way on our own."

"What do you think this is? The Oregon trail?" Augustus slipped into his blue travel duster and tied down his hat. "Well, Cousin, how about you? Can I interest you in one last Montana trail ride adventure?" But then, noting that Mr. Huntington and Dr. Lear had left camp to discuss their plans, he added, "Cousin, it looks as if you have no choice. I can't leave you out here as bait for the coyotes and wolves and those young rogues from Yale. Let's enjoy our last day in Montana and take a leisurely stroll. And see if we can find a steamer captain dumb enough to take that journalist off our hands. Otherwise we could be stuck with him all the way back to Philadelphia. Jeb, why don't you round up that mule that Mac keeps insisting is a horse? Poor animal will probably be relieved to haul a wagonful of Indian trinkets rather than carry that thing around." Augustus indicated the journalist clinging to the narrow band of shade cast by the chokecherry bush.

Augustus joined Cyrus Brody, who was resecuring the folds of canvas protecting the wagon's cargo. In spite of a career in the Capital, Mr. Brody had large, strong hands that appeared to be used to hard work. William stowed the bedrolls under the wagon seat.

"Are you certain two draft animals can handle all of this?" Augustus asked. "I've got plans for that mule."

"The wagon's not heavy," the man assured him, helping Jeb with the harness. "Conditions in that back country were the problem, not the load. And we were all exhausted. Even the horses. I'll let the boy handle them. He shouldn't have any trouble."

Jeb and Cyrus Brody pushed the recalcitrant mule into place and tightened the harnesses. Mr. Brody took a long drink from his canteen, then offered it to Jeb, who was as grateful for the gesture as he was for the drink.

"Think you can handle this?" he asked Jeb.

"Yes, sir," the boy exclaimed. He climbed onto the wagon's narrow seat.

"I'll be glad when we're rid of these remains," William said to his friend. "Something out here doesn't feel right."

Augustus stared at the smooth white canvas stretched tautly over the mound in the back of the wagon. "I thought you said you didn't have any remains in there," he said. "That you were carrying back artifacts from the battles."

"We transport artifacts," Mr. Brody confirmed. "That's why we're here. But there is so much out there, we have to be careful what and how much we decide to take. As you've seen, the going can get difficult transporting even this small amount, so we try not to get too distracted by trinkets, as you referred to them. When the battles are along the river, it's easy enough to ship whatever we find back home. But out here, well, you saw what we were going through."

"But I thought you said you weren't transporting remains," Augustus pressed.

"I said cavalry remains. These are just Indians."

"Sir, did you say you have bodies in there?" Jeb peered along the side of the wagon for any sign of uncovered bones.

"Bodies? I once tried sending home a couple of bodies, but even with salt, they get foul, and ship captains are reluctant to transport them."

"Yeah, like that time out on the Yellowstone," William said. The man laughed.

"I had one ship captain pull onto some deserted embankment," Cyrus Brody explained to Augustus. "Made me unload an entire shipment when he found out what it was. Had a whole list of complaints. First, he objected on the grounds of immolating the graves of the dead. That's the word he used. Next, he cited his fear of being injured by Indians. Third, he said the bones and bodies might be a problem if anything should happen to the vessel, although what kind of problem he never said. He was also concerned that the presence of the remains might incite the crew. Smallpox was his fifth objection, although how a box of bones could pass on the pox was beyond my comprehension and probably his. Regardless, he made me take the two bodies as well as all of the bones ashore. But he would have never known what was in there if that body hadn't started to stink."

The man took another drink from his canteen. "So now we leave the bodies alone and collect only bones," he said. "Mostly skulls, because they are lighter and easier to transport and don't foul the wagon the way the bodies do. Skulls are more interesting anyway, and the most telling of the remains."

"I found the skull of an Indian once," Jeb chimed in, "but Ma wouldn't let me keep it. Said it could've been a white man, so she made me put it back in the earth where it belonged. But it was an Indian, I know it, because I found it out by one of those burial things. There were bones scattered everywhere."

Cyrus Brody smiled at the boy's enthusiasm. "That's usually how we find ours, too." Another conspirator of sorts.

"You desecrate burial mounds?" Augustus inquired.

"They're not mounds," the man explained. "In this part of the country Indians build scaffolds to keep the corpses off the ground. If there's time, they wrap the body in hides and blankets and some of the deceased's possessions. I once found a full deck of playing cards in an Indian's hand. Sometimes when we come across them, the bodies are only half decomposed, which can pose a bit of a problem. It's not easy to remove a skull from such a body, although it can be done."

"And you do this for—" Augustus started to ask.

"We hope to have a complete collection of bones and artifacts before the end of the year when original material will be harder to collect. Remember, there won't be any burial scaffolds allowed on the reservations. There won't be a need for them. But this summer there are bodies to be found just about everywhere. It's a good time to be working out here, which is why I'm reluctant to head home, regardless of what happened to General Custer. If you're interested, I'd be happy to show you what we've collected so far," he said.

"Let's get this wagon out of here," Augustus replied. "I have no interest in bones."

☙

The trading post was three or four miles to the north and west of us, but because we were traveling with two wagons and a bear, and most of us were walking, it seemed at the time to be an indeterminate distance. Once on the road, Augustus chose to ignore what we were transporting, and instead focused on the land beyond the wagon, noting three grizzly bears rooting along a ravine and then a herd of more than one hundred antelope watching from a bluff along the west, their soft buff coloring almost imperceptible against the tan and golden rock.

"Cousin, I'm going to miss this place," he said.

He stopped to pick up a multi-colored rock, which he stuffed into the already bulging pockets of his duster. As he did so, he eyed something reflecting the light. As the others continued, Augustus clawed at the soft dirt, scooping up a plate-sized rock encased in sand.

"Will you look at that," he exclaimed. "It's a first."

Jeb, continually amazed by his new friends' discoveries, strained from the front of the wagon to see what Augustus had found. "What is it?" the boy wanted to know. "Another monster from the deep?"

Augustus held the discovery out in front of him with one hand, while brushing dirt and sand from its surface with the other.

"No monsters here," Augustus assured him. "Just peaceful creatures of the past." Augustus sighed with contentment as he carried the large ammonite over to the boy. "These beautiful, passive creatures lived millions of years ago when this very ground we walk upon was buried beneath the sea," he explained.

With the edge of his duster, Augustus rubbed one rounded edge of the shell to expose its surface.

"They did no harm. They were simply beautiful. Sometimes," he said, now placing the large shell, still encased in dirt, up to his ear, "if you listen very closely, you can hear the sound of the ancient ocean from whence it came."

The boy let out a real guffaw as if to let Augustus know he wasn't that stupid. He looked to me and then to his mother for confirmation.

"You stop putting those tall tales into my boy's head," Maggie warned Augustus. "I've got enough trouble without worrying about Jeb falling off a cliff looking for seashells. I'm warning you. You behave or I'll shoot you first chance I get." And then to her son she added, "Does this look like an ocean to you?"

The boy looked around the barren yellow and red expanse of shattered rock and dry creek beds through which we walked. To the east, large outcroppings of rock loomed like castles from an ancient civilization, while to the west, the land rolled off into hills and steep ravines. A rabbit bounded alongside the wagon and skittered away.

"I guess not," he said.

"Then don't you pay him no mind," Maggie warned. "You don't need no artists leading you astray."

Augustus shrugged, walking off with the dirt-encased shell held up to his ear. He leaned to one side, head tilted, as if listening to whatever it was the ammonite had to say.

❦

Large white clouds accumulated along the horizon and then shifted, carried by a hot, gusty wind. Thunder rumbled in the distance. The wagon road cut through a clearing that led to another bluff, where a rutted trail headed down a narrow ravine to the trading post on the river. More than one hundred tepees were pitched on the opposite shore.

"I wonder which one is mine," Augustus said, scanning the encampment with his glass.

A soft, sweet scent lapped over us with a rush of wind and then rain started falling, light and refreshing at first, enough to settle the chalk-like dust, and then harder and with such force that water poured in torrents through the once-parched creek beds, and cascaded off rocks and ledges and the brims of the men's hats.

Little Bear assured us that the weather would pass, so we took temporary shelter on the downwind side of the wagons. What he failed to predict was that, after the rain and the wind subsided, which it soon did, the rock-like earth would be transformed into a thick red mud through which it would be impossible to pass. As the storm cleared and we attempted to resume our descent, the wagon wheels spun long narrow trenches and the earth sucked all of us— horses, mules and people—deep into its mire.

"Now what?" Augustus asked of no one in particular, since, in theory at least, he was the man in charge.

"This, too, shall pass away," Little Bear assured him.

"How consoling in the depths of affliction," Augustus replied, quoting President Lincoln. "But in the meantime, my dear Indian leader and guide, what do you advise? If we linger too long, we will for certain be stuck, since we'll never find our way back to our camp in the dark."

"We stay where we are," Maggie announced. "It'll dry out soon enough. But if we push the wagons down the cliff, the horses will never make it. This mud can break an animal's leg. Break a man's, too, if he's not careful," she warned Augustus.

The storm moved east, carrying sheets of rain across the river. Waves of lightning pierced the blackening sky on the far horizon, booming back in our direction, but to the west the sky was blue, with only traces of clouds. The wind still moved in from the west, but it was hot again and fragrant.

"Well, I sure as hell don't care about a bear and a wagonful of dead Indians," the journalist said. "You can bury them all out here in the muck as far as I'm concerned. That fort's within spitting distance, so I'm walking."

Augustus looked to Little Bear, who shrugged.

"Hey, Mac," Augustus called out after him.

The journalist turned, stumbling as he did so.

"Don't forget to watch out for Indians."

The man shouted something foul back at Augustus, who removed his glass again to watch the progress of the journalist. The fat man picked his way between rocks and mud and flowing water, each progressive step more difficult than the last as his boots accumulated layer upon layer of the heavy mud. The man tripped and swayed and tumbled as he tried to keep his footing, but, undeterred, proceeded down the steep embankment, covering himself in the process with a thick coating of red. Five Indians watched the man from the front of the trading post wall. As Mr. McChesney stumbled closer, two of the Indians walked out to greet him.

The journalist, seeing two very large Indians approaching, changed direction, turning to enter the trading post enclosure from its far western side. As he did so, the Indians followed, now joined by the others. Having reached more solid ground, the journalist hurried as fast as the thick layer of muck on his boots would allow. With five Indians in pursuit, he broke into an awkward run.

"Do they take scalps?" Augustus asked Little Bear, sounding as if he were in earnest.

"Those Indians aren't interested in scalps," Little Bear responded. "Besides, the man has no hair."

"Too bad," Augustus said, losing interest. He turned his spyglass to the river. "Cousin, will you look at that," he exclaimed.

He handed me the glass and indicated a spot down by the river. I removed my spectacles and lifted the glass to my eye. I have never understood how to use such an implement to my advantage, but did the best that I could to adjust the lens. Two men were standing next to the water, one in a fringed leather jacket and the other in a long white duster. The one in white was looking at me with field glasses of his own. I squinted to see him better, but as I did so, the man blurred and then disappeared. I looked to Augustus to determine if the disappearing man was what he wanted me to see.

"Not there," he said, pushing the glass so that it was pointed in a more easterly direction. "There. Do you see it? It's a boat."

Again I tried to adjust the lens, and for a moment I did see a boat, or what appeared to be a barge with a white canopy stretched over one end, not unlike the covering topping Cyrus Brody's wagon. But then that, too, blurred from view.

"It's a boat, Cousin," Augustus said again. "We can sail back to our campsite in plenty of time."

"But that isn't a sailboat," I said.

"I stand corrected. We won't sail. We will float. We will paddle. We will drift with the current. All I care about is that we won't have to do this again." He indicated his mud-encrusted boots and filthy duster. Then he turned his attention to Maggie, hidden underneath her hat.

"Mrs. Hall," Augustus said in his most agreeable voice. "Could I trouble you to join us for a moment? Here, let me help you down from your perch." He offered his hand.

Maggie pushed back her hat and looked to me for confirmation, much as her son had done earlier, but I had no idea what Augustus had in mind.

"Do you perchance know the owner of that boat?"

He handed her the glass, which Maggie lifted to her eye. She held it there for a long time as if focusing on something she wasn't expecting to see.

"Not there," Augustus corrected, again pointing the spyglass farther downriver. "There. Can you see it?"

"Yes, I see the boat," Maggie replied, returning the glass to where she was first looking.

"Well?" Augustus queried. "Do you know the owner?"

Maggie concentrated on whatever or whomever she was focused on, as if not in the least bit interested in Augustus or his question.

"What's wrong with you women anyway? The boat, Mrs. Hall. Who owns the boat? I want to go for a ride." Augustus mouthed the words slowly, as if she were a child too young or stupid to understand.

Maggie hesitated but then turned her attention to Augustus, who was still standing next to her wagon. The bear poked its snout through the slats of its cage and grunted. Augustus reached out and petted the animal on its nose, like he might a friendly dog, and then pulled back his hand.

"What am I doing?" Augustus said with disgust.

"The boat," Maggie said, as if she were the one trying to coax a response from him.

"Now we're getting somewhere! Yes, Mrs. Hall, the boat. Who . . . owns . . . the boat?"

"John Bright," she snapped. Maggie climbed back onto the seat of her wagon and looked down on Augustus. "Ferries goods up and down the river, on the days when the steamboats don't run," she explained. "Or when they can't get farther upstream."

"Excellent," Augustus replied. "Excellent. Then he shall ferry us and my new Indian home back to camp."

As the sun beat down upon our party, the sky turned blue again and cloudless, and the thick, moist earth firmed back into a hard red clay, Augustus proclaimed, "'So foul and fair a day I have not seen. We should stand not upon the order of our going,' my friends, but go at once, before our dear Mr. Bright notices the change in the weather and ferries away without us."

∞

The trading post toward which we journeyed was a reclaimed fort, hastily constructed with a lopsided dock jutting into the river. A man named Jason met us at the gate and shook his head as if he might not let us enter. Even the Indians, who had returned to the wall alongside the post's exterior, watched with some suspicion.

"Maggie, what the hell are you doing out here?" Jason demanded to know as she and Jeb climbed down from the wagons. "There are Indians everywhere right now." The trader was a small, tight, compact man with leathery skin and copper-colored eyes. His clothing appeared to have never been washed, but his boots were well oiled and shiny.

"That is not a problem, my dear sir," Augustus assured him. "We brought our own." He indicated Little Bear on his horse.

The man's eyes narrowed as he looked at Augustus, but he did not respond. He did, however, swing open the gate so that our horses and wagons could pass.

"We're here to purchase a tepee that my friend, Little Bear, has ordered from his Indian colleagues. Cash money," Augustus announced, when the man looked as if he might continue to ignore him. "And we're looking for a gentleman by the name of Bright. We need to hire transport and we have money to give him as well."

Mr. Bright sat at a table picking his teeth and watching our party enter the compound. He was not any friendlier or more accommodating than Jason had been. There was no way John Bright was going to transport us back down the river, because he had no plans to go the way of Custer and his men.

"You know damn well," he said, "that those Injuns will hightail it to Canada, and will be crossing the Missouri by month's end. I'm not setting foot or paddle on that river 'til every last one of them is either herded up or shot."

At this pronouncement, the journalist staggered forward, lighting a cigar. His face and hands and clothing were still crusty with mud. "You see?" he said, puffing and blowing and waving the cigar in the air. "I told you so. I told you. They are savages. Each and every one of them. Thanks to this good man, I know all about it and am ready to submit my story. These are historic times," he proclaimed. "Historic times."

The journalist pulled a filthy sheet of foolscap from his jacket pocket and proceeded to read. "'Indians massacre General Custer and his men,'" he read. "'A party of our nation's finest was yesterday sent to the scene of the Montana massacre, to bury their friends and to mark where their officers fell, since their bodies have been transported to their loved ones back East. What these brave men discovered was a scene the likes of which any civilized person should never have to witness. More than two hundred fifty loyal comrades had been stripped of their clothing, their bodies so mutilated there was no way to tell the generals from the recruits.'"

The journalist looked up to ascertain whether or not we had been affected by his sordid prose. He blew a cloud of smoke, took a drink from his flask, and continued.

"'Scalps were taken. Heads were crushed. Arms and legs were

split open, or cut off and strewn around the sagebrush-covered field. And yet in all of this gore, not one Indian had the courage to touch our nation's courageous George Armstrong Custer. Wouldn't even touch his hair, since the brave general wore it in long golden curls which the Indians believe are sacred.'"

"Now, that's not what I told you at all," John Bright interjected. "I heard Custer was buck-naked as the rest. And that some Injun had cut off one of his fingers to keep as a souvenir."

"Well, I know that," the journalist conceded. "But you see, my readers will never believe that, Custer being a hero and all. These stories have to at least sound like I know what I'm talking about." The man laughed, a big foul-smelling laugh, his cigar held high overhead. "That part about the finger is a good story, though, and I'd include it if I could, just so I could paint a picture of Custer's finger pointing out of some savage's medicine pouch. Now, that is a good one, and I'll give you that."

"Perhaps someone would be so kind as to tell us how we might arrange for the hire of that big flatboat docked out there on the river?" Augustus tried to interject. "If not you, Mr. Bright, is there someone else who might transport us?"

But the journalist was not done. "You'll appreciate this one," the man continued, almost in a whisper now. He stood next to us, reeking of whiskey and cigars. "Not many will ever know this, 'cause they'll never want the public to panic, seeing's how we all love Custer and all, but my good friend over there assures me that them Indians shot his private parts full of arrows. And some squaw pierced his skull, ear to ear, with her awl." The man grimaced, letting out a small involuntary groan. The color rose in his already red-streaked face. "They sent me out to this godforsaken country to cover Custer, but thank the Lord I got here too late. Saved my skin, that's for sure. And thanks to my friend here, I can do my job and provide them with all the details they need." Again the journalist laughed. He was headed home.

"It's a real tragedy, what happened to the general and his men," the trader admitted, "but I doubt that it will have any effect on us here. You know how those reporters are. Anything for a story. Still, like I told you, Maggie, this is no place for women." Again he eyed the rest of us. "I wouldn't be wandering around right now unescorted if I were you."

As the man spoke, Augustus placed a pile of greenbacks on the table in front of Mr. Bright.

"We'll take the boat off your hands," Augustus said. "You can buy it back tomorrow if you want to come and get it. Or, as these men are my witnesses, if we don't make it out of here alive, the boat will be yours again, free and clear."

After the deal was struck, Little Bear helped Augustus carry his tepee down to the barge. Next to the river, a conical Sibley tent was pitched in a stand of cottonwoods, where three Indians sat next to a small campfire in spite of the heat. The Indians were handsome, brown-skinned men, with feathers in their hair and beads on their buckskins. They were not arguing, as it had first appeared, but laughing, slapping their hands on their knees, and pointing at one another.

One of the Indians acknowledged my presence and only then did I see why the three of them were laughing. The man in the white duster sat with them, smiling a wide, toothless grin. At this, the Indians laughed and slapped their knees again with even more conviction. The man turned back to his jocular friends, teeth in hand, and commenced snapping the ivories in their direction. The Indians pulled at their own teeth, hit one another on their shoulders and backs, and laughed and laughed until the man slipped his teeth back into his mouth where they belonged.

"Cousin, please, no flirting with strange men," Augustus called out from the river. "You have strange enough bedfellows at our own camp and we need to embark at once if we are to make it back before dark."

CO

The portrait that I kept of myself from that period is a watercolor Augustus painted of our journey down the river. In it, I am leaning back trailing my hand in the water, my hair is untied, and I am looking outward from the picture as if in a trance or lost in a dream. The dappled blues and greens of the sunlight on the flat, gray water and rocks, across my hair, and down the length of my dress give the appearance of all things on the water being as of one. The lightness of touch Augustus developed when using watercolors that summer seemed to suggest the translucent, almost transparent nature of the world. It was as if each brief moment he was able to capture with his paints was transitory, which in retrospect I suppose they were. He experimented later that summer with the same technique when applying oils but even though he was able to achieve a comparable structure with the layering of white and light blues, I don't believe he ever fully captured the spontaneity of the watercolors as they spilled across the paper. Of course, this, too, was just an illusion. Augustus worked hard at making those paintings look as if they had been completed with little or no effort.

I should admit, as well, that the portrait was never given to me by Augustus, although I often tried to convince him to let me have just that one piece of work. James Huntington also tried to convince him to part with it, and offered him quite a large sum of money, as I recall. But even though Augustus willingly sold a couple of other paintings to Mr. Huntington, this one he refused to sell. At the end of the summer, I took this one painting, along with another portrait Augustus had painted at my request. For that reason, I feel obligated to pledge them to you, along with the two landscapes in my possession, assuming they will join the others upon the day of my death.

∞

The world looks different from a boat. Augustus stretched out beneath the white canopy at the back of the barge and steadied the rudder, while Little Bear poled us away from rocks and snags. The horse and the mule were picketed side by side, and the bear was chained to the outside of its cage. From time to time the large animal scratched like a dog, rocking the boat, or snapped and grasped at dragonflies and other large insects as they flew by.

When we cleared a bend where the river narrowed into a deep ravine, white cliffs towered over us in wind-ravaged spires. Birds reeled in flocks overhead, or one by one chattered past us along the surface of the water. Little Bear stood silent, poling the flatboat away from the shore, watchful for the fallen trees littering the surface and for signs of submerged rocks, which could send the lot of us tumbling into the river. My guess is that Little Bear didn't care that much about his human passengers, who could easily swim to shore, but was more concerned about his bear.

Augustus, his face shaded by the wide brim of his straw hat, his body leaning back and into the shade of the tarpaulin, luxuriated in this quiet interlude. At first uncharacteristically silent, with nothing more than a sigh or a "Mmmm" of pleasure escaping from time to time, he reached over the edge of the boat and scooped up a handful of turbid water which he tossed into the air. The droplets reflected the light and were transformed, falling like shimmering stars back from whence they came.

"Ahhh, Cousin," Augustus sighed. "''Tis but a rotten carcass of a boat, not rigged, nor tackle, sail, nor mast; the very rats instinctively have quit it,' and yet, and yet . . ."

Augustus' voice trailed off behind him like the water rushing past his hand. He closed his eyes as the river and land through which it coursed opened and flattened, the towering cliffs giving way to an open stretch of grassland high above, punctuated down to the river with layers of red and brown and black and yellow earth. The only sound was the occasional whipping of wings as ducks and geese flew by just skirting the water, or the splashing of fish as they broke through the surface of the river before disappearing again.

We could hear the animals before we saw them, a muffled thunder of hooves and cries and wails and the soft thuds of bodies against bodies, flesh against flesh, as they neared the river in a wave. Little Bear's horse pulled back on its secured bridle, stomping and crying and rocking the flatboat up and down while the bear sat back on its haunches.

"Bring it in," Little Bear ordered.

Augustus, still lost in what appeared to be a laudanum-induced reverie, blinked and then squinted, trying hard to shift his focus from the light falling on the water to the dust rising in huge clouds along the far bank. As he did so, hundreds of animals started spilling over the edge.

"Bring it in," Little Bear shouted at him again, "over there." He pointed to an island-like sandbar where pelicans were taking flight in response to the deafening noise.

Augustus sat up, alert and alive, and pulled the rudder to the side while Little Bear pushed the boat across the deep current and toward the sandy bank. The fury of the pelicans' wings and the rustling of their heavy bodies engulfed us as they rose in unison, white feathers falling like snow.

Little Bear's horse cried out again and pulled hard against his picket.

"Hold him," Little Bear now barked at me. "Hold him down, and the other one, too, or they can take us with them."

I scrambled to reach the strap around the horse's muzzle, but just as my fingers closed around the leather, the animal pulled back so hard I thought I might fall. I grabbed for the bridle again and pulled the animal's head down, leaning into him so that he might be spared the sight of the animals rushing for water and the thick profusion of feathers and wings. With my free hand I took hold of the mule, which stood so silent and passive that it was hard not to assume that it, too, had taken some kind of soporific drug. Standing thus with my back to the front of the barge, the horse still trying to pull itself away from me, I did not expect nor anticipate our arrival on the sandy shore, which our boat struck as if it had hit a wall.

"Oh, Cousin," Augustus cried out as I fell. "Mercy on us! We split, we split!" he called. "Farewell, Cousin. We split, we split, we split!"

Momentarily dazed, I was half convinced that all was indeed lost and that Augustus' cries would be the last I would ever again hear. But then I looked up from the floor of the boat and watched as Little Bear led his horse and the mule onto the minute isle. With a few words whispered close to the animal's ear, he managed to calm the raging horse, after which he tied both animals to a large fallen tree. He returned to the boat for his bear, which stepped around me as I rose to my knees in its lumbering path.

Augustus, now silent and calm as if nothing had happened, stood up from his post at the back of the boat, pulled his watch from his jacket pocket, nodded to himself as if satisfied, and then stretched.

"Ah, Cousin, there you are," he announced, as I struggled to my feet. "'No more amazement. Tell your piteous heart there's no harm done.'"

He smiled as if what he said were true.

"No harm," he again assured me when I looked at him in disbelief. "No harm."

I picked up a rock and threw it at him, but I missed.

The tiny strip of sand and rock, fallen timbers and scrubby cottonwoods upon which we were standing was just upriver from the heavy flow of buffalo now forming a confluence of its own. Hundreds of animals continued to make their way over the edge, bellowing and mewling and sending up such a thick cloud of dust and dirt that the herd, one by one, disappeared as the animals slid over the edge and were engulfed in the choking black confines of it. Only when the buffalo entered the river and were swept downstream could we see them again, their heavy brown backs and heads bobbing and wailing as the animals struggled to make the opposite shore.

"All this for a drink?" Augustus asked.

Little Bear ignored him, leading his bear to a waterlogged tree stump where he sat down and placed his arm around the beast.

"So great and sanguine Indian guide, what do we do now?" Augustus asked. "It's going to be dark before we know it."

"This is buffalo country," Little Bear advised. "And buffalo rivers. We wait for them to pass."

Little Bear stroked his bear's thick fur and scratched the animal's head as if to reassure it. The bear licked its owner's face and hair, and then took Little Bear's hand into its mouth and sucked and rolled it around on its tongue as if the hand were a lump of candy. Little Bear leaned into the animal and closed his eyes. Augustus' eyes were wide in disbelief, but for once he was speechless. Or at least he kept whatever he was thinking to himself.

Downstream, buffalo were beginning to exit the river, some clambering up the steep wall of sandstone on the opposite bluff, while others wandered along the shoreline searching out an easier route. Yet others fought against the current and each other as they continued to spill into the water, only to be swept farther downstream.

Again, Augustus pulled his watch from his pocket. "It's getting late," he said. "This could take all day."

As the splashing and bellowing of the animals began to subside, or at least to appear more commonplace, the birds commenced their circling, some bobbing alongside the sandbar and others even floating back into the shallow water along the island's opposite side.

"I think of myself as an open-minded being, Cousin, and I certainly do not believe that the truth is written in any holy book, but I don't like your cavalier attitude when it comes to illustrating those birds." Augustus pointed to a group of white pelicans clustered together on the surface of the river, heads held high, their bills, long slashes of orange, held snug against their necks. "They look more like swans dressed for a masquerade than any distant cousins to your monster from the deep," he added.

The fat white birds drifted toward the sand and waddled ashore, comical and gawky, until one bird leaned forward and took to the air, white wings flashing to gray and then white again, followed by the others, one by one rising, skimming along the surface of the river until, satisfied that whatever had worried them into flight had passed, they returned to the water again, settling, ruffling, then turning, watching for fish. Three ducks followed closely behind, their wings whirring, bodies riffling across the water, distracting us for the moment from the larger animals downstream.

Just as Augustus appeared to be readying for an assault on evolution or on me, Little Bear patted his bear on the head, stood, and announced that it was time to go.

"The buffalo are happy," he said. "They won't bother us now."

Indeed, the thirsty herd did appear to be content, some easing their way through the water, others grazing on the far bank, and still others cutting a trail up and across the steep embankment.

Little Bear picketed the animals and pushed the boat back into the deepest, swiftest current of the river, where we were soon surrounded by buffalo, bellowing and mewling as the rushing river carried us all downstream. One buffalo, a large male standing in the shallows between our boat and a female on shore, moaned a long, rumbling threat in our direction.

"'Moon-calf,'" Augustus crooned to the upset beast. "'Speak once in thy life, if thou beest a good moon-calf.'"

The buffalo turned at the sound of Augustus' voice and bellowed at him directly, the animal's tongue wagging menacingly in the air, its eyes crazed and showing a readiness for battle.

"A critic, Cousin," Augustus beamed from the back of the boat. "There's a critic in the house."

Little Bear poled the boat even farther from the shore through a crowd of young animals swimming and lurching as they lost their footing in the quickening water. He turned briefly as if to warn Augustus, who shrugged his compliance before Little Bear could even speak.

"I'll be good," Augustus said, watching the animals' heavy heads and backs still bobbing alongside the boat. "I'll try," he promised again.

◌

The lone cabin depicted on the tepee with the glowing window and rising moon was James Huntington's library, which we discovered on that last stretch of river before we reached our camp. The library sat on a bluff, positioned so that its large window, which looked to the west, reflected the setting sun like a silvered piece of glass. As we floated around a bend, the reflection was so intense it was as if the sun itself had changed direction and had been transformed into a blinding star awaiting us upon the hill.

As the water carried us eastward and the sun settled into some clouds along the west, the sky turned pink, the edges of the clouds radiated a bright iridescent yellow, and the cabin appeared to retreat and then disappear along the horizon, which seemed to all but embrace it. It was then that we noticed the pale moon, rising above the bluff where we once saw Mr. Huntington's cabin, as if that exact moment in time was neither night nor day, or as if those arbitrary measurements marking the dark from the light, the future from the past, at least in this particular place on the river, ceased to exist or no longer held any relevance for any of us.

If you look closely at that diorama around the periphery of the tepee, you will notice that Augustus has painted himself into all of the scenes, first as the artist with brush in hand next to the tepee opening, then as the rudder man on the boat, and finally standing on that bluff, as one of two Indian scouts on horseback keeping a close eye on the mackinaw as it floats by. As I remember it, even the bear sports one of Augustus' eagle feathers over one ear. The final scene on the opposite side of the tepee opening is Augustus back in camp, hair and robe flying, his arms reaching out to the stars.

"I now have a favor to ask of you, my dear cousin," Augustus announced as Little Bear tied the barge up to the shore. "And it is not easy for me to ask this, after all that I have said. Don't make me go home with you. Please. I don't want to go back."

He said this assuming we would arrive back in camp to find that Patrick Lear and the students would be packed and ready to go. But as we both discovered, nothing went as assumed in Montana.

3. DRAWING, THE TOAST

We helped Little Bear unload the animals and scrambled up the embankment to discover James Huntington back in camp, searing marinated antelope steaks.

"Excellent," James Huntington called out when Dr. Lear's dog bounded out to greet us. "I was afraid you would not make it back in time to eat."

One of the Yale College boys pulled crusty potatoes from the campfire, while another opened cans of peaches and beans. The third was busy trying to coax the corks from three bottles of wine. Four candles flickered at the center of the camp table, dimly lighting the dusky shadow between night and day. A lantern placed at the end of the table was still unlit.

"Patrick," Mr. Huntington called out again. "They're back. Let's not ruin this meat by overcooking it."

Mr. Huntington flopped the steaks over one more time, pressed them with the back of a knife, and piled them one by one onto a platter, where the juices spread into a pool of fragrant red. He stirred a mound of wilted onions on the grill and spooned them sizzling over the meat.

"A feast, a feast," Augustus boomed as he entered the camp clearing. "My kingdom for a feast."

Augustus scooped water from the barrel and splashed his face. He rubbed his hands and forearms roughly with a towel, while closing his eyes and lifting his nose to inhale the sweet smell of onions and cooking meat.

"I hope we are not celebrating our departure," he said. "Not yet," Augustus added, pulling a chair to the table. "Not yet."

"On the contrary," James Huntington assured him, delivering the steaks to the table. "I believe Patrick has decided to stay. At least for another few days."

The youngest of the students retrieved cups and glasses from a crate and rinsed them in the barrel. James Huntington examined one tumbler, cracked but clean, and wiped it with a cloth. He filled this first one with wine and handed it to me. The boys busied themselves filling the rest of the cups, handing one to Little Bear after he, too, had washed the remains of the day from his face and hands.

Patrick Lear emerged from his tent on the opposite side of the clearing and walked stiffly to the head of the table. He did not look at the party assembled before him, but stared past us into the deepening night. Still standing next to the camp stove, Mr. Huntington raised a cup in his friend's direction.

"To Patrick Lear," James Huntington said. "Who will yet find what he is looking for."

"To Dr. Lear," we all chimed in, cups and glasses and bowls clinking over the wavering light.

Augustus, satisfied by the first taste of the wine, downed the remainder of his cup in one long swig. "Here's to what we're all looking for," he said, pouring another cupful and raising it in the air.

"I'll drink to that," James Huntington agreed.

Patrick Lear worked the muscles of his mouth and pursed his lips in and out several times before speaking. He wiped his forehead, trailed his hand through his hair, and rubbed at the back of his neck. He looked nervous and exhausted, as if just the energy to sustain this slim fragment of sociability was almost more than he could bear.

"We have two questions before us," Dr. Lear said, still standing. "First and most important is whether or not we should stay the course in Montana. I find myself in the awkward position of having to ask each of you for your preference, given what we know about . . ." His voice trailed off as his eyes scanned the horizon, where the stars were beginning to reveal themselves in the cloud-less sky.

Never one to stand on ceremony, Augustus stabbed a steak from the platter and piled some onions on top of it. "I'm not going anywhere," he announced. "I've just purchased a new home and I want everyone at this table to know I intend to live in Montana until the day I die." Augustus spooned beans onto his plate and speared a blackened potato. "In the meantime, though, you'll excuse me if I eat. It's been a long day and I have no intention of wasting away from hunger."

"Patrick, you don't mind if we eat while the food's still hot, do you?" James Huntington asked. "We can make more informed decisions on full stomachs rather than empty ones."

Patrick Lear grunted his agreement and looked back at his tent as if readying to retreat. Before he could leave, however, Mr. Huntington handed his friend a plate piled high with antelope, onions, potatoes, and beans. Dr. Lear held the plate out in front of him, as if uncertain what to do next.

"Eat," Augustus suggested. "One of you boys grab that tree stump over there for our leader. The man needs to sit down and eat."

Patrick Lear sat at the head of the table and pushed at the meat with his fork. He appeared to have no sense of the group's growing good will or congeniality, so removed was he from the simplest of human interactions.

"Oh, for heaven's sake, Patrick," James Huntington chided his friend as he joined us at the table. "It's not that bad."

"Not bad?" Augustus chimed in over a mouthful of meat. "This is great. We should be thanking those heavens that the news about Custer scared that other cook away before we all starved to death and someone tried to blame our demise on the Indians." Augustus shoveled beans and potatoes into his mouth, followed by even more antelope. "Food hasn't tasted this good since we were out under the stars in that sweet Maggie's care."

Patrick Lear looked up from his plate. "Mrs. Hall can cook?" he asked.

"Cook?" Augustus replied, now spooning out peaches. "The woman is like an angel with one of those camp stoves over there. Sage hens, grouse, sturgeon, catfish. She even bagged a turkey once while still sitting in the wagon. We had feasts like you would never have thought possible. None of the garbage that other so-called cook was trying to pass off as food."

Dr. Lear looked to me for confirmation.

"She's good," I agreed. "And Augustus is right. She can even bring down her own game."

"Well, Patrick," Mr. Huntington said, "looks like you have solved the problem of the missing cook."

"You won't stay?" Dr. Lear asked his friend.

"You know how much I enjoy this, but I can't," Mr. Huntington replied. "Although once I get the stonemasons under way, I'm more than willing to help out whenever I can. Sounds like the kind of hard work and attention to detail on which I thrive."

"And what about you two?" Patrick Lear looked at the two brothers. "How do you feel about staying?"

The older brother spoke for them both. "Sorry, Dr. Lear, but we're headed home, assuming we can get our hands on a couple of horses. This is more adventure than either one of us bargained for. My parents would kill me if the little one over there lost his scalp."

"Yeah, if you lived to tell about it." The younger student threw a charred bit of potato across the table at his brother.

Dr. Lear nodded his agreement. "Jack?" he asked.

"I'm staying if you are," the third student assured Dr. Lear. "Even if it's just an old buffalo, I'd still like to help you get it out of the ground. Might turn out to be like one of the horses with five toes that I heard Professor Huxley talking about."

"You're dreaming, Jack," the older student scoffed.

"Miss Peterson," Mr. Huntington said to me. "I know Patrick

is reluctant to ask you to remain, given the situation, so I will ask you on his behalf. Have you decided whether or not you are willing to stay should the party stick it out for the rest of the summer?"

I looked to Augustus, who was emptying the third bottle of wine into his cup. "I already told you, Cousin, I'm staying," he said. He washed down yet another mouthful of food and wiped his mouth on his sleeve. "I like it here," Augustus explained. He slapped himself hard on the face. "Even if the mosquitoes are as big as birds."

Both James Huntington and Patrick Lear awaited my response.

"As I said to you before, Dr. Lear, I made a commitment to both you and the Captain to document your discoveries in the field. I intend to meet that commitment before I return. That is, if you still want me."

Patrick Lear nodded, but said nothing, as if he were not certain what he did or did not want as far as I was concerned.

James Huntington took advantage of the quiet to open another bottle of wine and refill the emptying glasses around the table. Only then did he pass the bottle to Augustus, who spilled the dregs of the bottle into his cup. Dr. Lear, oblivious to the small human interactions going on around him, continued at last with his own thread of thought.

"Well, you see, that is of course the second difficulty I mentioned," he said. "This is not, if truth be known, my discovery. And this could create an awkward situation should we find anything of value where we uncovered that bit of horn."

He tossed the heavy fossil onto the table with a thud. The candles sputtered and hopped.

"You mean difficulty for me?" Augustus drained his cup and swatted at another bug. "I can hardly take credit for finding the thing. It was sticking right out of the ground. Even Little Bear and that animal he leads around like an oversized dog couldn't have missed it."

Little Bear sat so silently by the side of the campfire eating his meal that he had been all but forgotten by the others. As the group's attention shifted to him, Little Bear stood and added a log to the dying campfire. The wood sparked, sending a red light wavering across his chest. Pushing at the fire one more time to ensure that it would take, Little Bear placed his plate on the stump next to the stove and walked away.

"We still have one more problem," Dr. Lear continued, weaving the discussion back to his own concerns. "As you may know, we are supported as part of an endowment to Yale College. Everything we uncover here becomes the property of that college and its fledgling museum. As for recognition—"

"I don't need any recognition," Augustus declared, rising unsteadily to his feet. "What I need is to go to bed."

Augustus wandered off to our tent, wondering aloud who had put the bush in his way. His laughter drifted back through the night, followed by a long silence interrupted only by the occasional crackling and popping of the now fast-burning fire.

"Patrick, if you want my advice," James Huntington said when his friend did not continue, "even if this is something worth excavating, you can always mark it and come back next season if conditions become too dangerous. Either way, you give yourself the benefit of knowing exactly what you would or would not be coming back for."

Dr. Lear, his dinner still untouched, chewed instead on the inside of his cheek as he considered his friend's advice. He rubbed at his eyes with the back of his fists and then bowed his head, placing it into the palm of his hands. He sat there, eyes covered, until the rubbing once again commenced. He looked up and squinted as if trying to bring the table and those of us sitting there into focus.

"I don't know," he said. "Let me think about it."

He stood, stiff and distant, his shirt still crisp, his jacket buttoned. He inhaled as if preparing to speak, but instead pushed at his plate and left the table.

The students and I waited for James Huntington to give us some direction, but at first he said nothing upon which we could act.

"Let's clean up," he said at last, "and then we'll post a guard for the night."

"What about us?" the older brother asked.

"Whichever one of you is the heaviest sleeper should stand guard first so that you can sleep through the rest of the night once you're done."

"No, I mean about leaving," the student countered. "I don't want to be stuck out here any longer than necessary."

"I'm sure we can get Little Bear to take you downriver in the morning. Cow Island isn't far and there are troops stationed there. You can wait for the next steamboat, if that's satisfactory."

The older student slapped his brother on the back. Now they, too, were headed home. The two brothers rushed off to re-fill the large leather-covered trunk stored next to their tent. From time to time they cursed as they tripped or ran into one another in the dark.

Mr. Huntington stood up from the table. "Miss Peterson," he said. "Eleanor. I must tell you how happy it makes me to know that you're not leaving." He placed his hand upon mine, and then withdrew it so quickly I thought perhaps I had imagined it. "It's getting late. I'll heat some water for the wash."

As I stood to assist him, a lantern glowed within Patrick Lear's white-walled tent, revealing the shadow of a man, collapsed at a table. Then, as quickly as it was illuminated, the light went out again, casting the tent and its contents back into the night.

4. Fly Sheet from Yale College Museum

It rained hard that night, and a thin gray mist hung over our camp in the morning. Little Bear made a fire in our camp, and he and Augustus huddled next to it wrapped in blankets, arguing about whether or not it would be safe to erect the tepee next to the river where Augustus wanted it or up on the bluff away from river's shore. One by one the three students emerged from their tent, grumbling about the cold. They wandered over to our campsite, anxious for Little Bear's coffee and, for the two brothers, a trip to Cow Island, where they could catch the next steamboat home.

"Are we staying or leaving?" Augustus inquired. "I can never tell with that man." Augustus motioned to Patrick Lear's tent, which had yet to show any sign of life.

"We're leaving," the oldest student announced. "First thing this morning, if this gentleman here will agree to accompany us."

"Gentleman?" Augustus was still groggy from the night before. "Which gentleman?"

"I'll take them," Little Bear announced. "It's not far. But I will need the boat."

"What about us?" Augustus inquired again, as if he, too, were lost in the miasma that engulfed our camp. "I never know what's going on around here. Are we staying or leaving? Cousin? Do you know what is to be our fate?"

"Dr. Lear would like us to remain for the week, at which point we will make a more informed decision. I believe that is what was resolved," I said.

"I thrive on uncertainty," Augustus announced. He stood,

stretched, and looked down on Little Bear, still sitting cross-legged next to the fire.

"My dear Mr. Leatherstockings," he said, "you may take the boat, but only if you agree to assist with the erection of my new home. Down by the river, on the sandbank, if you don't mind."

With Little Bear and the three students gone, Patrick Lear apparently sleeping in, and Augustus preferring his own company as he trudged down to the river with his birds, I struggled to start a small fire in the main camp and commenced documenting the horn core still lying on the table where Patrick Lear had deposited it the night before.

"Ah, Miss Peterson, there you are," someone called from the edge of the clearing. "Hard at work, just as I would have expected."

Two men advanced from the west, leading their horses through the mist. At first I was convinced I must be dreaming, because the Captain joined me at the camp table as if he'd been there all along.

"And what have we here?" he demanded to know. The Captain lifted the heavy fossil and turned it from side to side. "Buffalo, perhaps?" He looked to his companion for confirmation, but the man in black was rubbing his long white hands in front of the sputtering fire.

"Put some wood on that thing," the Captain commanded. "And some coffee. I could use some coffee."

The man stacked wood from the still-wet pile onto the small fire, all but extinguishing it in the process.

"Sometimes I fear I have to do everything myself."

The Captain kicked the large logs to the periphery of the ring and replaced them with a few smaller branches. He blew on the glowing embers. The damp wood sputtered, crackled, and then burst into flame. He circled the brightly burning fire with the damp logs, suspending one log across the top to dry. The Captain rummaged through a box of food until he found the tin of coffee, scooped it into the pot, and then, after examining our barrel of river water, poured some from his own canteen instead. Placing the pot in the coals of the fire, and stacking another log alongside of it, he glared for a moment at his companion before turning his attention to me.

"Miss Peterson," he said. "I'm so glad to see you. I was afraid the news about General Custer might have frightened you away. The general often has that effect on people. He called on me once when I was back in New Haven, but I sent word that I was away. Thought him nothing more than an arrogant fop, if you know what I mean. But looks like I was mistaken about you as well. Pleasantly so, I might add. Pleasantly so." He took a long look around the campsite, not the way those of us who lived there did, but as if the land itself were in his employ. "So where are the others? Patrick and the boys?"

I was afraid Patrick Lear might still be sleeping but, not wanting to betray him, replied that I had not yet seen him.

"What?" the man bellowed. "He's still in bed? Patrick, what kind of game do you think you're playing out here?" He disappeared into Dr. Lear's tent and reemerged a few moments later. "He's not in there," he cried out. "But the Bible is, so he'll be back. And who is that?" he demanded to know as Augustus cleared the embankment from the river, his robe and scarf a blur of red and gold in the brightening morning sun. "I gave explicit instructions that this was to be a closed camp."

"My cousin." I started to explain about Augustus, but the Captain cut me off, seizing the journal from my hand.

"Not much to show for your time here," he said, noting the paucity of entries. "And what's this? There's a page missing from this book. I must warn you, Miss Peterson, about the dangers of holding anything back." He flopped the journal back onto the table, closing it with a thud.

"Coffee," Augustus proclaimed, joining us. "I could use a cup." He pulled the steaming pot from the fire with his gloved hand.

"I'll take that," the Captain demanded, but Augustus ignored him, pulling an empty jar from the crate next to the stove. Only after pouring a jarful for himself and stirring in a large scoop of sugar did Augustus turn his attention to me and the two men.

"Cousin, you have guests," he said. "Perhaps they, too, would like some coffee."

Augustus placed the pot on the table and, without another word, returned to the river. The man in black rummaged through the crate for additional cups, rinsed them in the water barrel, and poured a cupful for the Captain.

"You know," the Captain said, momentarily appeased, "I once went hunting for buffalo, back when I was in the field looking for fossils in Kansas, much like Patrick is looking here. But because I was from Yale College, the cavalryman who took me out expected me to stay behind and watch. Treated me like a child. So as soon as he left me in the ambulance with a pair of field glasses to take in the scene, I slipped the driver a five-dollar bill so that I might shoot a buffalo on my own. Shot a big one, right between the eyes. But when I climbed down from the ambulance to reclaim him, that sorry excuse for an animal stood and charged as I walked toward it all by myself across the plains. So I had to shoot him again, while the animal was in a dead run. Lost my hat, but that buffalo lost his head, so I guess it was a fair trade. Used my own knife and took the head right off there in the field. I have it with me to this day, mounted over the door to my study."

The Captain, satisfied by the effect of his story, paused to sip his coffee. I forced myself to remain at the table so that I would not pull away again, like I had wanted to withdraw from him on the first day we had met.

"You know, I believe that cavalryman who took me and the boys out in Kansas was a member of the Seventh. That was General Custer's regiment, as I recall. So we now know what happened to that sorry excuse for a military man. But what do we know about this bison?" He reached for the fossil, and fingered its ridges and the smooth broken end. "What can you tell me, Miss Peterson, that I don't already know?"

There was no reason to conceal information from the man who was supporting our stay in the badlands, but after Patrick Lear's comments, I wasn't sure how much I should freely admit. I told him that there was only that piece, and that Dr. Lear had instructed me to document it for the Captain's records.

"I am disappointed in you, Miss Peterson," the Captain announced. "It would appear that you do not know as much as I had once hoped." He threw the remainder of his coffee into the fire, which sizzled and sparked as if it, too, were somehow in defiance of the man.

"Jonathan," the Captain barked at the man in black, the first and only time I heard him use the younger man's name. "Get the horses. There's nothing to see here. We're going back."

"What shall I tell Dr. Lear?" I asked.

"Tell him to get to work," the Captain replied. "And assure him that there won't be any more of the likes of him admitted at my college if he can't find me something better than this." He stuffed the horn core into a satchel tied on the back of his saddle. "And while you're at it, give him this."

He pulled a fly sheet from the leather bag before cinching it back in place, and thrust the printed page in my direction. DIRECTIONS FOR COLLECTING VERTEBRATE FOSSILS FOR YALE COLLEGE MUSEUM, it read. Taking the reins from the man in black, the Captain pulled his heavy body onto the back of his horse.

"As for you," the Captain continued, looking down on me, "get your reports in on time. If there's nothing to report, and it turns out that I'm throwing my money away out here, I want to know that, too, or I can assure you that Patrick won't be the only one without a future. Not at Yale College. Not at the Academy, either. Is that clear?"

I assured him that he had made himself perfectly clear.

The Captain pulled at the horse's mouth and spurred the animal away from camp, the man in black trailing behind him. As the two men rode off in the general direction of where the horn had been discovered, Augustus returned for more coffee.

"You have interesting friends, Cousin." He filled his cup and removed his gloves. "I suppose this is one of your friends, too."

Augustus handed me his glass and indicated a whitish silhouette on the north side of the river. I removed my spectacles and raised the glass to my eye, trying to focus on the blur, but I was unable to ascertain exactly what it was I was seeing. I looked at Augustus, who retrieved the glass, focused it to his satisfaction, and then returned it.

Again I peered through the glass and could now make out a man in a white duster, standing on the bluff, watching as the Captain and his companion rode away.

"Know him?" Augustus queried.

"He was at the trading post," I recalled. "Entertaining some Indians."

"More outcasts awash in the badlands of Montana. I wouldn't worry about him, if I were you. There's plenty of room for us all."

5. PORTRAIT, LEAR DECIDES

"Peterson, do you know how to cook?" Patrick Lear asked as he reentered camp. "I need something to eat."

Without awaiting a reply, he disappeared into his tent while his dog sniffed around the legs of the camp table as if smelling for the identity of the visitors who had been there earlier that morning.

"Someone has been in here." Dr. Lear reemerged from his tent. "Peterson, do you understand what I'm saying? Someone has been in my tent."

Although the announcement was in no way meant as an accusation, Dr. Lear was visibly upset and I felt the need to defend myself and to explain about the Captain.

"He was here? This morning?" Dr. Lear stood stiff and unmoving as I told of the man's unannounced appearance in camp.

"Only briefly," I confirmed. "He took the fossil and left this for you." I indicated the fly sheet still folded on the table, secured under a rock. "And there was another man, too," I said. I pointed to where the man in the white duster had been standing. "I don't know what the other one wanted, since he stayed on the other side of the river. But he appeared to be watching me. And the Captain."

Patrick Lear chewed on the inside of his cheek and abruptly exhaled. Then, noticing my futile attempt at rekindling the fire to boil coffee and the canned peaches and beans I'd emptied out on a plate, his face softened.

"You do good work, Peterson," he said, and then he laughed, the first and only time I think I heard such a sound from the man.

When the remainder of our party gathered for a midday meal, Dr. Lear announced his intentions. Having made his decision, he looked relieved, relaxed even, although the stiffness of his clothes still imposed a severity on his overall demeanor.

"It is my understanding that all of you are willing to stay and help with this expedition in spite of the Indians," he said. As he spoke, clouds mounded along the western horizon and thunder rumbled, threatening rain. "Am I correct in my assumption?"

"*Stay* and *help* are two different situations altogether," Augustus corrected. "I, for one, am willing to stay. As I told you before, I'm not planning to leave. But I want it clear from the beginning that I am not willing to help. I'm a painter, not a desecrator of graves. However, being a painter," he added, "I am more than willing to stand guard, since I am envisioning a new series of landscapes, to make these badlands look good. My eye, therefore, will be trained on the horizon at all times, watchful for the slightest movement or shift of the light."

Patrick Lear looked as if this were too much information to take in at one time, so he turned his attention to me. "Peterson?" he said.

I hesitated, not at all convinced that, after what the Captain had said, I wanted to stay. I stuttered something about doing the best that I could to assist.

"I do not expect you to dig," he assured me. "Nor will I ask you to cook. I will, however, expect you to continue with your documentation and to correspond with the Captain on a regular basis. If there is something out here to uncover, he should be the first to know," he said. "And Jack? Are you still in?"

The student looked up from cleaning the dirt from his boots. "I'm in," the student agreed.

"Good man. Little Bear? Can I count on you as well?"

Little Bear sat on the ground rubbing the belly of his bear, which was rolling on its back in the dirt. "I buried bodies," Little Bear replied, as if that fact alone were all that Dr. Lear needed. The bear gnawed on Little Bear's hand and arm. "There's no reason I couldn't dig them up again. And the horses," Little Bear added. "I can care for the horses. Assuming we ever have any again."

Dr. Lear appeared satisfied. "I am not at all certain what kind of bones our friend Starwood has discovered," he announced, "but whatever is buried out there, it is significant. No matter where I sampled the ground this morning— and I dug trenches in a number of locations near that bit of horn—I inevitably hit an obstruction. I have heard of fossils being discovered all in one heap, so it could take us a while to uncover whatever is there. But I feel obligated to inform you that even if it should prove to be something new to science, the Captain will not provide any of us, not even you, Starwood, with any recognition for our work."

Augustus shrugged, as if such recognition were the last thing on his mind.

"We must all accept and learn to live with this one restriction," Dr. Lear continued. "It is the reality of the world in which we live. He who has access to the wealth can claim the prize."

"We're talking about a pile of bones and rocks," Augustus reminded him.

"True enough, Starwood, but these 'bones and rocks,' as you refer to them, hold the key to understanding the natural history of the world and man's place in it. Doesn't that interest you at all?" Patrick Lear stood, impatient for Augustus' reply.

Augustus, who had been working on the drawing in your list while pretending to pay no attention, stared back at Patrick Lear, trying to take a true measure of the man.

"'God said let the waters swarm with swarms of living creatures,'" Augustus said at last, "'and let fowl fly above the earth in the open firmament in heaven.' What else is there to know?"

"You're deliberately trying to provoke me, Starwood," Dr. Lear replied. "I won't have it."

"So you're saying that you believe in the writings of Charles Darwin?" Augustus pressed.

The color rose in Dr. Lear's face. "There is more to understand about creation," he snapped, "than simply declaring that man is just another ape."

"I didn't say that he was," Augustus countered, "although I have met more than my share of monkeys in my life."

Jack turned away, trying not to laugh. The humor others saw in Augustus' lack of respect only served to enrage Patrick Lear even more.

"I believe my body to be of the earth and my soul to be a gift from heaven. Thus, I am one with Mr. Darwin's discoveries, and separate from them."

"And you believe in miracles?" Augustus asked, refusing to back down. "That virgins can give birth? That men can walk on water?"

"I do not apologize for my faith, Starwood. Not to you. Not to anyone. That these bones have survived to tell me of what life was like millions of years ago is indeed a miracle. I would hope that all of us, even you, might benefit from their discovery."

"I'm sorry, Lear, but it does not interest me. I could not care less to whom the credit is given for such insignificant work. Now, if you will kindly excuse me, I have other, more pressing concerns." Augustus lifted his sketchpad by way of explanation and appeared to be willing to let the disagreement pass.

"I understand, Starwood, that this must all seem pointless to you," Dr. Lear replied. "Trivial even. But I can assure you that having worked in both the academy and in the field, pitting my brains against other men's money, it is discouraging to have one's efforts credited to someone who not only minimizes the work when it is completed, but then, when the work proves to be worthy after all, refuses to acknowledge your contribution and instead claims it as his own. And these days, because they control the very journals in which their work is published, there is little an independent scholar and collector can do to protest. It's as if you have prepared a canvas, identified a subject, and even applied the paint, only to have someone else sign his name to the work once it is done."

"It happens all the time." Augustus shrugged. "How do you think the great masters ever got anything done?"

"I'm not going to waste my time arguing with you," Dr. Lear snapped. "This region was once rich in life that exists no longer. If God has a plan, it is to provide us with opportunities just like these to seek out and answer questions about the history of the planet on which we live."

Then, to signal he, too, had more pressing concerns, Dr. Lear handed a bundle of cash to Little Bear and instructed him to rent or purchase horses. He should also inquire whether or not Maggie Hall would be willing to spend a month in his employ. He would also be willing to hire her boy.

"Tell Mrs. Hall that if there is trouble with the Indians, she and the boy will be safer with us," he instructed Little Bear, "than outside of town with horses and supplies to defend on her own."

Dr. Lear then handed a gun to Augustus. "Just in case," he said.

"In case of what?" Augustus asked me when Patrick Lear was out of his hearing. "In case I need to shoot my own food? In case I want to shoot myself in the foot?"

Augustus laughed at the thought of himself wielding a rifle, but then added in all earnestness, "You know, Cousin, I'm beginning to have serious doubts about this leader of yours. He seems to believe he knows more than his patron, or more than anyone else, for that matter. But he is floundering here, like those fish we saw in the river, running against the current, flopping around on the shore."

"But you will stay and watch the camp?" I pressed Augustus. "I can understand his concern."

"Of course I'll stay." Augustus looked at me as if now I were the one who had lost her way. "I've got work to do. Besides, Cousin, where would I go? Chicago?"

6. Map with Illustrated Border

When Dr. Lear, the student, and I reached the site that Augustus had discovered, the holes Patrick Lear had dug earlier that morning made it appear as if a small animal had been burrowing there. Bits of dirt and rock from the bluff behind the horn had also been removed, as if the animal had tried to determine whether or not to dig into the earth for safety or back into the side of the mountain instead.

"Start here," he said to Jack, indicating a long narrow trench he had excavated earlier. "What I'd like to do first is define a reasonable area where we should initiate our digging. I'm thinking from here to here, and then as far as that rock over there." He indicated where he had dug small test holes. "Then, Peterson, if you don't object, I would like you to measure the site and illustrate any bits of bone we should be fortunate enough to uncover from this particular grid. I don't know how far we can get this afternoon, but at minimum we should try to open this first square and see what is in there."

Without another word, Jack rolled up his shirtsleeves and, using one of the axes, proceeded to carve a narrow trench along the bluff. He turned at the corners where indicated by Dr. Lear until he had defined a rectangle. The two men then worked side by side, clearing the area free of sagebrush and other obstructions, as the wind raged across the side of the mountain, lifting the brush and dirt and sand and often flailing it back into their faces. They scraped away at the earth's surface and, when they could not dig any deeper, they defined an adjoining rectangle, where they again dug into the earth, uncovering what appeared to be the surface of several large fossilized bones.

Later that afternoon, the wind carried with it rain, which drifted over the ridge in thin, gray sheets. Jack and Dr. Lear at first ignored the weather, but when the rain turned to hail and the wind gusted so severely that the ice nicked our skin, the two men abandoned their tools and the three of us took shelter on the downwind side of the bluff where it partially obscured the excavation.

We huddled beneath an overhang of rock, waiting for the wind to transport the storm past where we were working. Patrick Lear daubed at the corner of his eye, where the adjoining skin had been cut by a chunk of ice, and stared silently toward the east where sunlight still illuminated the barren slabs of multi-layered rock. He appeared to focus on the farthest horizon, where the sky met the earth, both hazy and pale, blurred as if the one were becoming the other, the way Augustus often layered his earth and sky and water with the thinnest wash of white.

When the storm passed, the two men pushed away the icy remains of the hail, cleaned up the site according to Dr. Lear's specifications, and secured their tools, while I took some last-minute measurements, which I would use to document the site in the Captain's master journal. Once back in camp, I also transferred the dimensions of the excavation onto a larger map, like the one you asked about in your letter.

At first Augustus helped me apply the grid, but then, when I wasn't looking, he penciled in the illustration of the bear balancing a ball along the map's border, which, in Augustus' representation, appears to be a full moon surrounded by the firmaments, as you've noted. Dr. Lear inspected the map, still blank except for the grid and Augustus' drawing in the corner. He grunted to himself before disappearing into his tent.

Having received what he referred to as a critic's approval, Augustus sat with me for the next three or four nights and continued to decorate the map's border, adding first his tepee by the river and then the mackinaw tied to the shore. Next he penciled in my solitary workspace by the chokecherry bushes, which were beginning to develop fruit, and Dr. Lear's dog howling at the ball of a moon balanced above the bear. When still Dr. Lear did not protest, Augustus added characters from *The Tempest*, including Caliban and other monsters from the deepest recesses of his mind, and a few Indians on horseback who wandered homelessly around what remained of the border of the map. *Très mauvaises terres*, Augustus noted in the far right corner before signing his name.

7. DRAWING, GYPSY INVALID

During the day, while Augustus painted and pretended to guard our small encampment, Patrick Lear, Jack, and I returned to the bluff, where the two men worked to expose whatever was buried there. The surface of the fossils they struck with their shovels was fragile and crumbled whenever it was hit, so they switched to small spades and dug with their hands to clear the dirt and debris from the surface of the bones. Dr. Lear gave me permission to assist, so the three of us worked on our knees, uncovering the remains of what would turn out to be a creature that once lived on that very spot millions of years before.

I scooped at the earth with my hands and deposited the dirt behind me, letting it sift through my fingers, like sand marking time. The harder I worked, the more transfixed I became by the digging, my fingers pushing deeper and deeper through the dirt and sand. Soon I did not even notice or at least care about the heat or the intense light of the sun. When Dr. Lear tried to instruct me, I looked up but I could not see him. Nor could I see the landscape stretching out beyond us. I tried to focus, but everything in the foreground and the background appeared to blur into one cloth, a scrim obscuring a subject of much greater significance, if only I could see through it to the opposite side.

Two bright patches of blue passed overhead. Dr. Lear turned to track the birds' flight. Below us, a heron floated without effort above the trees, its wings flapping once, twice, and then a third time as it followed a narrow ribbon of water carving a canyon through the badlands into the east. The bird's call reached us from across the landscape like a trumpet heralding its passage from another time. I looked at the dirt still spilling from my fingers and then back to Dr. Lear. I opened my mouth to speak, but no words were emitted, as if I had been struck dumb, momentarily suspended between two worlds, neither of which I could see very clearly but which I felt certain existed on both sides of my hands. I blinked again and tried to focus. Then I closed my eyes.

"Peterson, are you unwell?"

Patrick Lear sounded concerned, but there was little if anything he could do for me. I tried to open my eyes, but it was as if they were permanently shut, trying to keep out the light.

"It's very hot," I said.

When next I awoke, Augustus was standing over me, wringing out a cloth. A stream of water pooled in the dirt at his feet.

"Ah, Cousin, there you are." He placed the damp rag across my forehead and over the top of my hair. "I was beginning to worry that we had lost you."

"Is she recovered?" Patrick Lear paced on the edge of our encampment, the scarred side of his face almost collapsed onto his skull. He was grim, but appeared to be more apprehensive than angry.

"She's fine," Augustus assured him. "Don't worry about my cousin. There's nothing wrong that a taste of some good whiskey, if you happen to have any, won't cure."

"Yes, of course," the man replied, his voice betraying his relief at learning there was something he could do to assist in my recovery. "Of course," he said again.

Patrick Lear hurried off and returned with an unopened bottle and a clean glass, both of which he had retrieved from his tent. Augustus poured out a large glassful before handing the bottle back.

"This is exactly what the doctor would recommend," Augustus said. "I'm certain of it."

"No," I managed to tell Augustus. "No, please."

"I myself have experienced heat stroke," Dr. Lear said. "It can be very disconcerting." He looked down on me, and then again to Augustus.

"There's nothing to worry about," Augustus assured him. "She'll be fine."

He watched Patrick Lear reluctantly return to his own encampment, and then he turned and smiled at me.

"No, what?" Augustus protested. "No whiskey? I wouldn't dream of it, Cousin. This is for me."

He took a sip and smacked his lips in appreciation.

"I need my strength and sustenance if I'm to nurse you back to health. You do look lovely there, my darling. So good to see that my little Gypsy cousin has returned." He adjusted the damp towel around my head and spread the ends of my hair out across the ground. "Excuse me for a moment while I get my paper and pens. This is an opportunity I cannot afford to miss. I must tell you that yours is a strange repose, Cousin. You appear to be asleep with your eyes wide open, standing, speaking, moving, and yet so fast asleep."

I distinctly recall Augustus working on the drawing you have listed as "Gypsy Invalid," although for some reason I thought he gave that particular drawing to James Huntington when he visited camp later that night. I recall that afternoon and evening well because Augustus made me lie on the ground, my head wrapped in a damp towel, long after there was a need for it. Whenever I attempted to sit, Augustus was quite resolute that I should not move, insisting that I was much too ill.

When James Huntington visited our encampment later that evening, he carried with him a special broth wrapped in a cloth so the bowl would not burn my hands. I tried to assure him that I was not ill, simply tired and overwhelmed by too much sunlight, but Mr. Huntington was not convinced.

"Even Linnaeus felt dizzy when he looked down the ages," Mr. Huntington assured me. "He said they passed like the waves in the sound, leaving worn-out vestiges of the passed world, and spoke to him in a whisper even when everything else had become silent."

Mr. Huntington sat on a stump of cottonwood and leaned forward. His entire world seemed to circle around me when he spoke.

"I, too, have experienced a similar sort of vertigo," Mr. Huntington confided. "Something you, who have studied anatomy, might appreciate if you have not experienced it yourself. For me, it happens when I look at a person's face. If I stop to consider the layers there—the skin, the muscles, the flesh, all the way down to the skull—I, too, can lose myself. If I'm not careful, I find myself becoming dizzy. Disoriented even. There are times when I allow my eye to move from face to face in a crowd and the more intently that I look, the more I feel myself falling through space if not through time. It is not a pleasurable experience, I can assure you, and yet I often force myself to complete the journey as I consider all of what I see while traveling there."

Mr. Huntington paused as if to recollect his thoughts. Stars blossomed overhead and what had once been but a silvery sky, with only an occasional pinprick of light, was transformed before our eyes into a globe of its own, its blackness brightened by stars and planets and galaxies. The heavens were awash with the light of these worlds, shining back at us through the darkness.

"'He looked at his own Soul with a Telescope,'" he said as if trying to regain his bearings. "'What seemed all irregular, he saw and shewed to be beautiful Constellations; and he added to the Consciousness hidden worlds within worlds.'"

He closed his eyes as if concentrating or trying to regain his footing.

"Is that also Linnaeus?" I asked.

"Coleridge," he replied. "I used to think the experience of exploring a person's face interesting, but not necessary," he said. "Now I have come to realize that it is both. There are worlds within worlds to see there."

I still felt overwhelmed, and could not comprehend a word of what Mr. Huntington was saying. He reached out and touched me, brushing my hair away from my face.

"We, too, are just bones, Miss Peterson. Nothing more than sinews and bone."

8. Illustration (Peterson), Fish in Pond

I completed the study of the fish the day I spent with Mr. Huntington. I had tried to assure Patrick Lear that I was fully recovered, but he would not allow me to accompany him, insisting
that he could not risk letting me work in the sun all day. Before I
could protest, James Huntington, who had stayed that night in
our camp, suggested that if I was up for a walk, both Augustus
and I might accompany him instead. He needed to check the
progress of the stonemasons, he told us, and he had something he
wanted us to see.

Augustus was preparing canvases for the new series of landscapes he was planning and so declined, saying he did not have
the time to be cavorting around the countryside, as he put it.

"But do me a favor," Augustus begged Mr. Huntington.
"Take my cousin with you. I have no need of her this morning,
and with nothing to keep her hands and mind occupied, she'll
spend the day sulking about being left behind, and do nothing
but get in my way. And see if you can't convince her to clean
herself up a bit. She won't listen to me anymore. Maybe she'll listen to you."

I never would have left with Mr. Huntington on my own like
that, but, unable to respond to Augustus' outright rudeness in
front of the man, I chose to ignore it, and turned to get my hat
and a small travel bag with paper and pens.

Mr. Huntington and I followed a rutted wagon road which
cut across a high plateau, punctuated by thick bunches of grass
and scrubby low-lying plants. Thin wisps of clouds skirted the
eastern horizon, tempering the glare of the morning sun, which

by then was casting shadows along the ridge. Antelope grazed in the distance, a few of them curiously raising their heads, but otherwise the animals appeared oblivious to our passing. At one point we inadvertently walked right next to a rattlesnake but it, too, was only remotely curious as it basked in the heat of the day.

We walked for at least a mile, maybe two, until we descended a steep ravine to the south, where five men loaded an open wagon with blocks of stone cut from the side of the ridge. The sixth man was harnessing the horses, preparing for their journey back to Mr. Huntington's land.

"We're just about done, sir," one of the men called out to Mr. Huntington, tipping his cap. "We'll have the rest of these down and ready by the end of the week."

"That's good news," James Huntington said. "It looks like we're going to get this house built in plenty of time."

"Yes, sir," the man said. "Ma'am." He tipped his hat yet again. "You and your husband are going to have the most beautiful house in the world. It'll certainly be the grandest one this side of Chicago. Or the Cotswolds."

Mr. Huntington led me over to the hillside from whence the blocks had been evenly cut.

"It's a rare talent they have, don't you agree?" he asked me, ignoring the man's misconception. "I had seen this kind of quarry operation before in Great Britain, where they say the sunlight of centuries is captured in the stone walls. I offered to pay these men's passage in exchange for the work they are doing here." Mr. Huntington ran his hand over the exposed rock. "But this is not what I wanted to show you." He moved his hand to my arm. "There's a place along that creek bed that I would like you to see."

The ravine where we were standing opened onto a wide, flat river bottom, an oasis of sorts punctuated by wild roses, honeysuckle, and groves of shimmery willow and aspen, before it narrowed again as it carved its way between two sandstone bluffs. We followed a pebble-strewn embankment until we reached a point where rock was breaking away in chunks, revealing dark cavities and small caves along the surface of the wall. Mr. Huntington turned over a large rock where it had fallen away from the cliffs. Hundreds of tiny silvery crystals glistened in the light.

"A woman I once met along the Schuylkill River chided me for removing rocks from their home. She insisted in all earnestness that stones need sunshine to live, inferring that I was in some way killing them when I removed them from the river and stored them in drawers. According to that woman, these rocks are breaking away from this mountain so that they can find their way into the sun."

He broke off a small chunk of crystals and handed it to me. He pocketed another piece for himself.

"I don't know about killing them, but I think you will find that they are most beautiful if you keep them on a window ledge where you can view them in the light," he said.

∞

"I am engaged to be wed," Mr. Huntington announced when we stood before his new home's foundation.

"Yes," I replied.

Although he was not asking a question, he seemed relieved by my response, as if knowing of his marital situation might somehow affect my opinion of his house and his plans.

"I hope you can sympathize, then, with how difficult it must be for a woman to be asked to leave the amenities and comforts of the East behind. Perhaps you could advise me of my prospects."

We stood on a flat, windy plateau, the same bluff Augustus and I had passed with Little Bear on the river. The site had been cleared, leaving an expanse of land, marked along the west and east perimeters by a line of transplanted trees and narrow gullies to allow for hand-fed irrigation. Enormous logs, some up to sixty feet long and over two feet around, had been milled into smooth, regular lengths and stacked into piles, waiting until the workmen completed the grueling task of laying out the foundation and lower-level walls. The rock was also being fashioned into a fire-place, as if they were moving the mountain and restacking it, piece by piece, hoping it might take root much like the trees.

After exchanging a few words of encouragement with the other workmen, James Huntington joined me in front of the foundation. He rocked back onto his heels, his thumbs in his coat pockets, his eyes narrowed.

"I know it doesn't look like much right now. . . ." His voice trailed off, as if in his mind's eye he were adding flesh and mus-cles and skin to the bones of rock piled before him. I don't be-lieve he was imagining the house as it might be, but rather envisioning it as if it were complete.

"It's beautiful," I said. "Your wife should be most pleased."

"That is my hope. But then I always have great hopes. Yet another of Huntington's follies is what I'm afraid she will think. Sometimes you make commitments that, unfortunately, have a way of catching up with you."

A cloud drifted across the sun, casting the clearing into shadow. Mr. Huntington scanned the horizon to the west as if looking for rain.

"We still have plenty of daylight left, and I'm sure Patrick will work until dusk," he said. "Would you mind staying long enough so that we can have something to eat?"

He retrieved his fishing rod and reel and pocketed a handful of hooks and artificial insects tied from feathers and fur. He dropped potatoes, onions, a crock of butter, and a small flask into a canvas satchel, and added a skillet and utensils. He looked ready to go, but he hesitated before placing another handful of potatoes into the bag.

"The river has never failed me before," he explained, "but I don't want us to go hungry."

We walked across the clearing, around an enclosure of nar-row, roughly peeled logs, and past the cabin perched on the bluff. Built on a rubble foundation, the squared-off logs were stacked with white mortar filling. On the covered porch, marked by a railing of weathered tree limbs, a barrel was upended next to a wooden bench, both of which were situated to look out across the river. Firewood was stacked next to the door.

Noting my interest in the humble structure, Mr. Huntington offered to show me his library when we had more time.

"It's not much," he said, "but it's more than adequate to meet my limited needs. I have several collections, both books and artifacts, which you might find of interest. I'm forever bringing my travels home through the things that I collect. My life feels so jumbled up and random at times, my collections help me capture the best of my experiences, and through them I try to bring some sense to my life. That's why I long for an heir. So that all that I once was, all the pieces that made up my life, won't be dispersed again."

I followed him down a steep trail leading to the river, where a creek merged with the Missouri. The wide shoreline was littered with broken cottonwood branches and chunks of driftwood, which Mr. Huntington gathered for the fire. I collected dried leaves and twigs and deposited them inside a shallow pit circled by an existing ring of stones, and then stopped to watch the path of a sandhill crane flying low along the water. When it alighted in the brush, two Canada geese were flushed from their cover. The birds skirted the water, one calling out to the other before the two of them settled and drifted away.

"Did you know, Miss Peterson, that those geese mate for life?"

"I'm afraid I know little about the natural world," I admitted. "I'm still not used to any of this."

"Not much on fires, either, are you?" Mr. Huntington laughed good-naturedly as he cleared the twigs and leaves I had deposited in the pit. "But that's fine," he added sensing my discomfort. "I enjoy this."

After replacing a few twigs and sparking the leaves into flame, he turned and reached his hands into the sky. He took in a deep breath and released it again. For a man who had traveled to so many of the world's great regions, collecting and exploring, it seemed as though he had walked through his own front door when he stood there on the river. He was completely at his ease and did his best to make me feel comfortable.

"What I was going to say before I inadvertently insulted you, Miss Peterson, was that I once had a great passion for bird hunting. I particularly enjoyed shooting waterfowl, which out here make for some excellent eating. About a month ago I shot one of those geese, but before I had a chance to retrieve it, its mate flew down to the body and pushed at the carcass with its head and flapped the air with its wings. It was as though the bird were trying to bring the other one back to life. I later heard what I'm convinced was the same animal, calling out from the top of one of those trees. It was crying for its mate, Miss Peterson. There's no other way to describe it. It was the most mournful, sorrowful crying I think I have ever heard. To this day I cannot escape the memory of it."

With a small fire now burning, Mr. Huntington turned his full attention to me. I could not look at him, so I lifted my arm to shield the sun from my eyes, and wrapped the other around myself in an awkward embrace.

"Oh, dear," he said. "I've done it again. I am sorry."

He pulled the stump of a log into the shade of some wild roses and placed his hand on my shoulder.

"This will keep you out of the sun," he said. "Miss Peterson . . ." he added, but then he hesitated. Now he was the one who was awkward, unable to find the right words. "I want you to know I have never shot one since."

The small fire sizzled and snapped as the crisp cottonwood leaves burst for a fleeting moment into flame. Mr. Huntington released me to add a second layer of twigs.

"Will you be all right?" he asked.

I assured him that I was fine and promised to tend the fire. I may not have been proficient at starting one, but surely I could keep a fire going once it was lit. To prove my point, I reached over and added two small branches to the brightly burning pile.

"Excellent," he said.

Mr. Huntington removed his boots and jacket, rolled up his trousers and sleeves, and picked his way through the shallows where the creek surged into the river. Soon his line was sailing through the warm air, sending water droplets shimmering like small iridescent jewels through the light and shadow along the creek. With each cast, he walked farther downstream, the fishing line rippling and cascading a fine spray of water over his head.

After landing his first trout, Mr. Huntington placed it in a pool dammed with stones and sand. After he returned to the water, I walked down to the artificial enclosure, where the trout circled and circled, its body shifting first from one side and then to the other. I completed a quick drawing of the fish, but soon found my attention drifting back to Mr. Huntington, knee-deep in the water, the dappled sunlight illuminating the tips of his yellow hair. His forearms were moist and they, too, seemed to glisten as his fishing line floated out across the water.

I reached out to touch the slick back of the fish, but it slid away from me, so I placed both hands underneath it and lifted the heavy trout gently into the air. Its large mouth opened and closed. Like Augustus with his ammonite, for a fleeting moment I was tempted to put the fish to my ear to decipher its strange language, but, fearing I might be discovered in such a compromised state, I slipped the fish back into the pool.

"Beautiful, aren't they?" Mr. Huntington deposited another trout into the small enclosure. "I will catch you two more if you promise to let me have your illustration. I'll even see if I can revive that fire."

"I'm sorry," I said realizing the fire had indeed died out. "I fear I'm not made for this." I indicated the water, the land, the sky, and now the fire much as Mr. Huntington had once before indicated them to me.

"It's simply a question of focusing your attention. Like you did with that fish," he said. He threw a handful of leaves onto the cinders and, once they ignited, added more leaves and twigs. He stared for a moment longer at the quickening flames. "I trust you," he said.

With two more trout in hand, Mr. Huntington cleaned them down by the river, replaced his socks and boots, and rejoined me by the fire. Gulls appeared out of nowhere, diving for the fish remains as they floated away.

Mr. Huntington pushed at the burning embers with a stick and built a platform with two logs upon which he balanced the pan. "Now, that's what I call a perfect fire," he said. "As my friend Patrick likes to say, you do good work, Peterson."

He sliced potatoes and onions into the butter and stirred the vegetables with his knife. When they started to brown, he pushed them to one side and dropped in two of the trout. Their tails slopped over the edge and sizzled in the flames.

"I either need to get a bigger pan or start catching smaller fish," he said.

"If I were you, I'd opt for the pan," I replied.

Mr. Huntington turned the browning fish and, satisfied, wiped his hands upon the canvas bag. Only then did he laugh.

"Why, Miss Peterson. I believe you told a joke." He laughed again. "You can be excellent company when you let yourself relax."

We sat in the shade of the roses, the air alive with the sounds of rushing water and of the birds as they noisily took flight from the trees. Mr. Huntington, who seemed to almost inhale his food as I had learned was his custom, appeared to hear nothing.

"I wish you could see the world the way I do," he said, as if we had been talking all along.

I nodded as if I understood and pushed the pink flesh of the fish on my plate away from the bones.

"There are times when I can see my life so distinctly," he said. "It's as if these rocks, this dirt and sagebrush, do not exist. But instead there is grass. Grass," he repeated as if to give the word color and form, "and horses with long, sleek necks and solid gaits. And six-rail fences along the horizon. And a stone barn. I can envision this barn." He stared off in the distance as if describing exactly what he saw. "I have traveled all over the world, seeking, and all along it was in my own country. Practically in my own backyard. Can you see it, Miss Peterson? Can you render a world as real in your imagination as that which surrounds us here?"

Butterflies flitted from plant to plant, and circled Mr. Huntington's shoulders and lingered around his hair. When one alighted momentarily on my arm, lazily airing its wings, Mr. Huntington reached out and cupped it in his hand. When he unfurled his fingers again, the insect was lying motionless in his palm.

"You killed it," I said.

Mr. Huntington held out his hand as if to reassure me. I wanted to touch the butterfly's wing, soft and black and dramatically edged in yellow, but before I could reach it, the insect righted itself and flew away.

Mr. Huntington took my hand into his and then he released that as well.

"It was not dead," he said. "I believe they pretend, to confound those who might wish to destroy them. Or perhaps they are just overwhelmed by circumstances."

More butterflies hovered overhead and he put out his hand as if to offer them a place to land.

"Miss Peterson, now what have I done?"

I looked out over the river as if at that particular moment nothing else mattered.

"It's not you," I assured him when I had regained my composure. "I think I need to go back home. This is not going to work for me here."

"But why? It's so beautiful."

I closed my eyes and opened them again, slowly, like the butterfly had closed and opened its wings, and then, as if this were what we had been talking about all along, found myself telling him about my own dream. The land on Staten Island, the apple orchards left for wild overlooking Raritan Bay, and the house, that sweet little clapboard house with its wide white porch collapsed on one side and its broken windows. And the storage shed with the salvaged barn door we would one day make into a study of our own.

Could I envision another world as real as this one? I could still see the mottled surface of boulders strewn along the shoreline, the narrow tidal creeks with their tumble of stones and clouds of buzzing insects, the sweet smell of decay alongside the marshes and the tall grasses which would brush my skirts and be crushed into pathways on my twice-daily walks, permanently staining my boots with their hay-like smells. And I remember the birds flushed from their cover, taking flight over the open hills, where they merged with a large stand of trees. And the boats. I could even picture the boats and the lighthouses signaling at night from the opposite shore. Sitting there with Mr. Huntington, those sounds and smells were more vivid, more tangible, than the surging creek and the flat, placid river next to which we sat.

"This was *your* dream?" Mr. Huntington leaned toward me, focused on my response.

I brushed an insect away from my face and, as I did so, tried to clear the images flooding over me like the river rushed over the stones.

"Yes, it was a dream," I agreed. "And like all dreams, it was not true. Or at least it was not meant to be."

Mr. Huntington picked his words carefully. "You mean in the sense of fate?" he asked. "That doesn't sound like the woman who documents the randomness of evolution."

"I don't believe in fate, Mr. Huntington. But I also know that randomness or chance or evolution, whatever word you choose to describe it, can be the result of sheer folly. When we first met, you said that after the war you could not go back to a day job as if nothing had happened. How could you expect it to be any different for me? Their leaders, with no regret or apology, sent men with little or no training into battle, where they were mowed down like animals. I have seen pictures, Mr. Huntington. There is no other way to describe it. And those who survived were demoralized, transformed into not much more than savages who would start at the slightest sound, no matter how benign."

Mr. Huntington placed a hand upon my knee. "I'm sorry," he said. "You have every right to be angry at me and all of the rest." Then he, too, stared into the distance. But these were not dreams he was envisioning now, but terrors.

"Inadequate training and preparation were the least of our concerns," he told me. "You suggest that men followed their leaders blindly, but there were very few men who were even able to lead. Half of the officers with whom I served were outright drunk most of the time, their men moving at random across a bloody, body-strewn field. I can assure you, Miss Peterson, that it was something none of us, North or South, were proud of at the time. And we're still learning to heal the heartache to this day.

"But that was a long time ago," he said at last. "You've obviously made your way."

He stated this as if it were just another truth, like his engagement, not requiring a response. And yet I sensed a question, too, as if he wondered how I could have landed on this sandy stretch of beach, yet one more disoriented bird. He opened the flask and poured us both a small drink.

"I wish you would continue," he said.

I told him how after the war I worked as an artist's mannequin, never particularly concerned with what I did or did not reveal. The students I sat for were from society, men and women with little talent, but they paid me well. Seeing them take art so casually, with so little to show for their work, gave me confidence in my own talents. I took to illustration, using discarded pencils and other supplies, copying from books or drawing for hours in the park. Anything or anywhere to focus my attention outside of myself.

The artist I worked for at the time recommended me to Benjamin Waterhouse Hawkins, who was establishing a shop in Central Park. I would like to believe he recognized my talent and wanted to encourage me, but it could very well be that he and his students were ready to move on to someone new. In any event, I was able to secure employment and, as New York underwent its own reconstruction, I felt as though I were building toward a new life of my own. One in which I would never have to rely on another human being ever again.

I could sense Mr. Huntington's curious mind trying to piece together all the disparate parts, the collections of artifacts and bones that had composed my life.

"You mean to survive?" he asked.

"Good women lose their men every day of the year," I replied. "I did not have the heart to go through it again. I needed something—anything, I suppose—which would allow me to make it on my own."

Mr. Huntington nodded. "But you stayed in New York," he noted. "I've always found it to be a city with too much intrigue and not enough charm."

But he was wrong. New York had been an exciting place after the war. I told him of how the Englishman had created a garden of ancient reptiles on the outskirts of London and had been hired by the commissioners of Central Park to accomplish a similar feat. The Crystal Palace of New York, was how it had been described, an island of tropical ferns and exotic trees under a great arched roof of cast iron and glass where visitors could see prehistoric American beasts. A forty-foot hadrosaur was under construction, using molds created at the Academy, and a carnivorous *Laelaps* would be displayed as if attacking the beast.

Men arrived like flocks of white-breasted birds, examining our progress and demanding to know the precise measurements of the belly of the beasts. They planned to host a formal dinner as they had in London, with tables inside the creatures before they were sealed. Fine food and wine would be served, with much toasting, speeches, and cigars. All of us, even those who were mere technicians, could not help but be caught up in the excitement, and in the realization that this was something unique for our country, new even to scientists like Professor Cope, who had studied the animals they were bringing back to life.

We all dreamed of what the museum would look like eventually, and how we would visit it in the years ahead. There was a young boy who made a few extra cents carrying buckets of wax and modeling clay. He told me he would visit the museum with his own children and show them the creatures we had constructed there in the workshop in Central Park. "I helped build that," he would say, and to emphasize his importance he stuck his thumbs into the imaginary pockets of his imaginary waistcoat and puffed out his imaginary chest. These dreams for the future were enough to keep the boy's heart and mind into everything he did. They even buoyed my own enthusiasm, in spite of the fact that the work itself was slow and the conditions under which we toiled must have been hotter and more humid than anything in which these dinosaurs ever could have survived.

But then a strange thing happened. One morning I arrived at work to discover wagons lined up in front of the workshop. Men I'd never seen before were tossing casts and molds into the beds of the wagons and hauling them away. A pit had been dug at the south end of the park to receive the remains. All of our work disappeared, buried in Central Park, never to be seen again. "Back to the earth from whence they came," was all that Mr. Hawkins could tell us. "Back to the earth from whence they came."

Mr. Huntington sounded alarmed as he asked how such a thing could happen, but in truth I could not tell him. It had something to do with politics, I explained. Something to do with power. All I knew for certain was that a new administration had restructured the department responsible for the park and, in the process, had fired everyone in charge.

"And the Englishman? What happened to him?"

"I think he was too upset at first to go home. He traveled to

Philadelphia, where he worked on reconstructing one of the Academy's hadrosaurs, and then to New Jersey, where he worked on a series of paintings for the college there. He hired me again to work as one of his assistants, but that project, too, proved to be short-lived."

"So you, too, were demoralized," he announced.

Again, he was not asking a question, but rather making a statement of fact. And yet, his concern was so genuine that I felt obligated to respond.

"He provided me with references and letters of introduction," I said, "and I was able to secure work in Philadelphia when they prepared the dinosaur for the Centennial display. And then of course the Academy was moving, so I had one more opportunity to resume the work that I had genuinely learned to love."

Mr. Huntington started to speak, but then shook his head as if trying to make the question go away. "Did you dissect chickens?" he asked.

I laughed until I thought I might once again cry.

"Yes, I dissected all sorts of birds. And worse, I often boiled their bodies first. There was a year in New Jersey when I ate nothing but soup."

"Another joke," Mr. Huntington announced.

"I can assure you I was quite serious at the time."

Still, Mr. Huntington seemed amused or maybe relieved by the lighter tone of our conversation. Once again geese were startled along the opposite embankment, but Mr. Huntington did not follow their flight this time but stared at the trees on the opposite embankment, trying to see something or someone on the other side.

"Thank you for letting us speak so informally," he said, turning his attention back to me. "Men and women should have more such opportunities to enjoy the natural world and one another's company." He took my hand in his. "But we should go. I don't want to give Patrick any more cause for concern. He has enough on his mind without worrying about our whereabouts and well-being."

He stood to extinguish the fire.

"I cannot pretend to understand the conditions of your employ, Miss Peterson, or what kind of life it may or may not resurrect for you. But I would urge you as a friend to at least give this beautiful part of the world a chance. The geese and the river and those trees could not care less about our tragedies or concerns. They will go on living as if we do not exist, and will continue to do so long after we are gone. I find that knowledge bracing. Freeing, somehow. I realize I am no one to advise you in this regard, but to paraphrase the poet, the past is a fine and private place, but I would not want to live there."

☾☽

We reached the excavation just as Patrick Lear and the student were preparing to return to camp. Both men were cutting limbs from adjacent shrubs and spreading them over the clearing.

"Peterson," Dr. Lear said, as if I had been standing there all along, "perhaps you could do me the kindness of mapping this before we go. As you'll see, where I estimated we would find additional bones here"—he walked us both over to where they had been digging—"I have found yet more obstructions. All of which appear to be of the same origin."

Patrick Lear punctuated each statement with a stab of his shovel, poking at the surface of the earth.

"As soon as we get more men, we need to start some exploratory digs back in this direction." He pointed with his shovel at the steep embankment rising behind us. "It could be," he added, scraping at the side of the mountain, "that we'll find even more fossils either here or behind there."

Mr. Huntington's eyes narrowed as he considered the implications of what his friend had said. Dr. Lear chewed on the inside of his cheek as he waited for his friend to respond.

"So what you're saying, Patrick, is that all of this"—James Huntington walked around the rock and sagebrush cover, considering—"might in fact be one piece of bone from the same animal? That's over five feet, Patrick." Again he paused to consider. "That would be enormous. Bigger than anything ever unearthed."

Dr. Lear clawed at the limbs and shrubs obscuring the excavation, animated in a way I had never before seen him. "This could very well be one animal," he replied. "You can see where we inadvertently broke off the top of this horn. Here, you can see where the broken piece once fit. We've been following that appendage down here." Again, he pulled more tree limbs away from where the two men had been digging. "We won't know for sure until we get down and around to the side of it, but this appears to be some sort of snout. And see here," he said with growing excitement, scraping away some loose dirt with his hands. "It looks like it could be a socket for an eye."

James Huntington stared at the ground where tunnels and exploratory holes had been dug into the earth. He squinted and held his head to one side and then another, as if to gain a better view, and then rocked back on his heels as he'd done when envisioning his house.

"What do you think, James?" Dr. Lear pressed his friend. "Am I imagining it?"

"I don't know what to think. But I wouldn't leave this out here without knowing. Not with that other one out there watching you."

Patrick Lear jerked back his head.

"What other one?" he demanded to know.

"I don't know who he is. But someone was watching Starwood and Miss Peterson. And today I think I saw someone down by the river watching us as well. What I'm saying, Patrick, is that I would be wary of leaving this for the season if you think this is a discovery worth claiming as your own."

9. Group Portrait, The First Supper

"The First Supper" was initiated over the next few days in celebration of Maggie Hall becoming a member of our party. With more wine and brandy requisitioned from Mr. Huntington's stores, and a meal of venison stew, tinned oysters, and fresh greens and onions spread out before us as if this were and always had been our daily fare, Augustus acted like a man who had once faced starvation but now was saved. Hand raised, white hair flying against the red silk of his best embroidered dragon robe, he sat at the head of the table and proclaimed, " 'Age cannot wither her, nor custom stale her infinite variety; other women cloy the appetites they feed, but she makes hungry where most she satisfies,' et cetera, et cetera, and amen."

"Is that Caliban, too?" Jeb wanted to know as plates and dishes were passed around the table.

"No, my son, that is your dear sweet mother, enchantress of the Nile, who has saved us from a fate worse than death."

"Monsters?" the boy pressed.

"No, a fate much worse than monsters," Augustus boomed, downing a full glass of wine and smacking his lips. "Dying of boredom from the company we keep and the food that we eat. But this, this . . ."

I tried to kick Augustus under the table, but by the look on his face I think I hit Mr. Huntington instead. He started, but did not protest.

"An epicurean heaven right here on earth," Augustus proclaimed.

"I'm going to say this but once." Maggie delivered a skillet of bread to the table and set it down with a heavy, attention-getting thud. "You start turning my son's head with your nonsense and big words again, and I'll murder you in your sleep. Have I made myself clear?"

"Why, my sweet Miranda, you have a touch of the Lady Macbeth. I admire that in a woman and can assure you, as these ne'er-do-wells are my witnesses, I would never dream of turning your son's head." With this pronouncement, Augustus poured himself another glass of wine and lifted it in Maggie's direction. "Only yours, my darling," he announced. "Only yours."

Patrick Lear cleared his throat. "Yes, that's fine, Starwood," he said, taking the plate being offered to him, "but at the moment I believe we have more pressing concerns."

"Mmmmm," Augustus agreed, shoveling stew into his mouth. "Much more pressing. Pass the salt, and the bread, too, if you don't mind."

"Mrs. Hall has agreed to stay with us through the month. I expect all of you to treat her with respect." Patrick Lear pronounced this to the table, but it was clear that Augustus was the one about whom Dr. Lear was most concerned.

"In awe and with respect," Augustus responded, raising his glass now in Dr. Lear's direction.

"As I said, Starwood, that will be fine," he replied.

Dr. Lear scooped up a spoonful of stew and stopped for a moment to savor it. "What I propose is this. We shall maintain a guard in camp both night and day. We cannot afford to lose any more horses or supplies. And we have women and children about whom we must also be concerned. Starwood, you will work the daylight hours along with Mrs. Hall, who will be in charge of our provisions. Since she will be busy most of the day, I expect you to stay out of her way, be vigilant at all times, and remain alert and ready for anything."

Augustus stuffed his mouth full of greens, wiped his chin on his sleeve, and smiled. "I am always ready for anything," he replied.

"Yes, of course." Dr. Lear scooped another spoonful of stew into his mouth and chewed thoughtfully. "The rest of us will share the responsibility at night. Little Bear has agreed to tend the horses and to assist with the dig. Jack will be my right-hand man. And Jeb? Will you be my left?"

Maggie looked up from the stove, where she was plumping dried apples in a pan. The sweet smell of browning sugar, butter, and spice softened the crisp night air.

"Yes, sir," Jeb proclaimed a bit too loudly, trying to sound as responsible as the other men. "I can do both. Shovel and guard."

"Good man," Dr. Lear replied. "The Captain has taken the trouble to hand-deliver a detailed list of instructions which will, to some extent, compromise our plans here. In addition to specific instructions about what we should carry with us into the field, and how we need to be more observant whilst there, he has reminded me once again of his interest in birds."

"Birds?" Now it was James Huntington who was distracted. "What does he want with birds?"

"As we have discussed, James, I am not at liberty to question the man and his peculiar passions. He has his motives, I suppose, as strange as they might seem to us mere mortals in the field. Perhaps he's interested in the drawings Peterson sent when she first arrived here. I believe, Peterson, we have already uncovered a good collection of bird bones, is that correct?" When I did not immediately respond, he repeated, "The birds, Peterson. As I recall, you have quite a collection of them in your possession as we speak."

James Huntington wiped his mouth with his handkerchief and looked closely at his friend. The others at the table, including Augustus, were transfixed by the food and wine and did not seem to notice the tension growing between the two friends. Jack swatted at a mosquito buzzing around his ear.

"And he said what exactly?" Mr. Huntington pressed.

"He said," Dr. Lear responded, pulling the fly sheet from his breast pocket and reading slowly, "'Small specimens are often more valuable than large ones, and should be carefully sought. Bird bones are usually small and very hollow, and should be preserved with great care.'"

Dr. Lear looked to his friend to ascertain his satisfaction. When Mr. Huntington did not respond, but rather wiped his plate clean with a crust of bread, Dr. Lear continued. "James, read it for yourself if you have doubts."

Patrick Lear thrust the paper across the table at James Huntington, but his friend ignored it. He poured himself another glass of wine instead.

"Surely you must understand that I am simply doing as I'm told." Dr. Lear repocketed the Captain's instructions when still Mr. Huntington did not respond. "I am not at liberty to set my own priorities as much as I might wish that I could do so."

"So what are you proposing?" Mr. Huntington knew perfectly well what his friend wanted me to do. As did I.

"I propose we continue documenting any birds we find just as the Captain has requested."

Augustus, who had been busy helping himself to a second plateful of stew and his third jar of wine, joined in. "I like birds," he announced as if this were earth-shattering news. "But could we give them to Maggie to cook first?"

Jack let out a loud hoot of laughter before realizing that getting involved in the discussion at this point might be a serious mistake. He cleared his throat and did the best that he could to turn his attention back to his dinner.

"Surely you're not considering . . ." Mr. Huntington stopped, apparently searching for the proper word.

"Let's be honest, James. The Captain thinks we're all idiots out here. We'll send him a few examples to prove that he's right."

"Now, wait just one minute," Augustus interjected. "The Captain may think *you* are an idiot, Lear, but he doesn't know that yet about my cousin. I don't give a flying fish head what he thinks of you, but the Captain has offered her employment which, as a woman on her own, she is most desperate to secure. As her protector here, I forbid her to look any more stupid than she already appears by getting involved in this charade."

"Forbid? That's a strong word, Starwood. How does your cousin feel about it?" Dr. Lear turned to me.

"I'm not stupid," I assured him.

Augustus tried not to laugh as he sopped up gravy with another piece of bread and washed it down with the last of his wine.

"I never said that you were," Dr. Lear countered. "And I'm the first to acknowledge the talents that you have brought to us here. All I am asking is that you continue illustrating bones as the Captain has directed. Are you willing to do that?"

"But Patrick," Mr. Huntington interjected before I could respond. "You cannot in good conscience ask Miss Peterson to send illustrations to Yale College as if she did not know the difference between the skull of a goose and that of an archaeopteryx."

"This is not your concern, James," his friend replied. He stabbed a piece of meat with his fork. "You know nothing of my situation here."

"But I do," Mr. Huntington pressed. "I've heard what they say about the Captain at the Academy. And I know perfectly well what he will do with any discoveries you uncover here. But I'm warning you, Patrick, as a friend, that you risk your own reputation if you draw Miss Peterson into the midst of a battle that is not her own. Even Starwood knows that."

"Excuse me, but may I say something?"

At the sound of my voice, the men at the table put down their forks and knives. Even Augustus was momentarily distracted from his third helping of stew, but it was Mr. Huntington who leaned forward, encouraging me to speak.

"You are asking me to defraud the Captain. I cannot do as you have instructed."

Dr. Lear pushed away his food. His jaw tightened. He said nothing but his face reddened, as he appeared to challenge us all at once.

"I'm sorry, Patrick, but she's right," Mr. Huntington said. "It compromises her. And it's just not done."

"It is the Captain who is the fraud," Dr. Lear snapped at his friend. "You know as well as I do that Peterson was sent as a direct insult to me. But now that she is here, I need time and she has the ability to buy me some. James, you're the one who insisted I cannot allow her in the field given her infirmity, and she needs something to keep herself occupied while we dig. I plan to continue with my thorough document of the excavation and will send in all the reports as requested. In the meantime, though, I am fully prepared to take responsibility for any misunderstanding the Captain's instructions have created. Do you have a problem with that, Peterson?"

For the first time since arriving in the Captain's camp, I felt myself drawn from a mere backdrop to the men's discussion, into the foreground as an integral part of it. This made me very uncomfortable, but now that I was there I was determined to hold my own ground. Perhaps it was Mr. Huntington's support that emboldened me, but I again told Patrick Lear that I was not willing to defraud the Captain or anyone else, for that matter, even if it endangered my prospects when I returned home.

"As I have already said, Peterson, I'm not asking you to defraud anyone." The man lowered the tone of his voice. "I'm merely requesting that you document any bones I give you as you have been doing all along."

"Do I have a choice?"

Patrick Lear leaned into the table as if he could not quite believe what I had just said. "I'm giving you a choice now," he replied, mouthing each word carefully. "My question to you is this. If I give you something to document, will you do it?"

I looked at Augustus, who was pleading with his eyes. This

is not your battle, he seemed to say. Be agreeable and stay out of their way.

"Yes," I answered. Dr. Lear's face relaxed. "But I will not lie about it," I added.

"I'm not asking you to lie," he replied, pushing away from the table in an unusual gesture that let his relief be shown. He sighed. "And James, what about you? Do you have a problem given what Peterson has agreed to?"

"No," his friend announced. "No problem at all." James Huntington downed his glass of wine and stood to take his leave. "Mrs. Hall, I congratulate you on this meal. It was, given our situation here, quite magnificent. Gentlemen," he added as a good-bye. "Ladies."

◎

Each night, over the course of the next week while the camp was readying for dinner, Augustus asked everyone in the party to sit for his own version of the Last Supper, the painting you have listed here. Jack and Jeb agreed, but only after Patrick Lear gave them permission to do so, saying in effect that he didn't care one way or the other. The two of them crowded together at one end of the camp table, the college boy oblivious to Augustus' directions to hold still or to look in one direction, while Jeb was so serious and immobile that Augustus had a difficult time getting the boy to move or look natural at all. He finally directed the stoic youngster to stand behind Jack, his arm upon the college boy's shoulder, to keep the fidgeting older student in place.

After completing studies of the two younger men, Augustus took to stealthier methods to capture the others in our group. As long as he kept silent, which he was wont to do when working anyway, no one except for Little Bear seemed to notice or care that Augustus sat under his netting, observing each of the individuals in our group. I remember in particular the study he completed of Patrick Lear, closing his mouth around a portion of meat, his fork suspended in midair. In the drawing, Dr. Lear's usually active facial muscles are relaxed as the man enjoys his food, but even as he does so his tightly buttoned shirt seems to hold him in place. He leans forward, and looks to his right, suspiciously watching for someone lingering just beyond his view.

During this same time, Augustus completed a series of studies of Maggie, whom he never tired of sketching as she stood at the camp stove or worked at the table kneading dough. In "The First Supper," Maggie's long hair falls braided in a thick yellow plait across one shoulder. She points heavenward with her right hand while delivering a pan of bread to the table with her left. She leans over to whisper something into Augustus' ear. Sweet nothings, if I know Augustus, although it's much more likely that she's threatening to shoot him if he doesn't behave.

Little Bear was the only one Augustus had trouble representing, since he rarely lingered in camp while meals were being prepared, preferring to sit with his bear down by the river or to use those early evenings right at dusk to supplement Maggie's supply of meat. Resigned that he would never adequately capture the would-be Indian, Augustus added Little Bear last, showing just his shoulder, the back of his beaded shirt, and the sweep of the man's long hair. As I remember it, he is leaning over to feed his bear, which sits on its haunches, begging for food, while Patrick Lear's dog chews on a bone in the dirt nearby.

For the first few days, while Augustus worked on the large study that would serve as his guide, he became unusually distant and self-absorbed. I'm not sure if it was the work that confounded him or if it was Maggie Hall, whom he had taken to following around like a lovesick dog until she hit him on the head with a spoon. I suspect such a love tap, as Augustus later described it, only served to excite his ardor, but he retreated to the river for the next few days, where he worked on his canvas.

"Cousin, the time has come for you to sit for me," he announced one evening after dinner. "I promise I won't keep you long, since I know how anxious you are to continue making pretty pictures of crows and vulture bones. But I can put it off no longer. I need you now."

I readily agreed because once again I found myself needing Augustus' counsel. The night before, when Jeb delivered a small bird cranium given to him by Patrick Lear for me to document, the boy also delivered a piece of fossilized dentary and a few bone fragments from what might have been the animal's skull. He pulled the fossils from the bottom of a cloth bag.

"Ma said I shouldn't get involved in any of this," he told me, looking around conspiratorially. "Says these bones have nothing to do with us and they could get us both in trouble. But I promised I would show you and I wanted you to see that I was telling the truth."

Jeb handed me the piece of a broken jawbone, and said there were more teeth scattered around the land behind the cabin where they lived. There were more pieces of skull, too, he said, which looked like the head of a giant bird. "Ma says birds don't have teeth, and made me go inside when I was getting this," the boy said, "but my pa sure seems to think so, 'cause I saw him putting the rest of the teeth in a box when he thought we weren't looking."

As the boy spoke, I rubbed away some of the loose sand in which the bone had once been embedded. The dirt pooled on my worktable, and I had that same disoriented feeling I had experienced earlier, as if the world were starting to unravel, one layer at a time. It took me a moment to respond.

"Your father is here?" I asked.

"He was," the boy said. "When he saw Little Bear riding up, he tried to shoot him, only his gun misfired and his hands got burned pretty bad, so he rode to town looking for help. We came here to the doctor's camp, so we haven't seen him since. But he'll be back."

I swept the sand from the table.

"And why is that?" I asked the boy.

"Because if he's interested in those teeth, he's really going to want the big bones that are lying out there on the ground next to them. Must be at least a hundred of them. And there's another skull, too. It's like a regular barnyard burial ground out where we live, only these aren't cows or buffalo, are they, Miss Peterson?"

I remembered the boy's question as I walked down to the river where Augustus was assembling his easel and attaching the large canvas umbrella. Behind him, hundreds of geese circled and called, landing on the water, twelve or fifteen at a time.

"Sometimes I miss the peace and quiet of the streets of Philadelphia, Cousin. At least in the city, when a man wants to talk to himself, he can hear what he has to say."

Still the birds' raucous calls filled the air, even noisier now as more and more geese flew overhead, with some of the birds waddling ashore, dipping their heads up and down in the air. Having adjusted his umbrella and secured his canvas, Augustus shifted his attention to about a dozen birds arriving later than the rest. Shielding his eyes as this newest group passed by, he watched them circle once more before they called out what might have been a challenge. Or perhaps their regrets.

"Now, those are my kind of birds," Augustus announced, watching the geese make their own way downstream. The same birds then flew back, setting off a shrill alarm from their companions on the ground. The new arrivals honked and circled and called, before they, too, alighted amid the crowd.

"I guess it's too much to ask for independent thinking amongst the birds," Augustus sighed. And then, looking back at me, he added, "Cousin, you look like a bird yourself, perched on top of that rock. I want you to sit over there, next to that tree."

I tried to make myself comfortable in the shade of a cottonwood while Augustus disappeared momentarily into his tepee, where he retrieved a red silk scarf. He draped it over my left shoulder and tied it loosely at my waist. He adjusted my hair away from my face, and then stood back for a moment and stared. He instructed me to lean into the trunk of the tree and to relax my shoulder and neck.

"Augustus, I need your advice," I said.

"My darling, that's exactly why I've asked you here. To give you some."

He returned to his easel and continued to stare, waiting, I suppose, for his eyes to adjust to the light. He was healthier now, and stronger, and his skin was copper-colored from the sun. He had long ago abandoned his ritual shaving, so what was left of his beard was long and wispy, making him appear like a mystic from the Orient, the voluminous sleeves of his robe flapping as he worked.

"I do not know your friend the Captain," he said at last. "Nor do I ever hope to have the pleasure, for a pleasure I do not think it would be. He reminds me of many of the men I have met in my long life in the arts, not normally constituted, arrogant, and destined for the hospital if he does not watch his step. But even so, I cannot condone this man Lear, a mere hireling after all, getting you involved in this game of theirs. I would be careful of him if I were you."

Augustus stopped to adjust the umbrella mounted on his easel. Satisfied with the patch of shade, he looked back in my direction.

"Cousin, you moved again. Lean into that tree, if you don't mind."

"I thought you liked Patrick Lear," I said.

"It's not a question of what or whom I like or dislike, my darling. It's all this plotting to steal the man's rightful place in his profession that I abhor. I don't care if the Captain outright purchased his position with someone else's money. Men buy places of power and reputation every minute of the day. This is how the world works. It's like a sacred trust, and men like Lear can't be creeping in from behind closed doors trying to upset all of that."

Augustus made a few more marks on his canvas and then stopped to consider his work.

"I'm the first to admit that if I were in Lear's situation," he continued as he worked, "I would probably do much the same thing. There's nothing worse than having your talents stolen as if they were not yours at all. I don't care who is paying your way. But I would not involve you in such a scheme. It compromises you and is not done, as your new friend Huntington insisted the other night."

Augustus stepped away from his easel and lifted my hair. He readjusted the red scarf to his satisfaction, slipping it across my breast. "Now look at me directly, Eleanor, and quit thinking about that Huntington fellow, too. He is no better than that friend of his. If I were you, I would divorce myself from them both."

I started to protest but Augustus would not allow it. "Eleanor, I resent your recent rebellious nature. It is not befitting a woman in your position. You should know that James is as good as married. He has told me so himself. It is not honorable for him to act otherwise with you."

The sun was slipping behind the cottonwoods, casting columns of light down the canyon and illuminating swarms of flies along the river. A V-shaped procession of geese flew honking overhead, just as the others were beginning to settle.

"There's so much noise in Montana, I can't even begin to think," Augustus said. "I'll never get any work done with so many distractions."

I decided now was not the best time to press Augustus for his advice. If he was right, and I was still at risk of losing the prize I'd traveled all the way to Montana to win, having access to those fossils on Maggie's land might significantly improve my chances. Not that I would defraud Maggie and her son, nor deceive Patrick Lear or even the Captain, for that matter. But knowing of other fossils might possibly help ensure my future. The Captain would pay for a find of this magnitude, assuming there was such a find. Maggie could have the money, if it would help ensure my own future at Yale.

"I'm warning you, Eleanor," Augustus snapped. "Remember what that preacher back in Utah said to you? He said no one is to be trusted, and acted as if these men were still at war. With any luck at all, Lear will come to his senses, do the honorable thing, and move you out of the line of fire. But if not, my advice is to lay low until all of this blows over."

The clouds behind Augustus took on a deep umber color edged in pink, softening the light.

"And for heaven's sake, Cousin, sit still," he said. "I've never seen so many fidgety models in my life."

⊘⊘

Later that evening, right before dark, Patrick Lear walked over to my worktable to inquire after the vulture skull and other miscellaneous bone fragments he had left for me to document. He held a lantern in the fading light, illuminating the illustrations as he compared my work to the corresponding bird remains. He nodded to himself as the light flickered across the small cranium he held in his hand.

"You do good work, Peterson," he said, shifting the light again, "but I think we can do better. James has an extensive collection of skulls, which he has agreed to let you document. If you can convince that recalcitrant cousin of yours to accompany you, I want you to relocate your camp. And his." He added this with emphasis before clearing his throat, as if the thought of moving both Augustus and his tepee were more than he could fathom.

"I want you to move over to James' land. It's a beautiful stretch of country along the river, and I'm certain that you and your cousin will be comfortable there. James has additional men in residence, as you know, and I don't believe you will be bothered should any Indians start to make their way north. I have instructed Little Bear to help you move. Mrs. Hall and her son will accompany you as well."

He placed the lantern on the table and stood directly next to it. "Jack, Little Bear and I will set up a camp of our own at the excavation and we'll make arrangements with the boy for the delivery of our meals. We will all be gainfully employed until we have our work completed, and I won't have to worry about anyone getting shot. Does this agree with you, Peterson?"

"What should I tell the Captain?" I asked.

He stepped away from the table, as if he needed to compose his response. Satisfied, he leaned back toward me. The lantern illuminated his face.

"I don't want you to worry about the Captain," he said. "I will correspond with him myself, and tell him of the illustrations I have seen here today. I will inform him that I have sent a small bird skull and bones, packed to his specifications. This news should appease the man, at least temporarily. And by the time the letter reaches him, followed by the package, we should be able to decide how best to proceed."

The wind picked up along the river, and the lantern shuddered. The man towering over me appeared to soften as the sunlight faded, his dark hair wisping around his face. Again he cleared his throat, as if waiting for me to respond, and then pulled at his collar. He wiped a trickle of sweat from behind his ear, as if rubbing away a pestering fly. He started to pick up his hat but, noticing the bit of jawbone, picked it up instead. Again he sucked on the inside of his cheek and looked out toward the eastern horizon. He nodded and returned the bone to the table.

"I appreciate your support right now, Peterson," he said. "And I'm not asking you to get involved. I just need a little time. As I said the other night, I will provide the Captain with full documentation once we leave here, and in the meantime, I will protect you from any of the other concerns that you might have. If you are willing to make duplicates of your illustrations, my guess is that James will pay you handsomely for your work. He has a genuine interest in these sorts of things, and collects both the artifacts and the illustrations, which he considers art forms in and of themselves. He will make it worth your while, technically and financially, I'm reasonably confident of that."

When I did not respond, he added, "I think you should know that someone else has been watching our camp." He indicated a man silhouetted on the opposite embankment, the sun setting behind the ridge of rock. The man was wearing a hat and fringed leather jacket. He appeared to be just sitting there, smoking a cigar.

"I would just as soon he wasn't watching you, too."

10. Cartoon, Monster from the Deep

Augustus agreed to move to Mr. Huntington's land without complaint, on the condition that I agree to assist him with one last adventure, and not ask any questions along the way. In his tepee, he dumped out all the pieces of fossilized bone and teeth he had collected on his rambles, mostly broken bits of what had once been bone, but none of any determinant origin. In particular he pointed out a piece of what might have once been broken from a jaw, and asked if I thought it would be of any value to Patrick Lear. I looked at the long, narrow ledge of fossilized bone, with no teeth or other defining characteristics, and had to admit that it would be of little interest to Dr. Lear, or the Captain, for that matter. I had already documented and sent off the first two teeth he had discovered, I reminded him.

"Good," he declared. "I don't want to compromise you more than you already have been, but I have plans for these bones."

With a burst of energy and sense of purpose, Augustus pulled gum from his supplies and stuck together his odd collection of teeth, herbivore and carnivorous, fossilized and extinct, to form an exotic dentary from the wedge of bone. He attached shards of bone to complete the look, adding a wash of yellowish paint and, while the composite was still wet, he rubbed it down with sand and dirt. Then, using a chisel from Dr. Lear's excavation tools, he fashioned yet another fossil into a shape that could almost pass for an eye socket. He considered attaching that to the wedge, but decided against it. "He can't be that stupid," he said.

While the specimen dried, he sketched the skull of a horrific-looking beast, with mouth agape, assorted teeth threatening. He dated the drawing, as he might an official documentation, and added a map of a spot along the river, although he would later forget to leave behind this drawing with his man-made piece of skull.

"Augustus, what is this for?"

"For science, my dear. If an artist can't contribute to the world and how we see it, who can? But remember. You promised. No questions. We've got to hurry, though, if you expect me to join you at your new home with James Huntington."

He bagged the smaller excavation tools and his imaginary monster from the deep, and crept from his tent. When he decided it was safe, he motioned me forward. We walked to the bluff overlooking his tepee, where Dr. Lear had earlier pointed out the man wearing the fringed jacket, watching our camp.

"Start digging, Cousin," Augustus announced much louder than necessary as he handed me a spade. "Right here is where I saw it."

I started to laugh, but he shushed me, and told me he was quite serious. Without complaint, I helped dig a trench in the sandy soil while Augustus worked with great concentration, shoveling and moving a few rocks out of the way.

"I've had enough, Cousin," he said at last, even louder this time, admiring the shallow pit carved into the bluff. "I'm too old for this. But I swear to you there was something up here. I saw it."

He sat and placed his head in his hands, and as he did so the monstrous jawbone slipped from his bag. It rolled into the deepest recess of our narrow ravine, followed by the orbital cavity, which lay on its side. He kicked at the bag, scattering more bits of fossilized bone into the hole.

"Mark this place, Cousin," he called out to me. "We'll bring your friend Lear up here when he gets back."

"Augustus—" I protested, but he would not hear me out.

"Just mark it," he demanded again. "We're going to need more help if we're going to get this out of the ground."

He shoveled a few scoops of earth back into the hole and turned to go. "Coming?" he asked, before hurrying off the ledge.

I caught up with him at the river, where he was skipping rocks across the surface of the water. "Augustus, what are you doing?"

"Skipping rocks. I used to do this as a boy," he said.

"But we can't show that to Patrick Lear," I protested, but Augustus cut me off.

"No questions," he warned, letting loose another rock. "Can you do this, Cousin? Skip a stone across the surface?" He handed me a flat, smooth rock. "Try it. It's not as hard as it looks."

I tossed the stone into the river with a splash.

"No, not like that," he yelled at me. "Like this."

He spun a stone onto the water, where it arced six times, almost reaching the other side. He picked up two more stones and, satisfied that they were what he was looking for, handed one to me. "Don't look now," he whispered, "but someone has found our monster." Returning to what I realized now was his stage voice, he yelled at me again. "You're not trying hard enough, Cousin. Watch how it's done." He skipped another rock across the river.

On the ledge, the same small man in the fringed jacket crouched behind some bushes where we had been digging and then disappeared from view. Dirt and rubble cascaded toward the river, and then the man could be seen again, slinging his pack onto his shoulder. He looked back, making it hard to miss the fact that both of his hands were wrapped in white. He scurried along the embankment like a small rodent and was gone.

Augustus took in a deep breath and exhaled with satisfaction.

"Cousin, I like it here," he said. "I suddenly have an overwhelming urge to read some Shakespeare. But first let's pack up and see what kind of monsters we can find buried out there on Mr. Huntington's land."

11. Drawing, Man with Guitar

The pen and ink drawing of the man with the guitar was most likely done the afternoon and evening Augustus and I moved our camp to James Huntington's home site on a bluff overlooking the Missouri. The man in question, Ian Hacker, floated down the river as Augustus and Little Bear argued about the wisdom of setting up the tepee on a small island where the Judith joins the Missouri. The island was not much more than a pile of rocks and dirt where a few shrubs and trees had taken root, not far from where Mr. Huntington earlier had been casting for trout.

"Music," Augustus cried out. "'Where should this music be? In the air or the earth?'" Lifting his ear in the direction of the sound like an animal lifts his nose to a detect a scent, he cried out again, "'But soft, now it sounds no more.'"

A rowboat floated into view with a compact Chinaman in a wide-brimmed hat at the helm. The man was leaning back, keeping the boat on course with one of the oars, while at the bow a man with shaggy brown hair strummed on a guitar. The two men might have floated on by, not even seeing us, had the boat not drifted through the shallows and slowed.

The Chinese oarsman pushed at the rocks to keep the boat from being stranded, but it was too late. The boat grated to a halt. His passenger looked up blinking, as if awakened from a deep sleep only to discover himself in yet another, even stranger dream.

"Gentlemen." Augustus waded out to greet them and to help them climb out onto the land. "I feared such sweet sounds waited upon some god of the island, so I am here to make my claim."

"Ah, right," the man with the guitar replied. He climbed out of the boat as if he had reached his destination. "And you, my dear sir, must be Prospero having brought us here without the benefit of a storm. Very kind. Very kind indeed. And this, I take it, is your magical isle."

The man splashed through the water, hat in one hand, guitar in the other. Replacing his hat, he offered his free hand to Augustus.

"Ian Hacker," the man announced. "Englishman, miner, aeronaut, and musician for hire. And this gentleman here is my good friend Chen." The Chinaman nodded but would not venture closer, wary of Augustus in his red robes. "Like myself, a second son who has left his homeland a free man in the hopes of finding Gold Mountain."

"Welcome to my island paradise, Messrs. Hacker and Chen." When Chen ignored his offered hand, Augustus swept it overhead. "You will discover no gold here, I think it fair to advise, but the island is a treasure trove of wonders nonetheless. Let me introduce you to my own man and Indian guide, Little Bear, whom I have freed from a rock so that he might assist with the construction of my humble home. And this is my dear, sweet Cousin Eleanor who, like me, has been banished to spend the remainder of her days upon this remote isle."

The Englishman looked as if this little pile of shrub-covered rocks in the middle of the river were a dreamland beyond his ken, a notion only slightly assuaged when I assured him that I did not live on the island, and that even Augustus was only temporarily camped thereon. "Right," he said, as if he understood it all. Even the bear, which was flailing around in the water searching for fish, was accepted by the Englishman without question.

The Chinaman in his company was a neat, fine-boned man, who knew how to use his compact size to his advantage. With little effort, he pulled their boat onto shore and secured it. He then joined us, carrying a bottle of Scottish whiskey and a pickle barrel filled with sawdust and ice. He cracked the barrel open, spilling a pool of water at his feet.

"Oysters!" Augustus exclaimed. "Can I interest the two of you in being my guest here on the island for the day?"

But the Englishman needed no invitation. He had already located a shady spot beneath a cottonwood, where he commenced strumming on his guitar and telling us his tales. He and Chen were both hard-luck miners, he said, having arrived in the Territories long after the easy gold had played itself out. Chen was particularly unfortunate, since there were laws and taxes to discourage miners like him, and ruffians to run him away from any claims he might try to make should he choose to ignore those laws. Mr. Hacker then told how he, too, had been faced with a similar fate when his hot-air balloon burst into flame before a planned celebratory trip on the Fourth of July.

"An unsolved mystery," he announced. "One of the many mysteries of Butte. Best not to stick around to clear my name since I'd already been paid in advance. Handsomely paid, I should add." The two men had therefore linked their fates and were headed for the Black Hills of the Dakotas to see if they could discover any new luck there.

Mr. Hacker continued to strum his guitar as if perfectly content to let the Black Hills gold and a change in his fortune wait for yet another day. As Chen pried open oysters and the whiskey was passed from hand to hand, I believe the rest of our party would have been happy to let him, if two events had not changed the direction of the afternoon.

The first was when another boat, a mackinaw like the one Augustus had purchased, floated into view. At the front of the barge stood the man in the white duster, who, because of the wind, did not at first hear the guitar. Nor did he see us, so intently was he inspecting the embankment where it was breaking away from the north shore of the river as he drifted by. The face and bare arms of the other man on the boat glistened with a thick coating of grease to ward off the bugs, but even so I recognized him at once. He was the man at the station in Utah. The one who had given me the fossilized leaf.

This second man, who sat at the rudder, was apparently asleep, for, as the flatboat rounded the bend, instead of directing it to one channel or the other, the man did nothing, letting it drift toward the banks of our sandy shore. In fact, had the boat not hit a snag, creating a loud enough thump to startle the man in white, who in turn alerted his helmsman, they, too, might have been marooned.

Hastily poling the boat to the northern, deeper channel, the two men floated by. The standing gentleman tipped his hat as he passed, while his companion, the one from the station, placed his coat over what appeared at first glance to be nothing more than a pile of rocks.

"Gentlemen," the man in white greeted us from the water. "Ladies," he added. "Would you be so kind as to inform me if this is the way to Cow Island?"

"Stay the course," the Englishman called back. "Stay the course," he called again.

"Thank you," the man replied as he drifted out of range. Lifting his hat high over head in a final salute, he then placed it upon his heart and bowed in our direction.

"Good man, that," the Englishman said as the boat floated downstream. "Lovely chaps. Gentlemen, to be sure."

Augustus peered out from beneath his netting. "You know them?" he inquired.

"I met them, yes. In Fort Benton. The tall chap, the one in white, was purchasing fossils from some ruffian." The Englishman plucked absently on one of the guitar strings, adjusted it, and then plucked it again. "Dreadful fellow, that," he said, as he continued working the strings of his guitar, plunking and tuning. "Had hands wrapped in bandages, one arm all the way to the elbow and the other almost to the wrist. A Montana outlaw who can't even handle his gun."

The Englishman chuckled as he recalled the man in question, his laughter followed by the sound of six strings strummed in unison. Satisfied with the harmonious result, he looked up at Little Bear, who was sitting with his back against a tree. His bear rummaged with his nose through a pile of leaves.

"Odd country, this," the Englishman said.

☙

Later that afternoon, we waded through the shallows on the downriver side of the island and followed the narrow path back up the bluff to James Huntington's home site to see if we could help with the preparation of our dinner. Emboldened by the drink, we also hoped to convince Maggie to feed an extra couple of mouths. As we climbed the embankment, we could hear the pounding of hammers and other sounds of construction, followed by the barking of Dr. Lear's dog, which ran out to greet us along with Jeb, who lagged not too far behind.

The hammering, it turned out, was not from the Welsh workmen, who had returned to the quarry, but from Mr. Huntington, who was working on the corrals. Even now I blush at the thought of revealing this, but with his shirtsleeves rolled to the elbow and his hat pushed back to reveal the golden streaks in his hair, he appeared to me as godlike. Or at least as someone from another, more ancient time.

Maggie was standing at the camp stove set up next to Mr. Huntington's cabin. She started to complain about the visitors, but retreated to the storage shed when Augustus headed in her direction, a hungry look in his eyes. Augustus, temporarily deterred, started to erect his umbrella, netting, and stool in the shade, when Maggie reemerged, demanding that he wash the filth from his hands and get to work chopping vegetables. Augustus smiled as if his attentions were again being welcomed and, abandoning his netting, proceeded to splash water about himself in a benediction.

"She likes me," he announced, chewing on a carrot.

"And keep your hands out of your mouth," Maggie chided.

"Oh, Maggie, say it isn't so. ' 'Tis an ill cook that cannot lick his own fingers.' You know that." He reached for another carrot but she hit his hand hard with a spoon.

"And stop that other nonsense, too. Bring home all these extra mouths to feed, you better get to work if you want anything for supper."

The Englishman, fearing he, too, might be thumped if he did not make a contribution, picked up his guitar and strummed, humming quietly to himself.

"Feels just like home, doesn't it?" Augustus asked. " 'Sounds and sweet airs, that give delight, and hurt not.' " He chopped vegetables and, when Maggie wasn't looking, popped another piece of carrot into his mouth. " 'Sometimes,' " Augustus continued, " 'a thousand twangling instruments will hum about mine ears.' "

"I'm warning you," Maggie said without looking up from the stove.

Ian Hacker, more confident that not only would he escape censure but he and his man might actually be fed, picked up the tempo and the volume of his strumming. At the sound of the music, James Huntington restacked the last of the poles, stripped off his shirt, and proceeded to wash at the water barrel situated next to the cook stove. He did not seem in the least bit concerned by the women standing nearby watching, Maggie more discreet than I was, if Augustus' words of warning to me later were true.

"I once heard guitarists in Europe perform music like that," Mr. Huntington said. He pulled a freshly laundered shirt over his head and slicked his wet hair away from his face. "There were dancers, too. Women in big skirts, with flowers in their hair, and men with high-heeled boots. You're not here to pick our pockets, are you, Mr. Hacker?"

Ian Hacker was at first stunned by the question, but realizing it was asked in jest, replied "Ah, yes, right." He laughed, revealing a mouthful of too many teeth. "No, we are not Gypsies, but mere second sons, castaways from society in search of a fortune of our own. We wouldn't refuse a bit of dinner, though. That is, if it were offered."

"He brings whiskey and music," Augustus announced. "I vote we invite him to stay."

"Mrs. Hall?" James Huntington inquired.

"I already have too many mouths to feed," she announced, and turned her back on the lot of us. She stirred grease into a pan.

"Oh, Maggie," Augustus protested. "Say it isn't so."

"If you would let me finish, I was going to say two more aren't going to make any difference. Besides, we don't want them wandering out there by themselves. There are Indians about."

"Right, then," Mr. Huntington said. "As our friend Mr. Starwood, here, would say, 'If music be the food of love, play on.'"

"A gentleman and a scholar," Augustus declared, dumping a pile of chopped potatoes, onions, and carrots into the pan sizzling on the stove. "And madam, while you may be prickly, you are without a doubt the country's most enchanting wild rose." He bowed deeply to Maggie. "But now you must excuse me, for I have important work to do."

Augustus retreated beneath his netting, while Little Bear chopped a pile of wood he had collected down by the river. I sat on the uneven porch step leading up to Mr. Huntington's cabin, waiting as he disappeared inside to retrieve a skull he wanted me to document for his personal records.

"I realize this isn't a bird," he said, joining me on the step, "but I was wondering if you might be willing to work on this until Patrick arrives and gives you better instructions for how to employ your time while you're here. This one is a particular favorite of mine, and it would please me very much if I had a proper illustration of it."

He handed me a small tortoise skull, which he said he found

while retracing the journey of a man he had met by chance in the British Museum.

"The man was there to inquire after the collection he had donated from his journey down the Amazon with Alfred Wallace," Mr. Huntington explained. "The way he described the lands, and the thousands of species new to science they encountered, I knew at once I must see it for myself. I discovered this little fellow during my journey there. I don't believe he is prehistoric in the sense of what you and Patrick are interested in here, but he is old nonetheless."

I held the skull in the palm of my hand and examined it closely. With its beak-like mouth and my renewed humor, which had been helped immensely by Mr. Hacker's whiskey, the animal appeared to be whistling along to the Englishman's tune. I sat the skull in my lap and stared out across the clearing. A freshening wind blew in from the west.

Mr. Huntington pulled a chair and a small table onto the porch of his cabin and provided me with a heavy leather-bound journal and a set of pens for my personal use. He disappeared into his cabin again, and reemerged with a gilt-backed volume of *Naturalist on the Amazons,* by a Mr. Bates, which he said I might also enjoy perusing as I had the time.

To an outsider, the scene that afternoon at Mr. Huntington's home site might very well have appeared like any other domestic situation. Dr. Lear's dog dozed at my feet and birds called back and forth to one another across the clearing, competing with the cheery strums of Ian Hacker's guitar. Little Bear continued to chop firewood, which Jeb stacked neatly next to the stove, while his mother worked at stirring up one of her masterful stews. All of us, it seemed, were trying to contribute by staying out of each other's way and giving each other small pleasures while we waited to eat.

12. Portrait, Indian Surgeon

In our complacency, none of us paid much attention when Patrick Lear's dog roused itself from its slumber. The dog sat up and tilted its ear to the wind, much like Augustus had done on the island. It bounded out past the corrals just as Dr. Lear galloped into the home site, leading Jack's horse. The animals kicked up dust and debris as they ran.

Jack was slumped in the saddle, looking lifeless as he clung to the neck of the large animal. The student was bootless, and blood seeped from one of the legs of his trousers, in spite of the strips of cloth tied across the young man's thigh. The far side of his saddle was black with blood.

In a flurry of activity in which everyone seemed to know what to do without having to be told, and time seemed to be suspended even though the world around us whirled out of control, Mr. Huntington and Dr. Lear lifted the young man off his horse, while Little Bear, Jeb, and I cleared the table. Maggie poured water into pots and placed them in the fire, while the two men laid the student upon the table, like one would place a corpse, for a corpse the young man appeared to be. His face, only hours before the color of honey, was now pale, and his hands were white around the fingertips and cold to the touch. Mr. Huntington cut the student's trousers along one leg and pulled the sticky fabric away from the flesh, revealing a blunt hole and a gaping gash that had torn the thigh.

"Indians," Patrick Lear announced with contempt. "Can't even shoot straight. Look at this mess."

"I've seen worse," James Huntington replied, "but I'm not

sure I know what to do about it. If we were in the field, they would simply cut if off. But I don't think I have the stomach for that."

"We are in the field, man," Patrick Lear shot back. "What else can we do?"

The two men eyed one another carefully. "This isn't war, Patrick," Mr. Huntington said.

"Tell the Indians that," his friend replied.

Needing to take some kind of action, Patrick Lear stormed off with the two horses and pulled the saddles from their backs. Both animals bolted to the opposite side of the temporary corral as soon as they were released, kicking up even more dust, which was picked up and carried in the wind.

"The bleeding isn't as bad as it looks," Mr. Huntington announced as if to himself. "Let's take a look at it after it's clean. Jeb, can you get me some rags? And soap. I'll need some soap."

Augustus emerged from his tent of netting and stood at one end of the table, sketchpad in hand. He stared at the lifeless body covered with blood stretched out before him, and then walked out to the ledge above the river. He looked as though he might be sick.

Little Bear washed his hands in the barrel. He tore a sheet of cloth into rags and deposited them into the pot simmering in the fire. He pulled a heavy woolen blanket from the storeroom and handed it to Jeb, wordlessly instructing the boy to cover the student. Looking as if he might burst into tears, the boy did as he was told, careful not to interfere with Mr. Huntington.

"This leg would go if he were a recruit," Little Bear said, standing next to Mr. Huntington, who was washing blood away from the wound. "It's easy enough to do. But if he were an officer, we would save it."

"Can you?" Mr. Huntington inquired.

"I can try," Little Bear replied, again without any sign of emotion.

I could not watch, but was later told that Little Bear expertly cleaned the surface of the wound, cut it even deeper with his knife, extracted two bullets, one of which had lodged in the student's femur, and the other which had skirted the bone and torn through the flesh. He cleaned the wound of even more debris, and sewed the gaping hole into a long tight slit marking the front of the student's leg. The entire surgery took only a matter of minutes, after which the student was bundled up and put to bed in the cabin.

The only true likeness Augustus captured of Little Bear that summer was this portrait, initiated after the would-be Indian saved Jack's leg and probably his life. Augustus worked on it later that evening, after Patrick Lear had retreated to the river to consider his next move. He was willing to risk his own life, Dr. Lear announced, but he could not accept responsibility for any others.

Little Bear wasn't convinced that Indians were the cause, saying only that the wound wasn't made by an Indian's gun. James Huntington pressed him for an explanation, wanting to know, too, how such an unlikely man had developed such precise surgical skills.

"I've been told all the old guns from the war have been traded to the Indians," Mr. Huntington noted. "I've even seen a few. They never were worth much, but I can assure you they still work."

"Perhaps," was all Little Bear would say. When Mr. Huntington waited for him to continue, Little Bear added, "If an Indian had wanted to kill the boy at that close of range, he would not have wasted two bullets. He could have easily done it with one. I'm afraid it's members of our own race who don't have much skill when it comes to shooting one another."

The two men exchanged a look of recognition, after which Little Bear quickly lowered his eyes to the fire.

"You were in the war, weren't you?" James Huntington asked.

Little Bear stood as if to excuse himself, but Mr. Huntington would not, or could not, relent.

"A medic?" he asked.

The early evening light reflected off the underbellies of birds as they wheeled through the sky. Little Bear pushed at the dirt with the soft toe of one of his moccasins, but still he did not respond.

"May I ask what happened?" Mr. Huntington pressed.

Little Bear wiped the palm of his hand across his mouth and down his chin, and turned his attention to a buckskin tie on his vest. "I was told flat out I was unfit for further duty as if I had been diseased. I was sent home to recuperate, or least that's what they said."

His face grew hard and contorted as he was forced for just that moment to remember. Seeing him then, withdrawn into another time or place altogether, it was not difficult to imagine him in military dress looking out over a field devastated by battle.

The wind moved across the clearing, lifting small clouds of dust. Dr. Lear's dog ran after the spinning dirt and then, spying a flock of ducks hovering together in the water, ran straight down the embankment, sending birds protesting into the dusty air.

"I was more than fit," Little Bear continued. "That was the problem. I made the mistake of cooperating with a government commission sent to prepare a report on the conditions under which we were trying to work." He laughed, but he did not think it funny. "How could I not cooperate after what I had seen? Men suffering from want of sufficient food and water. Men lost to severe exhaustion due to undisciplined marches and lack of sleep. And when men were sent into battle, there was no strategy but that of unleashing a hungry, angry mob."

"I never heard of such a report." Mr. Huntington made the announcement as though questioning himself, rather than Little Bear.

"Oh, there was a report, all right. It was scathing, which was why they condemned me as well. The officers threatened to resign if the charges were made public. They said the report would discourage recruitment. Even the surgeons refused to continue if the report was released."

"You would think the medical staff would want to improve—"

"You would think a lot of things," Little Bear interrupted. "But these men do not think. Not in war. They were promised blankets and bandages and baked and canned goods. That alone was sufficient to purchase their silence."

Mr. Huntington looked at Little Bear, not believing what he had just heard.

"They were promised more, of course. Funds for medicine and surgical supplies. But most of that went to purchase brandy and wine. The spirits tipped the balance, keeping the officers and their charges in line. None of them were content, but they were resigned to see the war through to the end."

Little Bear had a distant look on his face, as if he were trying to disappear into himself. I'm certain Mr. Huntington could tell his questions were difficult and not welcomed, but still he pressed to learn more.

"And you?" he asked. "What happened to you?"

"I don't know," Little Bear replied, the familiar flatness returning to his voice. "I was never injured, but at some point my spirit fled my body. I was no longer the person I had once been. It was the result of one of the battles, but I can't even tell you which one. All I can remember is the constant sound of gunfire. And one man crying out into the night, 'Oh, the dead and dying on this bloody field.'"

When it looked as though he had nothing else he could tell us, Little Bear continued. "I don't believe in souls. Not life after death. Not any of it. But all that was left of me after the war was a hollow frame of bones and muscles and flesh. The rest of my body or soul or whatever it was that contained all of the man I believed myself to be had deserted. I was empty. There was nothing left."

"So you came out here to fill it again?" Mr. Huntington's

voice sounded sympathetic but the question was too pointed. Little Bear recoiled.

"Mr. Huntington, please," I interjected. "This has been a difficult afternoon. For us all."

Again Little Bear wiped his thick hand across the corner of his mouth, as if wiping away blood.

"Filling it up again," he continued, in that same inexpressive way of his. "It's never that easy, is it? I lost the desire to intermix with others of my kind. Out here, at least for the most part, I don't have to. And with this dress . . ." Little Bear looked down at his mismatched buckskins and moccasins. "Let's just say people tend to leave me alone."

Augustus walked up to the table with the half-empty bottle of brandy that Little Bear had used during the surgery. He poured a large splash into a coffee cup and offered it to Little Bear. Then he poured a cupful for himself.

"They left you alone, that is, until we barged into your life," Augustus noted.

Little Bear laughed again, this time as if appreciating a private joke. "A man's got to eat." He lifted the cup to his lips and then paused. "And drink," he added, nodding in Augustus' direction.

13. Drawing, American Trail Riders

Later that evening, with two or three hours left before dark, Patrick Lear asked Little Bear to accompany him to the temporary camp he had established next to the dig site. Mr. Hacker, eager to earn his keep, volunteered the assistance of Chen, who, the Englishman claimed, was an expert at handling mules, although the Chinaman did not look very comfortable sitting on the back of one. The drawing in your collection is of the three men as they trailed down the embankment, Dr. Lear straight and stiff in his saddle, Little Bear relaxed and almost one with his blanketed pony, and Chen perched atop the back of a mule, his long black queue bobbing up and down underneath his hat as he bumped along, leading two of Mr. Huntington's pack animals.

"All I can say is, God bless America," Augustus said as he watched the three of them disappear down the canyon. He made a few quick sketches in his notebook. Only then did he turn his attention to me.

"It's getting serious now, Cousin. I believe it's time for you to go."

Of course he was right. We were in essence circling the wagons, preparing for an assault, one which we were ill prepared to survive should we be attacked. Little Bear could very well be right that we were not threatened by Indians but, whatever the threat, there was no point in staying any longer if I did not live to return home.

"My suggestion is that we put you and young Jack on the next steamboat out of here. Might be able to link up with that friend of yours in the long white coat or the little rat with the fringed jacket and have a real adventure. But either way, I don't want to be held responsible for some redskin deciding you'd make him a good wife."

He laughed at the thought of it but then stopped to consider. "Now that I think of it, you probably would."

"Augustus, please."

"No, of course you're right, Eleanor. I apologize. You would no doubt be some poor Indian's worst nightmare." Again he laughed to himself, shifting his attention to Jeb and Mr. Huntington, who were working again on the pole corral. Maggie walked over to her son and slipped an arm around the boy's shoulder. Jeb listened with great earnestness to whatever his mother had to say. She smiled and tousled her son's hair.

"What about you?" I asked Augustus.

"I'm surrounded by the walking wounded," he replied. "But I think she has what it takes."

For the first time since the operation, Augustus looked directly at me. The strain of the day, coupled with an excess of brandy, had ravaged his face. He looked as if he had aged overnight, or just that afternoon, into a very old man. He turned his attention to Maggie as she moved in her brisk, no-nonsense way to the cabin. She said something to the Englishman before disappearing indoors to check on Jack. The Englishman nodded and smiled to himself.

"'The fair, the chaste, the unexpressive she,'" Augustus sighed, his eyes still lingering on the door behind which Maggie had disappeared. "I wonder if she would pose nude for me."

"Augustus!"

He shrugged as if dismissing a jealous suitor, and walked back to the camp stove to help with cleaning up. Watching his slow, plodding gait as he carried a stack of plates back into the storage shed while Maggie reemerged from the cabin, scurrying here and there accomplishing three times as much, I realized that Augustus was capable of building a new life for himself here. And if he was, why couldn't I?

Patrick Lear, Little Bear, and Chen returned later that evening, walking their horses and mules along the edge of the river. The moon shifted from behind a cover of cloud, casting eerie shadows in among the cactus and brush as one by one the men and their animals walked up the embankment like phantasms rising from the earth in a wash of blue light.

"Any sign of the Indians?" Mr. Huntington called out as the men drew nearer to camp.

"Not a sign," Little Bear answered. "I rode out onto the plateau and looked around just in case. I didn't see a thing."

Little Bear and Chen walked off with the horses and mules, while Jeb ran ahead to open the corral. Patrick Lear watched them trail off across the clearing.

"Jack's doing better?" Dr. Lear inquired.

"Remarkably better," Mr. Huntington reported. "He's asleep now, but earlier he was sitting up, eating some soup that Mrs. Hall prepared. Says he doesn't even want to go home, although I'm not convinced his staying here would be in anyone's best interest. I wouldn't want the responsibility of him in his condition. Maybe you should contact his parents and ask them what they want you to do."

Mr. Huntington turned his back to the fire and lowered his voice to keep the rest of us from hearing what he said next, but the night air was so still I could just make out that he was informing Dr. Lear of Augustus' plans to send me home with the boy.

Patrick Lear stared down at the campfire. "Where is Starwood, anyway?" he asked.

"He and the Englishman are sleeping out on the island. They both insist they're not afraid of Indians, and I tend to agree with them. There's not much worry of them coming around here."

Dr. Lear removed his hat and held it in front of him. He fingered the soft felt around the brim. "The excavation has been tampered with," he announced.

"What would Indians want with a bunch of fossils?" Mr. Huntington replied.

"It wasn't Indians. Little Bear was right. Just some crack-brained lunatic who wasn't much of a shot. Must have liked the looks of Jack's boots, since we found his old ones in the ravine next to where he left the boy. This is a horrible country. They'll shoot you for your belt buckle or the sugar in your pack if they think they can get away with it."

"But fossils? Surely you don't think—"

"I don't know what to think anymore," Dr. Lear interrupted. "But whoever it was, he was interested in what we were doing up there. Didn't even look at any of our gear, and I had my tent and cookware and tools all free for the taking. If it had been an Indian, at least the knives and pans would have been gone. Whoever it was ignored all of that and just poked around where we were digging. He obviously wanted to know what it was we were uncovering."

"What are you uncovering?"

"I don't know." Dr. Lear chewed thoughtfully on the inside of his cheek and then pursed his lips. He ran his hand over his chin where the beard was now all stubbly. "There appear to be bones buried everywhere, but they're all back in that bluff. I don't think I can get it out of there without some assistance. And if that fossil I showed you before is a skull, it's so big I'm not sure how I would transport it even if I could get it out. And now with Jack out of operation . . ." He stopped to consider. "There's no way I can do this on my own."

"You could always contact the Captain for more help."

"You know that man would have me out of here in a heart-beat, moving in as if all of this were his. I'd rather have more in hand first. Not that there's any guarantee that I can protect myself even then." Again he let his voice trail off as he took the cup of coffee Maggie offered.

"But they are his for the keeping, Patrick."

"I know that," Dr. Lear replied. He sounded resigned, all of his anger and wariness a thing of the past. "He can have the fossils. Store them away in drawers or in the museum. It doesn't matter to me. But just this once I'd like an opportunity to establish myself. Otherwise all I will have to show for my life is the success and accomplishments of others. I know under the circumstances I will never amount to much, James, but I must have something of record to show for all the work I've done."

Having unsaddled the horses and stowed the gear, Little Bear and Chen walked over to the camp stove for coffee.

"There's always Little Bear," Mr. Huntington suggested.

Again Dr. Lear pursed his lips and sighed. He rubbed his face and placed his hat back on his head as if to leave.

"I know I won't be of great assistance," I could not help but chime in, "but I am willing to do whatever I can. The Captain sent me here for the summer and I would like to complete the assignment and demonstrate that I'm worthy of his trust."

"Since when do you care about the Captain?"

Augustus walked up from the river, wearing nothing but his red robe and his boots. When everyone stopped as if to ask where he came from, he explained, "I smelled coffee and thought it might be morning." He looked at the stars and the moon partially hidden behind a wisp of cloud. "Wrong again." He shrugged.

"I don't want to go back, Augustus." I stood so that the men weren't all towering over me. "I want to finish what I started here."

"Now, listen, Eleanor, we've been through all of this." Augustus sounded annoyed, but he was clearly exhausted. "There are Indians out there and I can't be held responsible for you under those conditions."

"I'm not asking you to be responsible for me, Augustus. Besides, there are no Indians."

Augustus dismissed me with a laugh and shuffled over to the camp stove to get a jar of coffee.

"Ask Little Bear," I challenged him.

"What does he know?" he dismissed me again. "He's no Indian."

Augustus' demeanor changed when he approached Maggie, as if all his harsh edges softened in her presence. He smiled directly into her face. She frowned at him but handed him his coffee. He smiled again, dipping his head to one side.

James Huntington stepped back into the light of the campfire. "May I interject here?"

"This is none of your business, James." Augustus stood at the edge of the circle of light. The gold dragons on his robe appeared to leap across his chest.

"Augustus!" I pleaded, but he ignored me.

"James, you're a good man, and you're building a decent life for yourself here. But don't be breaking my cousin's heart with promises you can't keep. I agreed to accompany her here, and I must insist that she be allowed to return in one piece. For heaven's sake, man, we're in the middle of nowhere surrounded by savages."

"But Augustus," I insisted, "they say there are no Indians anywhere near here."

"Don't be stupid, Eleanor. I'm not talking about Indians."

"Augustus, what has gotten into you?" I tried to lower my voice, but everyone was silent, staring at us.

"I'm tired, Cousin. And with all this commotion it's difficult to sleep. But in case you have missed the obvious, a young man almost died today. This is no longer a simple childish amusement of digging in the dirt. I want you to go home. And preferably not in a box."

"I'm not going, Augustus," I said, trying again to whisper but finding it difficult to keep my voice down. "Not if the others are staying."

"Well, that's settled, then," Augustus exclaimed, handing his half-empty cup back to Maggie. "But I want everyone here to know that I will no longer be held responsible for this woman's well-being."

"Since when have you ever been responsible?" I challenged him again.

"We'll talk about this in the morning," Augustus replied.

Noticing the others still standing speechless before him, Augustus bowed. A gust of wind lifted the border of his robe and rippled it like a red silk ribbon around his bare knees.

"'Blow, blow thou summer wind,'" he said before shuffling back to the river. "'Thou art not so unkind as woman's ingratitude.'"

14. DRAWING, READY FOR WAR

The two Crow Indians in military dress represented in this drawing arrived at Mr. Huntington's home site the night of the same day Jack was shot. Maggie, Jeb, and I had made beds on the floor of Mr. Huntington's cabin, where we slept across the room from the student, while Augustus, Little Bear, Ian Hacker, and Chen all slept out on the island, in or next to Augustus' tepee. Mr. Huntington and Dr. Lear stayed up late, talking by the fire.

It was hot in the cabin, and I could not sleep, so I took to examining the contents of Mr. Huntington's library as a candle burned itself out on his desk. Shelves of books were stacked along one wall, with titles from astronomy to the ancient philosophers of Greece. Skulls of animals and birds stared blankly from a ledge along another wall, and in the corner, Indian blankets, beadwork, and other artifacts Mr. Huntington had collected during his explorations around the world were displayed. I can still recall a headdress decorated with row upon row of iridescent green beetles strung across the band like beads, and a ceremonial spear with ribbons of black beetles, each of which was almost as big as my hand. On his desk were stacked flat wooden boxes topped with glass under which were pinned exotic butterflies and strangely colored moths. Two more boxes were displayed on the wall as if they were great art. One contained a brown and yellow butterfly at least a foot across, and the other held an equally formidable moth with markings which, at first glance, made it appear to be a snake.

Fearing my restlessness was keeping Maggie and the others awake, I took a buffalo robe out onto the porch and watched as the sky cleared of clouds and deepened into a blue-black awash with stars. I could hear the river moving through the landscape down below me, the surging sound of the water heightened in the hot summer air. The horses in the corral shuffled in the dark. An owl's cry pierced the darkness. And then another.

It was well past midnight, and still Patrick Lear and James Huntington sat by the fire. The tension between them seemed to have subsided, replaced by a mutual concern about what should be done next. Although neither seemed to be particularly worried about Indians, their demeanor suggested that they might have other concerns. As the two men talked, their voices rose and fell against the rushing of the river and the gusting of the wind. Sometimes I could hear every word they said, other times I could hear none of it. But it was reassuring to have them there, their voices weaving in and out of the night like the bats dipping and weaving around the cabin.

I must have fallen asleep, for the next thing I remember was the rasping sound of the word "whiskey" and two Indians towering over the fire. They seemed to appear out of nowhere, slipping into camp under the cover of night. Even the dog didn't hear them until they entered the ring of light, the two Indians looking down on James Huntington and Patrick Lear, both of whom hastily stood to greet them. If the two men feared the intruders, they gave no indication. Perhaps it was because the Indians wore military-issue boots and blue woolen jackets, only partially hidden under the blankets in which they were wrapped. Or they might have been able to tell just by looking at their angular, handsome faces that both Indians were Crow, a tribe allied with the U.S. government.

James Huntington greeted the young men in their own language and offered them drinks. After downing in one swallow the finger of whiskey Patrick Lear was willing to share, the two drank bowls of coffee sweetened with sugar and milk and then, without ceremony, sat by the fire as if intending to stay.

It was unsettling to watch the two of them from a distance,

turning from brown to black to red and then to brown again as distorted shadows played across their flat, thin faces and chests. When either of them leaned momentarily away from the fire, it was if they disappeared altogether, only to flicker again into view as if they had just crawled out from the belly of the earth. In spite of Mr. Huntington's apparent ease with the visitors, I could not help but wonder if I should alert Maggie and Jeb, or try to slip down to the river to arouse Augustus and Little Bear. And then it occurred to me. What if Augustus and Little Bear and the Englishman and Chen were already dead? Murdered by the Indians in their sleep. I pulled as far as I could into the safe confines of the buffalo robe, trying to make myself invisible, a shaggy mound immobilized by what was in the end an irrational fear.

I later learned that if it hadn't been for the whiskey, the Indians would have been far more afraid of the two men sitting next to the fire than any of us could have ever been of them. Sitting Bull and the Sioux were moving north through the area, and they were terrified of being out on their own. They had been drawn to the white man's fire, as they called it, for protection from the night and the possibility of finding food.

James Huntington set them at ease with his knowledge of their language, and soon discovered that the two men were scouts for General Crook, the same unit the men from the Smithsonian and the foul-mouthed journalist had been following. The Indians claimed they were discharged from duty, but Mr. Huntington said later he was certain they had deserted and were trying to make their way back to their families. Normally their tribe gathered along the Missouri for the summer hunt, but the young men had not been able to locate them. And without horses, the two Indians were unable to travel far. They were enthused when Mr. Huntington said he knew of their families, but devastated again when they learned he did not know where they had gone.

The Indians matter-of-factly told Mr. Huntington that our

encampment had horses and a boat, both of which they had considered stealing, but said they feared the medicine man who lived out on the island. They had been watching the one with the long white hair, they said, and he was a man of great power. They were afraid that if they violated him in any way, they would have a formidable enemy to contend with either now or—worse, if they were forced to kill him—in the future. Best to leave men like that alone, they explained. Mr. Huntington said something about Augustus which, from the tone of his voice, was meant in jest, but the Indians were not amused, taking the prospect of killing and then encountering crazy men in the afterworld quite seriously. As Augustus would later point out, since most of the men in our party were only interested in digging rocks from the earth, it would appear that our collective safety, at least among these superstitious Indians, was guaranteed.

Patrick Lear offered the Indians something to eat, which they devoured as if they had not eaten in days, and then offered to let them stay the night. The young men took their blankets and crawled under one of the wagons, while Dr. Lear and Mr. Huntington laid out their own bedrolls next to the fire. I would later learn that the two friends traded off a weary watch, just in case, fearing petty theft more than more heinous crimes. I, too, slept fitfully on the porch, but when I roused myself early the next morning, I could hear one Indian snoring, the rhythmic rumbling of his sleep softening the frantic sounds of the ducks rising along the river. Tired, hungry, and scared, the two Indians were not unlike any other young men of their age.

Of course, Augustus, still ornery from the night before, did not agree.

. "Indian scouts unable to find their own people," he said, after downing his first cup of coffee. "They have good reason to be afraid of me. Where are they now? I'll put the fear of God into them."

But the two Crow scouts already had left, along with James

Huntington, Patrick Lear, and Little Bear, to revisit the excavation. Dr. Lear had questioned whether or not it would be wise to provide the Indians with horses, and to travel with them into open country where they would have such an obvious advantage, but Mr. Huntington assured him that the worst the scouts might be capable of would be to ride off with their mounts. So Dr. Lear gave them but one, a packhorse large enough to more than adequately carry the weight of the two young men, but incapable of running off, at least not without being recaptured again.

Augustus, still dressed in his robe and boots from the night before, held his hands in front of the campfire. The remaining eagle feather fluttered in the band of his hat. He looked exhausted, in spite of sleeping in past midmorning, and was disinclined to pursue our disagreement from the night before. Having watched the Indians appear out of nowhere, I was much more sympathetic with Augustus' fears, particularly those he claimed to entertain on my behalf. But in many ways, it was simply too late to go back.

"What would a couple of Indians want with a pile of old bones?" Augustus asked. His voice sounded as worn out as he looked, and uninterested in the response.

"They asked for food and work if we had it," I explained. "Dr. Lear wants to see if they would be willing to help him dig. He described the site to them, but from the way they looked at one another, I think they assumed they would be desecrating graves. So he's taking them out there to show them and put them to work if they're willing."

"And Little Bear? What does he think about these new arrivals?"

"I don't know. He hasn't said much about anything since the surgery. But he wasn't wearing Indian dress. And he left his bear in the care of the workmen."

Augustus poured himself another cup of coffee, as if all of this information were more than he could digest. He said nothing, but waited for me to continue.

I told him that when Little Bear had checked on Jack earlier that morning, Little Bear was wearing work pants and the worn-out boots he and Patrick Lear had found in the ravine next to where the student had been shot. I might not have paid much attention to the pants and boots, but he was also wearing a collarless shirt with the sleeves rolled to below the elbow. When I asked about it, he said it was because he had volunteered to help with the dig and he didn't want to ruin his clothes. But he'd never bothered with what he had on when working before, I said to Augustus.

"Too many changes for an old man." Augustus looked around the clearing. "Where is my sweet Mrs. Hall? It's long past my mealtime and an old man needs to eat."

I pointed to the remaining pan of biscuits sitting on the edge of the stove, just as the Englishman walked up the embankment from the river, carrying a ceramic pot and a tin of tea. His hair was wet, forming dark ringlets dripping around his face and wet patches on the shoulders of his shirt. He greeted us with his broad toothy grin.

"Ah, there you are, Gussie, my good man. And Miss Peterson. Capital morning. Capital. Took your advice and floated downstream like a log on the river and watched the birds watching me. I do believe I've died and gone to heaven here."

"Morning, Ian," Augustus said without much enthusiasm, shoveling more than half the biscuits onto a plate. Only then did he offer the remains to the Englishman.

"Actually, I was hoping for a cup of tea," the Englishman replied, still smiling. "Might I trouble you for some hot water?"

"No trouble at all. Where is that Mrs. Hall?"

Augustus was disconcerted to learn that Maggie and Jeb had also left that morning, saying they were going to pick up supplies. But I told him I thought she might also be checking on her cabin, and possibly removing some things of value to keep with her here.

"You mean she left without me?" Augustus sounded incredulous.

I assured him that she'd be back, but then added, "Honestly, Augustus, you should give that poor woman some room to breathe. She's got enough to worry about right now without fending off your attentions."

"She likes me," Augustus countered.

"Of course she likes you. But she's got her hands full. And if the look in her eyes meant anything when examining that outfit Little Bear was wearing, I think she has more than her share of worries right now."

The Englishman, resigned that there would be no hot water forthcoming from either one of us, poured himself some coffee from the pot simmering on the edge of the fire. He sniffed at the cup and, closing his eyes, ventured a small sip. He grimaced, popped a bite of dry biscuit into his mouth, and then swept a trail of crumbs off the front of his shirt. He took another sip of coffee, coughed, and downed the rest of the biscuit, brushing more crumbs as he chewed. Again he sniffed, grimaced, sipped, coughed, chewed, and brushed. Somehow he managed to nourish himself in this methodical fashion.

Augustus, oblivious to the antics of the Englishman, shifted his awakening gaze upon me. "What worries?" he asked.

"There was something about that man with the bandaged hands that she found disturbing," I explained.

"Of course she was disturbed," Augustus replied, growing more impatient. "That woman is trying to build a life out here for herself and her child, and these are the kinds of men who are going to be in charge in this part of the country. Even I get upset thinking about it. Furious, in fact."

But he was missing my point. When still he tried to dismiss me with another offhanded remark, I lost my patience. "Augustus," I said, "I think she recognized those boots Little Bear was wearing."

15. ILLUSTRATION (PETERSON), RAVEN SKULL WITH GREEN WASH

Augustus left later that morning with Chen and an extra mule, ostensibly to intercept Maggie and Jeb, to protect them from any Indians they might encounter, and to help them transport any possessions they wanted to move. But I had the feeling Augustus was even more unsettled by the story about the boots than I had been. Refusing to let me accompany him, he left me in the protective care of the Englishman, the student, and the Welsh workmen, who were finishing the last of the stonework before moving on to assembling the logs. Mr. Hacker, content to be left behind and to serve as my protector, strummed his guitar in the shade of the cabin while the workmen rhythmically hammered away.

Jack awoke around noon and, with my help and that of Mr. Hacker, hobbled out to sit on the porch. Maggie had changed his bandages and done the best that she could in the way of a bath, so he looked healthier, albeit still weak from the surgery and dazed from sleep. She had also washed out his hair, which, like mine, suggested the color of rust, although in the noontime light both his hair and beard glowed almost red. His face looked better, too, with renewed color spotting his cheeks and lips. The student propped his leg on the low porch railing, leaning back so his face and upper body were exposed to the sun. He closed his eyes and relaxed his mouth so thoroughly that the muscles and skin of his face seemed to collapse. If I had not been able to detect the slow, methodical rising and falling of his chest under his shirt, I'm sure I would have checked to see if he was dead.

I worked that morning on the documentation of the four

views of the raven skull you have listed as one of your miscellaneous illustrations. I remember this distinctly because when Jack roused himself later, he expressed an interest in my work and was particularly drawn to the layering of muscle I added to one view of the skull. Afraid he would be unable to help with the digging, and unwilling to be sent home, he asked if he might be able to assist with this kind of documentation. His uncle was a lithographer, Jack informed me, and he had often helped with projects during the summer months, mostly preparing preliminary sketches and tracings based on other men's work. He had tried his hand at ink wash illustrations as well, he said, although those tended to be nothing more than simple sketches from nature, rendered mostly for his own amusement to while away the time. Still, Jack seemed genuinely interested in the process of documentation, and by discussing the details and challenges of working in the field and then translating that work for publication, we were both provided with a much-needed distraction from the uncertainty at hand.

Placing my chair next to his, I showed him the illustrations of bones and bird skulls I had completed to date, explaining how red sable brushes and lampblack could be used to highlight the bone. He in turn pointed out places where lithographers would take exception to the excessive use of my pencil and where I'd applied pressure to indicate minute details. Jack also explained how the printers would consider my work nothing more than a preliminary design, a starting point to copy in reverse, which they would then transfer with a greasy crayon onto limestone prepared with a solution of nitric acid and gum.

"It is a shame, though, when you think of it," the student added. "So much of the work you do capturing anatomical details is lost in this fashion. I understand that publishing is a critical component of modern science, but it does seem an indignity to the illustrator that so much detail of character and artistry must be sacrificed along the way."

"One can hope," I countered, "that the illustrations might

live beyond the reproductive process, if nothing else as documentation of Dr. Lear's work in the field."

"There's always hope, Miss Peterson," the student said, without sounding all that hopeful about this or anything else, given his condition. "But I know the Captain from campus. He is not what anyone considers an honorable man. I doubt that anything will survive from this experience, except that which promotes the Captain's reputation. I can assure you that the Captain will take your work and Dr. Lear's and treat it as his own."

Jack leaned back and closed his eyes, the wind ruffling his hair. He rolled his head to one side, enjoying the warmth and movement across his face. When it looked as though even this brief exchange might have already become exhausting, the student looked down at his swollen leg before turning his faraway gaze on me.

"The only person I've ever met who appreciates the kind of work you do is Huntington," he said. "You may not have noticed, but he has a fine collection of natural history illustrations tucked in with his books. But then, he's not like most men you or I will ever have the pleasure of knowing, Miss Peterson," the student continued. "In or out of the sciences. Huntington seems to know by intuition how to appreciate even this bleak landscape. He's like a child in many ways. Believes the world is a fascinating and wonderful place. All of it. What a shame there aren't more people like him."

While Jack dozed again in his chair, I worked on the four views of the raven skull, to one of which I added a pebbly layer of skin. Without feathers and a sense of scale, it was easy to see how birds might have developed from the early saurians, growing smaller and more agile until they took flight. To the final view I added a light wash of green which, layered over the pencil and ink, gave it an otherworldly feel, like an ancient creature from the deep, as Augustus was fond of calling them.

Since the war, these studies had been enough to keep my heart and mind occupied and, like Little Bear, I had sealed the rest of myself away from others of my kind. Sitting there on the porch of Mr. Huntington's cabin, with a warm wind rising off the river, I allowed myself the fleeting pleasure of envisioning a new life and a world in which the house across the clearing might have been constructed for me. I smiled when I remembered how I had once so despised the land that surrounded me here. Jack, of course, was right. Mr. Huntington was indeed a remarkable man.

I took out the mandible fragment Jeb had found, with its multi-layers of teeth and the bit of bone that might have once been part of the nasal cavity. Because it reminded me of the hadrosaur teeth I had worked on while helping with the reproductions for the Centennial, I wondered if I could make the various fragments fit the general profile of that creature's reconstructed skull. To complete the public mounting of that hadrosaur, the scientists had constructed a replica of an oversized iguana skull, which they painted green. As I handled the cranial pieces, trying to place them in some sort of logical order, I could not help but wonder why, if the creature had a pelvic structure so similar to a bird's, it wouldn't have had a similar-looking skull.

I placed the raven's skull next to where I worked and, using it as a model of sorts, constructed a realistic-looking skull with the fragments of bone that I had in hand. I placed the dentary far back in the mandible and then pieced together an extended nasal cavity lying flat above and beyond that. As I constructed this strange-looking version of a bird, one flat piece of bone appeared to fit as a rounded extension of the nose, as if it were in fact nothing more than part of a wider duck's bill. Realizing I was getting carried away, I placed all the pieces in a pile, intending to start again.

Before I could try another configuration, however, the Englishman sauntered up from the river. At first I assumed he was singing, but as his voice grew nearer, it was clear he was talking with great enthusiasm, presumably to himself, a personality trait in total sympathy with the Englishman. I would have thought nothing more of it if I hadn't heard a voice responding to his. I looked up from the bones just as the Englishman and the man in the white linen duster approached the cabin.

"Look who I found," the Englishman called out.

Mr. Hacker stumbled across the home site, attempting to use two thick-limbed tree branches for support. He pointed with one branch to the visitor, a tall, thin man with an unruly beard, who seemed as unaware of the Englishman bounding alongside of him on makeshift crutches as he was of the large, quarrelsome mustang he was leading by a rope. He focused his full attention instead on the clearing, his eyes seeming to take in every square inch.

Without encouragement or invitation, the visitor tied his ill-tempered horse to the porch railing and stepped up to the table where I worked, scrutinizing the jumble of bone fragments assembled there. He pushed at the fossils, as if such trifles could be of little interest, before picking up the piece of dentary to take a closer a look. When he returned it to the table, he placed it not where he had found it, but back behind the nasal cavity as I had done earlier. He stepped back for a moment to get a better view of the effect. Only then did he turn his attention to me.

"You must be the Miss Peterson I have heard so much about?" the newcomer asked. He offered me his hand.

"Yes, that's right," I responded. "Mr. . . . ?"

"Edward," the man replied. He held my hand too long and too firmly in his own. "I see you are fascinated by skulls."

He released my hand so that he might push at one of the bone fragments, making the skull look rounder, more like that of a reptile than a bird.

"Mr. Hacker says you are illustrating a collection of bones. He showed me the drawing you did of a saurian displayed in that tepee down by the river. Not unlike this one," the man added.

He examined the illustration of the raven skull, which I had covered with skin and a wash of green paint. "You have a good eye, Miss Peterson. A very good eye. You don't discover talent like this very often in the Territories. But you do seem to be forcing some of this, don't you agree? Still, I have noticed that the Dinosauria approximate birds, and possess several peculiarities in common with them. If pressed, it would be my advice to place the class somewhere between birds and the Crocodylia."

Before I could respond, Jack let out a sharp gasp in his sleep. He turned his head and wearily opened his eyes. Realizing he was not alone, he eyed the visitor carefully before stirring himself and attempting to sit.

"Ah, Jack," Ian Hacker said. Then he, too, joined us on the narrow porch to assist the student as he struggled to sit upright. "Found these branches down by the river," the Englishman announced. "Thought they would make excellent crutches to help you with moving about."

As attention was turned to the student, I folded the loose pages of illustrations back into the Captain's journal and started to return the skull fragments to the box, but as I did so the man placed his hand upon mine. His was a large, powerful hand, but soft to the touch. I could not help but notice that unlike mine, both his hands and fingernails were immaculately clean.

"Wait," he said. "Don't put those away yet. I might have something that will interest you."

From a large leather satchel he pulled another piece of dentary not unlike the piece with which I worked, although his piece was broken along one side, revealing three rows of closely packed teeth, one row stacked upon the other.

"I believe if you put a piece of bone like this here . . ." His voice trailed off as he situated the bit of fossil teeth to form the lower mandible. "See how that looks? And that bit there," he added, taking a rounded piece of bone and adding it to the skull as if it were a crest, "probably goes here. See how nicely that fits?"

Again, he stepped back from the table to get a better view. He nodded to himself as if satisfied with the results.

"Interesting," he said, returning his own piece of fossilized dentary to his bag. "Very interesting."

The visitor leaned against the porch railing, as if being in Montana with three total strangers were the most natural thing in the world. "I appreciate creativity in our science," he said, "since we have so few established rules and such limited information with which to work. I believe, Miss Peterson, that if you will allow yourself to look at the world with new eyes and describe what you see and not simply report what the others say is there, you could make some startling new discoveries. Even here, in the middle of Montana.

"I am not suggesting you pursue just any concept that leaps into your head," the man continued as he sorted again through the jumble of bones. "That's what artists do, and science is more than art. But we must be creative in our thinking nonetheless." Again he pushed at the bones on the table and stopped to consider.

Satisfied with the shape of the strange outline of a skull he left lying on the table, the man pulled a watch from his pocket. The Englishman helped Jack make his way off the porch using the crutches.

"We were thinking of tea, Miss Peterson," the Englishman called back over his shoulder. "Do you think you could accommodate us?"

"Tea? No, that's most kind, Mr. Hacker," the visitor interjected, "but I fear I do not have the time. I promised to meet my colleague on the river within the hour, and he tends to worry about Indians if I do not make it to my appointments on time. I keep telling him I'm much more likely to fall off a cliff or be shot in the head by your employer, Miss Peterson, should he be fortunate enough to find me alone in this part of the world." The man laughed quietly as if at a joke only he could appreciate. "Fortunately, I am now headed back to the States."

Again the man looked at the bones on the table. "Miss Peterson," he said, offering his hand. "This has been a most enjoyable respite from my journey."

"Mr. Edward," I replied.

When I spoke his name, the visitor questioned me with his eyes, holding my hand again for a moment too long.

"Ah, right," he said, as if mimicking the Englishman. "I would be delighted if we could continue this conversation at a later date. At the Academy, perhaps, when you return to civilization. I would welcome your company there and regret we did not meet earlier. In the meantime, it has been a pleasure. A pleasure indeed."

16. Drawing, Man with Bandaged Hands

When Chen arrived later that afternoon with a mule and two packhorses loaded with gear, there was not a sign of Augustus or Maggie and the boy. He asked for water for himself and for the horses and, after picketing them in the shade, commenced unpacking, his wide-brimmed hat bobbing up and down around the horses and the mule. Ian Hacker bobbed and weaved with him, his shaggy head emerging first on one side of a horse and then on the other as he tried to elicit a response about what had happened to the rest of our friends.

"Dragon bones," the Chinaman replied. He stacked bedding and other supplies neatly against the cabin. As he worked, the wind fluttered his loose shirt around him like enveloping wings. "They transport dragon bones to the river."

"Chen, my good man," the Englishman countered, "just like there is no gold in these mountains, there are, alas, no dragons. A sad fact to contemplate, I know. But true nonetheless."

"Mr. Augustus knows dragons," Chen replied. "He's a very powerful man, with thirteen dragons."

"Ah, right. You mean Mr. *Starwood's* dragons," the Englishman said, nodding his head. "So, my good man, are you saying that they took Mr. Starwood's bones to the river?"

Chen stared at the Englishman. The wind lifted the brim of his hat, revealing the top of the Chinaman's head. His scalp had been shaved, leaving just enough hair to braid into a long black queue. At first the man said nothing, but uncinched the leather straps from the belly of one of the horses. The heavy saddle fell to the ground at his feet. After pulling off the last of the saddles and stacking them next to the cabin, the Chinaman squatted down on his haunches and filled his pipe.

"Now, my good man," the Englishman insisted after Chen sat for a few minutes contemplating his pipe, "what have you done with our friends? Did you leave them for the Indians or what?"

"I believe your Indians are related to my countrymen," he replied. "We saw three Sioux and they looked like men from my home." The Chinaman exhaled a cloud of smoke.

"Yes, and so they must be," Mr. Hacker agreed, "but did they take our friends?"

"I have already told you. They are moving dragon bones. A wagonful of bones."

"Well, of course they are. Just as I expected," the Englishman replied, scratching his head. "But tell me, then, where might they be taking these dragons?"

"Down to the river to meet a man. And to catch a boat."

At this, the Englishman turned to me in exasperation. "I apologize, Miss Peterson. I can't seem to get a thing out of him, man of the inscrutable East that he is. Do you want to try?"

"Mr. Chen," I said. "Were the dragon bones they transported like this one?"

I held out a piece of the jawbone Jeb had given me. Chen would not take it when offered, but stared at it intently. When he was certain of what he was seeing, he turned his eyes on me, so completely absorbed that I thought he might sit there forever, freezing me in his stare.

"The bones, Mr. Chen. Were they like these?"

"Yes," he replied. "Mr. Augustus recognized them. He and the lady were taking them to the river."

"Do you know whom they were planning to meet?"

But this was more information than he was prepared to give, and Chen returned his attention to his pipe. Mr. Hacker shrugged as if to warn me not to expect any more information, but when I did not move, Chen continued.

"There was a man with bandages," he said. "And the boy. But there was someone else, too. A man in a long white coat, who was on his way home. He's the one Mr. Augustus said they were going to meet. They plan to signal the boat at Fort Claggett if they can catch it before it goes."

With that short announcement the Chinaman stood, satisfied that he had met his obligation both to me and Mr. Hacker. He nodded and started to lead the horses and mule over to the corrals, but I asked him to arrange for a horse for me. I wanted to be of assistance to Augustus, but I also wanted to know what was to become the fate of those bones.

Seeing my determination to go with or without him, Mr. Hacker agreed to accompany me. He did so with grave reservations, he insisted, certain that we would be of little or no assistance to Augustus, no matter what kind of trouble he was in, and that we would therefore be safer waiting for his return. When still I would not defer to his good counsel, he enlisted Chen to saddle two of Mr. Huntington's horses, suggesting that it might be safest if the Chinaman stayed at the cabin with Jack while we were gone.

When I asked Chen to give me a horse with one of the small men's saddles like the one Maggie used, the Englishman raised an eyebrow, but he did not protest. He did, however, dramatically holster a gun, as if my eccentric behavior might force him to defend me from ruffians on the road.

The trading post at Fort Claggett wasn't far, and once we were en route, Mr. Hacker proved to be an enjoyable and loquacious companion, entertaining me with tales of his travels throughout the West in a futile search of riches and fame. He bounced alongside me on his horse, an unusually large and spirited black mustang.

"When I left my homeland, I was still very young," Mr.

Hacker shouted as his horse ran past me on my left. The English-man pulled back on the reins and the mustang came to an abrupt stop, sending the man hurling forward. Having regained his bal-ance, the Englishman smiled, waited for me to catch up, and then continued.

"Some would say I was very stupid. I know for certain that my family believes that to be true."

Again the horse lunged forward and stopped when Mr. Hacker pulled back on the reins. And again, the Englishman set-tled into the saddle.

"My father agreed to finance my passage regardless of his reservations because I was able to convince him that unless my older brother met an untimely death, I was destined to live a long and impoverished life, proving to be a millstone around the necks of both my brother and his growing family, who would have had no choice but to support me into my declining years."

As he spoke, Mr. Hacker let the reins fall slack and the mo-ment he did so his horse bolted again, this time kicking at me and my placid-gaited mount. My horse turned to avoid the big black's fury, protecting us both from the animal's hooves, but Mr. Hacker was not so fortunate. He went flying, first to the right of the horse, and then to the left, with only the heels of his boots in the stirrups keeping him from falling from the back of the beast. As first one and then the other of the Englishman's legs fell onto the horse, the irregular blows to its flanks serving to enrage the beast even more, and sending the wild animal forward in irregu-lar bursts.

Mr. Hacker, flailing first from one side of the animal and then to the other, jerked hard on the reins, bringing the horse to an abrupt halt, almost unseating himself again. But the English-man regained his composure and waited for me up the road, stroking the furious animal's sweating neck.

Now it was my horse's opportunity to misbehave. As it trot-ted to rejoin its corral mate, the mare lurched to a stop and re-fused to venture any farther. Thinking it was the animal's understandable reluctance to get close to a horse with such an unpredictable temper, I urged her to the left, onto the far side of the road, thinking we would travel around Mr. Hacker and his horse and then he in turn could follow. Still the horse refused to move.

Mr. Hacker, holding the reins tightly, turned his horse to determine the problem. As he did so, the mustang sensed what mine had already seen: an enormous rattlesnake sunning itself on the far side of the road. The snake, stirred by all the dust and commotion, was now coiled and ready to strike. The Englishman's horse, up for any excuse to get into a froth again, stomped at the ground and then rose straight up onto its hind legs, and commenced pawing menacingly into the air.

"Whoa," Mr. Hacker called, pulling hard on the reins with one hand while trying to hold on to the saddle with his other. "Down, boy, down."

The mustang hit the ground hard with its two front feet, sending Mr. Hacker up onto the animal's neck and then falling back into the saddle as the horse ran past me, again kicking up a thick blanket of dust along the road. Mr. Hacker's feet, although still in the stirrups, were now flailing somewhere around the mustang's neck, while the man's shaggy head bounced up and down near the animal's tail. He jerked back on the reins, his free hand searching for the saddle.

"Whoooaaa," he shouted as the horse turned and stampeded down the road, headed in my direction.

Again, without instruction, the mare moved out of the way as the Englishman's horse ran up beside us and came to an abrupt halt, sending Mr. Hacker flying. But this time, anticipating his flight, the Englishman wrapped both arms around the horse's neck and held on. The mustang's eyes were wild, its breath coming in short, panicked gasps.

Once he realized the animal was through, at least for the time being, the Englishman looked up, cleared his throat, and smiled.

"Ah, Miss Peterson. You must remind me to commend Mr. Huntington on his choice of animals. I like a horse with spirit."

The Englishman righted himself in the saddle and, keeping a firm grasp on the reins, turned his exhausted horse around to face in the opposite direction.

"Now, where was I? About to leave for California, as I recall. In search of adventure. But if you'll excuse me for a moment, I think I'd like to go back and get that snake as a souvenir."

☙

When we reached the clearing just to the east of the trading post, we could see a wagon perched high on the bluff on the opposite side of the river. Maggie and Jeb stood off by themselves, holding the horses and three pack mules, while Augustus stood next to a team of mules harnessed to the wagon. His blue linen duster was unbuttoned, and flapped around him in the wind. A man I had never seen before but assumed was Maggie's husband sat in the wagon, barking orders at the mules or maybe at Augustus, who was trying to coax the animals down the steep incline. The animals were wearing blinders and should have been oblivious to the dangers below, but Augustus could not get them to budge. The man in the wagon, thinking he knew a better way, started beating on the animals, trying by this more direct method to move the mules.

Augustus, oblivious to our presence, continued to tug at the animals' harnesses without success. With the wind and rush of the river, we could not hear what he was saying, but he appeared to be yelling at the man in the wagon to lay off the whip as he tried to urge the mules across the hill rather than straight down the steep incline. Still the animals balked, digging their hooves into the ground and bracing their legs. It was then that they started to slip, as the loose shale along the ridge gave way underneath them.

The two mules at the front of the team were the first to lose their footing, sliding stiff-legged into Augustus, who scrambled back up the ridge to get out of their way. As the front animals started to slide, they pulled the other two with them, sending the wagon and its heavy cargo listing over the edge. The man in the wagon stood up and beat at the mules, trying to get the team to run with the momentum of their sliding, but instead of moving forward, the animals continued to balk, stalling the wagon, which was now tipped on the side of the ridge.

Again, Augustus rushed forward, trying to get the animals to move down and across the ledge, but first one and then another mule lost its footing until the wagon's cargo did them in. As the wagon teetered on the side of the ravine, the left side was so much lower than the right that the weight of the fossils, which had been secured and covered with a tarp, pulled the wagon over, first onto its side and then onto its back, causing the wagon's wheels to spin in the air. Augustus clambered back up the embankment and out of the way, just as the mules slid onto their sides, and then they, too, flipped onto their backs.

At first there was no sign of the driver, who must have been buried beneath the wagon. Augustus, Maggie, and Jeb all scrambled down to help him, but as they did so, the mules started kicking to right themselves, and the wagon slid again, this time flipping onto its wheels and pulling the animals back over, only to start the process again, the wagon and the mules toppling over and over again as they plunged down the steep ridge. As they rolled, the mules drew their feet up close to their chests, and then extended them as they righted themselves. The animals and wagon flopped and tumbled until they reached the bottom of the incline, where the mules landed on their feet as if nothing had happened.

The wagon and its cargo were not as fortunate. The bed of the wagon smashed broadside into some boulders, breaking loose from the mules. The cargo tumbled into the river. The mules, freed of their load, ran downstream about a hundred yards, dragging the tongue of the wagon and the shredded remains of the tarp, which flapped like a sail. Then, as quickly as they had started, the mules, too, came to a halt, as if satisfied that they had reached their destination.

Seeing the fate of his wagon, the driver, who had been thrown free of the wreckage, ran down the side of the ravine until he, too, lost his footing and toppled end over end, only rolling to a halt when he reached level ground. Badly shaken but not hurt, he forded into the river, trying to scoop up the heavy rock-like fossils before they merged with the deep current and were carried away. It was then that I noticed the fringe on his jacket and the bandages on his hands.

"Get down here," he screamed at the others, who were leading their horses and the pack mules at a diagonal across the steep embankment. "Forget those damn horses. Get down here and help."

The man waded into the water and floundered with his bandaged hands, trying to identify and catch what must have seemed like nothing more than oddly shaped rocks as they tumbled by.

During all this commotion, Mr. Hacker and his horse were not idle. With the dust and rocks flying across the river, the black mustang reared on its hind legs, sending the Englishman first forward, grasping at the animal's neck, and then back again as the horse lurched forward. When the wagon burst open upon the rocks, the horse headed straight for the river, where it held its ground, pawing at the edge of the water as if readying itself for a fight. Mr. Hacker pulled back on the reins, keeping the mustang's head drawn close to its chest, as he dismounted. The horse, sensing an opportunity for one last bit of mischief, kicked its back legs at the Englishman, but Mr. Hacker had the reins wrapped around his hand so he was able to stay close to the horse's neck and avoid its wrath.

While the man in the fringed leather jacket was swept farther downriver in search of the fossils, Maggie and Jeb were rejoined by Augustus, who helped them lead the other horses and pack mules down and across the ridge in an upriver direction.

These animals seemed content to follow wherever Augustus wanted them to go, but then they weren't packing a ton of rocks behind them, either. Augustus made his way upstream just opposite Mr. Hacker, who was spinning in circles as the mustang attempted to deliver at least one good kick. Again my horse demonstrated her manners by walking down to the river, keeping a good twenty feet away from Mr. Hacker and his horse.

Augustus shouted at us across the river. He would travel farther upstream where the river was divided by a narrow strip of land. Shallow riffles strewn with rocks and sand would make it easier to cross.

Seeing his party desert him without even raising a hand to assist, the man in the river shouted again. But other than a small hesitancy on the part of Jeb, who looked over his shoulder before his mother urged him on, the three acted as if the man did not exist and continued their journey upstream. Screaming with rage, the man scooped and flailed, disappearing from time to time underwater, dislodging his hat, which floated from view. Then the man himself was cast adrift, merging with the swift and deepening current, his head bobbing to the surface just once before he was pulled downstream and around the bend, another bit of debris afloat in the river.

17. PORTRAIT, CHINAMAN WITH SNAKE

Augustus initiated a series of drawings the evening we returned to James Huntington's home site, after he and Ian Hacker had spent a good part of the return journey swapping tall tales and a bottle of the Englishman's whiskey. Skinning and preserving the snake was Mr. Hacker's idea. After hearing of Augustus' adventures encountering desperadoes on Maggie's land, and then taking his life in his hands by agreeing to help load and transport the bones to the river to meet a man in a boat, the Englishman decided in his inebriated condition that he, too, wanted to be a collector of bones. He would commemorate the day, and his own bravery, by preserving the rattlesnake he had shot.

As he told of his plans, Mr. Hacker waved the snake at Augustus, who drew back with exaggerated horror at the size and strength of such a beast. He then warned the Englishman to be careful because rattlesnakes had been known to bite the hands of unwary travelers long after the rattlers were dead. To emphasize his point he took the snake from the Englishman and waved it back at him, making a combination of hissing and snapping noises in the man's face. The Englishman showed his crooked teeth in a hiss-like laugh and helped himself to another tumbler of whiskey.

"Chen, how are you at skinning a snake?" Mr. Hacker wanted to know.

The Chinaman gave him a look of utter disbelief, but said nothing, clearly not believing most of what had transpired since he had tied his fortunes to that of Ian Hacker. Chen pulled a narrow knife from its sheath and commenced to slice open the belly of the snake and expertly peel away the skin.

While his companion worked, Mr. Hacker turned to me for advice on how to preserve the animal's skeleton for display.

"Shall we boil it, Miss Peterson? I want to show my compatriots the horrors of traveling in the West."

"No boiling," Chen interrupted, looking up from the specimen, which was now nothing more than a five-foot hunk of flesh stretched out on the camp table. "Boiling's for soup."

Mr. Hacker looked again to me for advice, his eyebrows lifted, while Chen scooped out the reptile's internal organs and set them aside. He sliced and pared the snake flesh into long strips and stacked them neatly next to the entrails, as if both were a rare delicacy, which the Chinaman apparently considered them to be.

"So, my dear Miss Peterson, now shall we boil the snake?"

I started to explain that boiling would indeed loosen the remaining flesh and muscles, making it easier to pull them away from the bone. However, having tried several different methods on birds, I knew that even mild boiling sometimes distorts a carcass, altering the structure of the bones. Boiling can also weaken the ligaments, which I assumed in a delicate specimen like a snake would be needed to keep the vertebrae in place.

As we talked, Chen efficiently cleaned the carcass, using his knife to cut closer and closer to the bone. Satisfied that he had recovered all the edible flesh, he lifted the long narrow skeleton in both of his hands and offered it to Ian Hacker.

"Bury it," Chen advised.

"No, you miss the point, my good man. I want to keep it. For display. To terrify my friends."

"Then you should bury it," Chen repeated.

Again, the Englishman turned to me with an exasperated look on his face. "What do you advise, Miss Peterson? Obviously there's some celestial superstition about bones going on here. He'll eat the foul creature but he won't let me keep its bones."

"Actually, I think he means that you should bury it," I confirmed. "We used to do that when I was a child. We would bury seashells, and the insects would pick them clean. Much more effective than boiling."

"Right, then. Bury the bones it is."

While we discussed the merits of burial versus boiling, and Augustus sipped more whiskey and completed the portrait of Chen, Maggie and Jeb unpacked their meager possessions and established a camp of their own to the south of Mr. Huntington's cabin. Since the men in camp were becoming indisposed by drink and Mr. Huntington and Dr. Lear were gone, I offered my assistance but Maggie would not accept it, saying she and her son needed the time together to rebuild their lives, now represented by a well-worn cavalry-issued wall tent and two rickety chairs. Then, in what must have been an act of defiance, since she never expressed any humor in the gesture, she dramatically raised an American flag in front of her tent as if laying claim to that small piece of ground. When I asked about her husband, all that she would say was that if he'd worked as hard clearing the land as he had digging up worthless rocks, she and the boy would be rich by now.

That evening Augustus also did a quick study of Maggie as she unsaddled her horse. In spite of his inebriated condition, Augustus seemed to capture all of the woman's strength, dignity, sadness, and fatigue in a few quick strokes of the pen. He also sketched Jeb as he helped his mother unload their gear and feed and corral the horses and mules. After dinner, during which we all were encouraged to sample Chen's cooked snake, Augustus presented two of the drawings to Maggie with great ceremony as if they were rare portraits in oil. Since they are not part of your collection, I can only assume she kept these drawings for herself, although she did not let on that she was impressed with the portraits at the time.

18. WATERCOLOR, THE BATHERS

I was surprised, I might even say shocked, to see this watercolor described as part of your collection, since I did not see this particular painting when I prepared Augustus' work for transport, and was never led to believe that he had seen Maggie and me while we bathed. And yet, as you have described the scene, one woman stretched out soft and golden, looking almost ripe in the last light of a summer day, and the other wading through the river, pushing at her clothes, it leaves me no doubt that Augustus had been watching us.

After dinner, Augustus and Mr. Hacker, having polished off more than their share of whiskey, staggered down the embankment for a swim. When they disappeared into the bushes downriver to disrobe, Maggie walked up holding two blankets and a cake of soap. Her hair was almost brown with dust from the trail, and her overalls and sweater were covered with dirt and grease. I could not help but notice that she smelled of horses, and wondered if the day had had a similar effect on me.

"I was hoping that you might be willing to accompany me while I bathe," she said. "Too many men about to be on my own." When she sensed that I might refuse her, she added, "Dipping a cloth in a water barrel's not the same as dipping your body in."

I followed her down to where the Judith joins the Missouri, and found a place to sit next to an upended tree. Maggie sat beside me, and unlaced and removed her boots.

"That cousin of yours is nothing but trouble," she told me, rubbing her pale feet in the pebbly sand. "I don't know what to do about him. When he came across that worthless husband of mine digging around in the dirt, if your cousin would have had a gun, I think he would have killed him dead, right there on the spot. So instead, he offers to help the idiot just to get rid of him."

"I'm sorry," I replied. "I know this cannot be easy for you."

"It's not that," she said, already indifferent to the events of the day. She untied her hair and let it fall across her shoulders. She closed her eyes and combed her hands through her hair. "I love it here. Even that filthy old Missouri never ceases to fill me with hope."

She stared at the river without emotion, and then stood to dip her hands in the clean running water of the Judith. She rinsed her hands and pushed the water up around her sleeves before stepping from her workmen's overalls, pulling off her sweater, and depositing them both into a pile.

"He told me I have what it takes," she said, stopping to look down at her pale body, small-breasted, slim-hipped, and muscular. She shrugged. "No one has ever said that to me before."

Soap in hand, she waded knee-deep through the cold water. When she reached the pool formed where the two rivers merged, she slid forward until fully submerged and then stood back up again, shook out her hair, and wiped at her slick skin with soap.

"Get in here," she called out, tossing the soap onto the shore. "You can't hide under all that dirt forever," she added, before merging again with the water. She floated along on the surface of the water, head back, eyes closed, hair a tangle of yellow like petals around a flower, exactly as you have described it.

Watching Maggie so alive in the moment, so at peace with herself and the river in spite of all she had been through, I remembered that James Huntington had waded through that same stretch of river right before he had urged me to picture a world even more vivid than the one which I looked upon now. One in which a man could break from the past and the horrors that held him, and build a new life for himself in a new land. One where it would take nothing but the strength and clarity of the imagination to add flesh to a pile of rock and logs, like a painter adding color, shape, and form to what would otherwise be nothing but an empty expanse.

Although it was late in the day, sweat swelled along my forehead and under my arms. Moisture pooled on the backside of my knee and broke loose, trickling down my leg. Flies buzzed greedily around my face, drawn to the moisture and the salt and stench of sour flesh. My filthy field clothes, which had seemed like such an extravagance when we first purchased them, appeared not much of an improvement over Maggie's workman's attire.

As Maggie floated without effort around the shallow pool, kicking at the water from time to time, I realized that I, too, had to immerse myself, and be open the way that Maggie was to the river and all that it promised. Before I could give this impulse much thought or deny it, I stepped from my dress and undergarments and placed them, one by one, upon the water. They floated flat and dull upon the surface as if two-dimensional, clothes made for rough-cut dolls. I brushed the soap free of sand and bits of rock and waded out after my clothing, until, filling like sponges, one by one each piece collapsed. I ran soap up and down the filthy lengths of them and pushed the cloth back into the shallow current. Then I slid the thick block of soap under my arms and down my legs and across my face and behind my neck, and then I, too, pushed through the icy water and soaped up the thick mound of my gritty hair. After scooping up my clothes and placing them on a rock to dry, I waded out toward Maggie.

Maggie did not acknowledge me as I approached, but rather just floated there, the corner of her mouth softened by what might have been a smile. I stretched onto the river's surface as she had done and let the water buoy my body as it rushed by. I'm certain we both would have floated there indefinitely if we had not heard Ian Hacker calling out Augustus' name.

Maggie righted herself with a sigh of resignation. "Why do

men always have to spoil everything?" she asked. She shook the wet hair from her face and wrung out a thick yellow coil. "We can wait them out up there," she said.

We retrieved our clothing and blankets and retreated into a grove of aspen, just as Augustus and Ian Hacker waded into view, both of them naked as the day they were born.

"Look at him," Maggie said, indicating Augustus, who was kicking up water as he walked. "Just like a child. It's no wonder my boy adores him." Ian Hacker pushed into the deeper pool where we had just been floating and paddled around with his hands before his face like a dog.

"Still," she added, eyeing Augustus closely, "it's good to see a man again. Even that sorry old excuse for one. It's been too long." She wrung more water from her hair and pulled on her dusty sweater, while I braided my own hair like Little Bear's, mind, body, spirit, together into a whole.

"He's smitten, you know," she said at last.

"I know he is," I replied, struggling back into my wet under-clothing and hastily rebuttoning my dress. "I'm sorry if he's been a bother but he's happy here and I think he wants to stay."

"Not him," she said.

Maggie watched Augustus and the Englishman cavort, still drunk and yet energized, too, by their time in the river. She stepped into her overalls and toweled her hair, before pulling her hat back down around her ears.

"You look better," she said to me, having returned to her usual demeanor. "Keep wearing your hair like that and there's a good chance you won't lose him."

19. PORTRAIT, WOMAN WITH DOG

The woman with the dog arrived later that same evening, in the company of an elderly aunt who served as her companion. The small dog yipped across the clearing, upsetting everything in its wake, particularly Augustus. As their driver helped the women down from the wagon, the dog skittered over to the cabin, stopped to sniff at the steps leading up the porch, and lifted its leg. Spying Augustus sitting under his netting, the dog turned and started barking again.

"Where's your gun?" Augustus asked Ian Hacker.

Mr. Hacker, who had consumed even more whiskey after his swim, rummaged around in a bag. He pulled his pistol from its holster and waved it over his head.

"Shall I shoot it, Gussie?" he called out. "Shall I, old man? Just say the word and it's doggy stew."

By this time, however, the dog had barked its way over to Maggie and Jeb's tent, where it once again lifted its leg, dampening the pole upon which Maggie had raised the flag. Jeb pitched a small rock at the dog, which howled as if it had indeed been shot. It scooted back to its owner with its tail between its legs.

The two women looked around the campsite as if they had been transported to an outpost beyond the farthest fringe of civilization, which in many ways I suppose they had. As the younger of the two scooped up her howling dog, I walked forward to apologize for my companions and to attempt to make the visitors feel, if not comfortable where they had landed, at least welcomed.

The older woman intercepted me as if defending her charge. She wore a light woolen travel dress of the same soft gray color as her hair, and a black straw hat that flapped in the wind. As she advanced, she held on to her hat with her left hand while using her right in a futile attempt to keep the hem of her dress out of the dirt. I offered my hand, but the woman ignored it.

"My dear," she said as she approached. She looked at me through slightly narrowed eyes and raised chin, which gave the impression of being talked down to, although I was a full two inches taller than the woman. "We are looking for a James Huntington. Our driver insists the man lives here." She looked around the clearing. "But clearly there has been some sort of mistake."

The younger woman started to join us as well, the dog draped over one arm, but hesitated as two bright yellow butterflies circled her hat. She waved at them with her free hand, trying to get them away.

"Perhaps you would be so kind as to provide us with the proper directions if you have heard of him. My niece is engaged to the gentleman in question, assuming we aren't lost or he hasn't disappeared on us altogether."

"No . . ." I started to say, but found I could not continue.

The older woman clutched at her flopping hat and turned to go. "I was afraid that we were lost," she said.

"No. I meant . . ." Again I hesitated.

The younger woman looked with disgust as one of the butterflies alighted on the seat of the wagon. She cradled the small dog in her arms as if it were a child.

"You're not lost," I said at last. "What I meant to say is that this is Mr. Huntington's cabin. But he's not here. At least not at the moment."

"Oh?" The woman viewed me and my still-damp costume with renewed interest. "And who might you be, then?"

"I'm a friend. Or an associate, I guess you might say. Well, neither, really. In any event, this is his land. And that is his cabin."

"Julia," the woman called out to her niece. "You need to hear this."

The woman looked questioningly at her aunt but did not move.

"Julia," the woman repeated.

The younger woman grimaced and handed her dog to the driver, who tossed it into the bed of the wagon as soon as the woman had turned her back. As she made her way over to her aunt, Augustus decided it was time for him to intervene on behalf of his own charge.

"What seems to be the problem here?" he demanded to know. "Did my cousin not properly welcome you? Let me be the first, then."

The woman pulled back as Augustus approached. Instead of offering his hand as I had tried, he wiped his hand on his robe and pushed at one dirt-encrusted fingernail with this thumb. He cleared his throat.

"Eleanor," Augustus said as if just noticing me. "What have you done to your hair? You look utterly transformed. Remind me to paint you one last time before you leave."

As the younger of the two women joined us, she turned to her aunt, demanding an explanation while fanning at the air as if to warn other insects to keep away.

"Julia, the driver was right. This is Jim's home. And these people . . ." she started to say, but hesitated as if uncertain how to best introduce us. She narrowed her eyes to take in not only me and Augustus, but also Chen and Mr. Hacker, who was still holding on to his gun. Jack, who had heard the wagon arrive, hobbled out onto the cabin porch, while Maggie and Jeb waited across the clearing, standing guard over their American flag. They looked prepared to defend it with their lives if need be. The woman cleared her throat as if in parody of Augustus. "And these people," she tried again, "are his associates."

"But there must be some mistake."

The younger woman sheltered her eyes with her hand, her gaze drifting to the still-unfinished house illuminated in the last, bright light before nightfall. In the shade of the rock chimney,

the workmen had tied the bear, which sat on its haunches looking at the woman looking at it.

"I was led to believe that . . ." The woman faltered, as if not
certain what exactly she had been told or what she now believed.

"Mr. Huntington is with his friend Patrick Lear," I tried to
explain. "But only for a day or two. They didn't take much in the
way of supplies, so they will return soon. It's getting dark, so perhaps you would care to join us in the meantime. We can make
you something to eat. And some tea. I'm certain Mr. Hacker
would be more than happy to share some of his tea."

At the sound of his name, Ian Hacker staggered forward,
waving his gun.

"Tea," he exclaimed. "Yes, of course, my dear ladies. We
shall have a proper cup of tea. We may be wild out here in the
West, but I would not want you to think us inhospitable."

When James Huntington, Patrick Lear, and Little Bear did
not return to camp that evening, there never was a question that
something might have happened, or that the two scrawny Indians, as Augustus referred to them, might have done them harm.
As far as Augustus was concerned, James Huntington had probably learned of the women's arrival and was reluctant to return
home. Still, someone had to take responsibility for these new visitors, Augustus informed me the next morning, and it wasn't
going to be him.

He pointed to the young woman stepping onto the porch.
She sat at my worktable and leaned forward so that her face was
washed in the early morning sun. Unlike the night before, she
looked confident in her surroundings, as if by waking up in Mr.
Huntington's cabin she had realized the strength of her position,
or staked her claim, one which she was now chary to concede.
Her dog scurried across the clearing, and it, too, marked everything in its way, keeping its distance only from Maggie and Jeb's
little campsite and their flag.

The older woman emerged from the cabin, and made her
way with a single purpose across the clearing. "I've been speaking

with my niece, Mr. Starwood, and as you must appreciate, we cannot remain here under these unusual circumstances, even though the strange paraphernalia in that cabin indicates we've found the correct place. Still, contrary to what my niece believes, we would be irresponsible to remain here on our own without knowing for certain that James is still in residence here. And, given the apparent transitory nature of his situation, if he indeed even wants us to stay. So I respectfully request that you escort the two of us and our driver to James so that we might ask him ourselves."

With this announcement, the woman turned and marched over to the driver, who was preparing for his return to town. She tapped the edge of her parasol on the wagon to get the man's attention, but apparently he did not hear her, for he turned his horses to go.

"I will not travel with them on my own," Augustus informed me as the driver pulled away from the clearing. "I'll get Jeb to harness up the horses before that woman turns that umbrella of hers on me. But I want you to ride along with us, Cousin. I don't trust that man Lear, but whatever it is he's up to out there, I think you need to see it for yourself. And then I want you on the next boat out of here. So you can take a proper bath."

As he spoke, the young woman ventured out onto the edge of the porch and leaned into the railing. Her hair lay thick and lush around her shoulders, her clothes were neat and pressed, and her face was clean and shiny, ready for another day. For that fleeting moment, she seemed entirely content to stay exactly where she was.

"I have to say I'm even beginning to question the good judgment of our friend Mr. Huntington," Augustus said. "She is a beauty. I will give him that."

Ian Hacker walked up to the water barrel and announced that if Augustus was traveling to the excavation, he wanted to ride along. "I need to get a good look at those dragon bones," the Englishman said. "Chen assures me they are good for what ails me." He scratched at his hair, still wet from his morning dive into the river, as if attempting to massage out the deleterious effect of the night before. "Not feeling too well, if the truth be known. Not well at all."

Augustus dipped his silk scarf into the water and wiped his face one more time. Dipping it again, he tied it, dripping, around his neck.

"My guess is, Cousin, that after seeing that there is nothing up there worth waiting around for, you will be ready to go home."

20. Study, The Illustrator of Bones

Having discovered the site in the first place, Augustus led the horses and wagon across the expanse of sandstone and sagebrush that stretched for miles behind Mr. Huntington's land. The two women, still accompanied by the small dog, shielded their faces and hair against the wind, but neither of them complained. Even Augustus and Mr. Hacker had little to say, as both appeared to be recovering from the night before. In fact, the Englishman was feeling so shaky that when Chen had stepped forward with the black mustang, a horse Mr. Hacker insisted he still admired, he asked instead for the bay mare. "I fear, my good man, that I don't have the stomach for that one this morning," was all that he said.

Our party climbed the final ridge just after noon to find ourselves on an open expanse interrupted by scrubby grass and shrub-covered mounds, sharp ledges of shattered rock, and gullies and ravines which might once have held rivers and streams but were now lined with tufts of sagebrush and water-washed stone. A herd of antelope grazed along the horizon, looking almost white as they stood in the glaring heat and wind. Other than an eagle circling overhead, there was no sign of movement. No horses. No men.

"We aren't lost, are we?"

The older woman looked at Augustus, while her niece looked around, uncertain where she was.

Augustus removed his hat and wiped his face with his scarf. He stared out over the ridge where he had once tossed his hat. "No, that's where they should be. Unless they have found another site altogether." He wiped his face again and replaced his hat. "They could be lower, I suppose. Behind that embankment, or down in that ravine. I don't know," he said as if to himself. "I don't know."

Augustus leaned into Ian Hacker, who looked even grimmer than the young woman, as if he had been consumed by all that he had himself consumed the night before.

"Still have that gun, Ian?" Augustus asked.

"Gun?" Mr. Hacker replied. "Ah, right. My gun. It's here, Gussie." Mr. Hacker patted the bag hanging off the back of his saddle.

"Let's take a look, then," Augustus said, telling Jeb to keep the wagon where it was until he called.

"How will we know?" the older woman wanted to know.

"Don't worry, you'll know," Augustus replied. "Hang on," he advised Ian Hacker, slapping his horse. The two men rode out across the clearing, their horses kicking up even more dirt.

"What seems to be the trouble here?" The older woman turned to me as the two men made their way across the plateau. "What have they done with James Huntington?"

I looked at the woman and then at her niece, unable at first to respond. I suppose I should have reassured them, but I was not all that assured myself. Not about Mr. Huntington. Or about these two women.

"I don't know," I replied, just as Augustus had done. "I don't know."

An Indian stood atop the far bluff and raised what I assumed to be a gun. Augustus and Mr. Hacker slowed their horses, dismounted, and then disappeared, their horses obscuring our view. At such a distance it was difficult to tell if they were walking forward to meet the man or preparing to shoot back. Then, as if by magic, the Indian also disappeared, and Augustus and Mr. Hacker led their horses around the bluff until they, too, were gone from view.

"That was an Indian, wasn't it? My eyes aren't so old I can't still see at a distance," the aunt announced. "Julia, there is something wrong here. I don't know what these people have done with James, but I don't intend to allow them to do it to us as well."

When her niece did not respond, she turned her attention to Jeb.

"Boy, take us back," she demanded.

Jeb, who had been sitting stone-faced ever since Augustus and Mr. Hacker had left our party, looked to me for guidance. I spoke to the woman instead.

"You're welcome to go back but I need to get out first," I said. "I can't leave them here. Not without knowing." I stood to exit the wagon, but as I did so my path was blocked by the woman's niece.

"I need to get out, too," the younger woman announced. "I didn't come all this way to be turned away now." She stood as if fully prepared to walk across the open expanse of barren land on her own, if need be. It was then that I could sympathize with Mr. Huntington's desires. And his plans.

Jeb stared straight ahead, waiting for the adults to work out their differences.

"Julia, don't be stupid," the older woman protested. "This is not a lark. Do you have any idea how many people those Indians have killed in this part of the country? This is not New York City, in case you have missed the point."

"I'm not going back," her niece replied, as if it were settled. "I have to see Jim."

As she prepared to exit the wagon, Augustus reappeared from behind the bluff and waved his hat in the air. The aunt looked annoyed if not outright furious by the situation, but she did not protest. Instead she waited, resigned to see the journey to its inevitable end.

The ride across that gray rock-strewn expanse was one of the longest I have ever taken, then or now. It was as if the air had been suspended, or that our horses were pulling the wagon through water. Julia and her aunt sat stiff-backed and unmoving, staring straight ahead as if they, too, were suspended in time. Only Jeb was animated, leaning forward and urging on the horses, anxious to be reunited with the men.

When we reached the bluff where Augustus was now standing, he helped Julia and her aunt disembark from the wagon while I clambered out from the opposite side. Jeb secured the horses in the shade, and we followed Augustus through a narrow ravine along the backside of the bluff.

"Well, at long last, Cousin, you get to see your monsters from the deep. You won't be disappointed."

As we walked forward, Patrick Lear blocked our advance. He looked ravaged by this short time in the field. His usually crisp shirt was rumpled and torn, his face was unshaven and streaked with dirt, and his curly dark hair was filthy and uncombed.

"Ladies," he said, intercepting us. "Given our circumstances, I cannot turn you away, but I must insist that you take a vow of secrecy about anything you might see while you are here today."

Julia and her aunt stared at Dr. Lear as if he were crazed.

"I apologize if my behavior seems rude, but I must insist," he said. "You, too, Peterson, although I understand that your situation is unique."

"What have you done with James Huntington?" Julia demanded to know. She stepped forward to meet Dr. Lear, standing before him stiff and uncompromising. Her aunt appeared shocked by her niece's forthrightness, but relieved, too, that the question had been asked.

Dr. Lear hesitated, as if he did not understand what this woman wanted or what his friend had to do with the situation at hand.

"Nothing," he said at last. He looked confused, dazed even, uncertain how he should respond.

"Then take us to him." The aunt stepped forward, emboldened by her niece. "And stop all this nonsense this instant."

Again Dr. Lear hesitated. "I'm sorry, but I must first have your word."

"Don't be ridiculous, young man. Of course you have our word. Who would we tell? Who would care? Now take us to Mr. Huntington, or we shall return to the fort and send the cavalry out here to find him for us."

Patrick Lear turned his attention to me. "Peterson? I understand that this compromises you, but I must insist. At least until it is time."

I nodded my approval. Given all that Augustus had quipped about monsters, I doubted that we would see anything of value to report anyway.

Satisfied, Dr. Lear led us down the ravine into a shrubby gully where the dirt along the embankment had been dug away. At first we saw only the ends of one or two isolated bones, large tibias or femurs from the looks of them, but as we pushed our way through the shrubbery and around large piles of dirt and sand, it became clear that the entire hillside was being excavated and that something large, very large, was being uncovered.

"Whoa!" Jeb exclaimed, as we entered the next clearing, hidden deep behind the mound where one of the Indians still stood guard. In front of us, and in a cavern carved deep into the embankment, a partial skeleton had been exposed, pale and helpless against the earth, transfixed now in stone but otherwise lying in the dirt just as it must have done when it died. And there was a skull, the orbital sockets and nasal cavity of which had been exposed. There appeared to be a fin of sorts, or a shield, that lay crumpled or deformed back behind the animal's head, and three horn-like structures adorned the snout. The horns were of various lengths, one of which had been broken off where it protruded above the eye. Although not fully exposed, the skull was easily six feet in length. It was the remains of the largest animal, living or dead, that I had ever seen.

"It's not a jumble of bones at all," I said, turning to Dr. Lear.

"You can understand, then, why I was reluctant to inform the Captain until I knew for certain what was here," Patrick Lear said. "Now at least I have the time I need to submit a full report. I needed this opportunity, Peterson. And in return I will recognize the contributions of us all, including your documentation."

I could hear Dr. Lear's words, but I was too transfixed by the animal's blank stare to pay him much mind. I stepped forward to meet it, a living animal reaching out to one long dead, and touched its narrow snout where the surface of the bone had been chipped and broken away. I ran my hand over the animal's dusty brow and along the broken piece of horn, and I could feel the dust of the creature's very being transferred to my own warm flesh.

"Mr. Augustus, you should see what's in there," Jeb exclaimed, climbing out from the cavern. "There really are monsters from the deep, Mr. Augustus. Huge monsters."

Jeb was followed by James Huntington, who climbed out from the earth as if he, too, had been uncovered there. His clothes and hair and body were streaked with dirt and, like the silent skull, he beckoned me forward to greet him.

"Miss Peterson," he said. "Just who I was hoping would arrive. I have something you must see."

He took me by the arm and turned to lead the way back into the cavern, but as he did so he saw Julia and her aunt standing in the shade of the grassy bluff. In spite of the wind and the dust, the young woman's hair was neatly pinned, her face free from the ravages of the sun, her clothes still pressed and flawless. In such a setting she must have looked at first like a vision from another world.

"Hello, Jim," she said.

"Julia," he said. James Huntington shook his head as if trying to clear it, uncertain what time or place he had crawled back into. "Julia," he said again, as if by saying her name he might make her appear real. "Julia, you can't be here. Didn't Patrick tell you? There are Indians."

One of the Indians, the younger one, still looked down on us from the crest of the bluff, while the other Indian and Little Bear climbed out from the excavation, two more buried animals coming back from the dead. They stumbled as their eyes adjusted to the bright light.

James Huntington rushed over to the woman and her aunt as if to push them back through the brush, to return them back through time to that part of his memory where they both belonged.

"But Jim," the young woman said. She stopped, still uncertain of her surroundings. "Aren't you happy to see me?"

"Of course I am." Mr. Huntington went to take the woman's hand but then, looking at his own, decided against it. "But I can't let you stay," he said. "We can't have women here. Tell her, Miss Peterson. There are Indians only a day's ride away." Mr. Huntington turned to the aunt. "Sarah, surely you must understand the situation."

The older woman said nothing, but stared straight ahead as if she, too, were inhabiting another world.

"Patrick, I'm taking the wagon," Mr. Huntington announced. "I'll bring it back later. Jeb, can you help me with the horses?"

As Mr. Huntington led the two women away without ceremony, Ian Hacker called out, asking if he might ride along. "I think I'm seeing things," the Englishman announced. "But just in case these are the dragons that Chen keeps telling me about, I'll take these bits back to aid in my recovery." He rubbed a small piece of horn core across his forehead as if trying to transfer its powers, and then pocketed two or three chips of bone broken away from the surface of the animal's skull.

"Perhaps now you would be so kind as to arrange for my cousin's departure as well," Augustus said to Patrick Lear. "Although she may not think of herself as a lady, I believe she is a woman nonetheless. If those are Cheyenne or Sioux you are keeping an eye out for, I don't want her here."

"I'm only asking for one more day, Starwood," Dr. Lear said. "Maybe two. I just need enough information to complete my report. Then we'll all have to leave anyway because we're going to need more men, money, and time if we want to get this out of here. It's much too big for a party of this size to handle."

"There's never enough men, money, or time, Lear, you know that," Augustus replied. "I will assume whatever is left of her responsibilities, but only if Eleanor is sent back home with those other women. Surely you must realize that this so-called science of yours is no longer a game."

Patrick Lear grimaced and started the instinctive working of his mouth. He looked down the ravine as if waiting for someone or something to appear. Augustus doodled in his sketchpad, impatiently waiting for the man to speak.

I was the one who broke their awkward silence. "You said I would know if there was something worth staying for," I said to Augustus. "It's looking at us now. And you were right about another thing, Augustus. This is not a game. I may not be a scientist, but I came here to illustrate bones. And there are bones here for me to illustrate."

I turned to Dr. Lear, who looked both relieved and grateful, and asked him where I should start.

21. LANDSCAPE STUDIES, BADLANDS OF MONTANA

The final drawings on your list, studies for the landscape Augustus planned to entitle "Very Bad Lands," were completed that afternoon and the following morning as he sat on the bluff with his eyeglass at hand, watching for signs of Indians making their way north.

Little Bear and the two Indians helped with the excavation, digging the dirt and loose rock away from the fossilized bones, while Jeb carried away buckets of debris. During that first afternoon and into the evening, Patrick Lear and I worked on mapping and documenting the dimensions of the massive wedge-shaped skull with its thick horn cores, and then I sketched both a lateral and dorsal view of the parts of the skull that were exposed, including a fan-like shield splayed out but crumpled behind it. Although the skull was nothing like a bird's, in spite of the rounded bone which closed over the predentary like a beak or snout, the illustrations I had completed that summer prepared me in a way that made me feel as if I had been working on this kind of creature all my life. I completed the rough sketches to an approximate scale, with the massive animal's head translated to the Captain's journal just as I saw it there in the ground, glaring at us across the eons of time. Even Patrick Lear appeared to be satisfied with the results.

"You do good work, Peterson," he said later as we huddled around a lantern, wary of lighting a fire.

That night, while we ate a meager dinner of cold beans and succotash direct from the cans, Little Bear did his best to make small talk in Crow. The two Indians said little as they shoveled their food into their mouths and kept an eye on Augustus, who was watching them as he sketched.

As the two young men ate, they started arguing among themselves in their native language, which sounded to my ear like the rush of water over stones.

"Wolfbox thinks the bones in the cavern belong to giant horses which live underground," Little Bear explained, "and that we've killed them by trying to bring them into our world. He's upset and wants to leave for fear that the animals will come to life and kill him. That other one, Horse Guard, says his brother is a fool. You can't kill animals that are already dead, he told him, but if they go back to the cavalry they will be killing men just like themselves who are very much alive."

"Tell them they can both go," Patrick Lear said, sounding sympathetic to their concern. "But not until tomorrow. I will give them dried meat and apples and one of the horses, but only if they stay until we're through. If they leave now, they will end up in the arms of their enemy, who they know as well as we do is very nearby. Tell them that."

At this announcement, Horse Guard stood and looked down at the rest of us huddled around the weak light. "Tell me yourself," he said in perfect English. He looked past us as if challenging the night. "Tell me why you make us dig into this rock, while you keep us away from the rest of our land. There is nothing you can give to me that is not already mine own. I shall vanish and be no more, but this country is ours and we intend to keep it."

Augustus stood to meet the young man's challenge. "I am surrounded by ingratitude," he said. He tried to look at the Indian, but the young man avoided his gaze. "'I pitied thee,'" Augustus said. "'Took pains to make thee speak, taught thee each hour one thing or other, when thou didst not, savage, know thine own meaning.'"

"That's enough Starwood," Patrick Lear protested. "Sit down."

Augustus ignored him. "'Thou wast deservedly confined into this rock,'" Augustus boomed, "'who hadst deserved more than a prison.'"

"Starwood, I said that's enough."

Patrick Lear stood to face the two men. Augustus towered over them both but Dr. Lear held his ground. "That's unacceptable and I will not allow it," he said. He turned to the two young braves. "Horse Guard, I will gratefully give you the horse. It will be a gift. But I want you to know that I will not allow you to steal it."

The Indian looked at Augustus and then to Patrick Lear. "My brother and I must eat," the young man said without any sign of emotion, "but we will leave you in the morning. We will take your horse, only one, whether it is offered or not. And then we will rejoin our family."

Without another word, the two young Indians picked up their blankets and retreated to the bluff overlooking the ravine.

"I think you put the fear of God into them," Little Bear said.

"More likely the fear of Shakespeare," Augustus replied.

He sat down and did his best to make himself comfortable in the dirt.

"I apologize," he said at last to Patrick Lear. "I'm tired. And worse, I'm losing my sense of humor."

"We all are, Starwood." Dr. Lear picked up the lantern, which illuminated the stress and fatigue in his face. "I think it's time for all of us to start thinking about home," he said, then he turned and walked off into the darkness.

"Don't worry," Augustus said to Little Bear. "I'll make it up to our lost Indians in the morning."

"Just the same," Little Bear replied, "I think I'd better sleep with the horses tonight."

The following morning, Little Bear bridled the packhorse and Patrick Lear presented it to the Indians along with a generous supply of food.

"I hope you find your family," Dr. Lear said. He handed the rope bridle to Horse Guard. "And know that I wish you and them well."

The Indian nodded and swung onto the back of the horse. His younger brother followed. Augustus held out the portrait of the two Indians in uniform but the older brother looked past Augustus as if he did not exist. Augustus examined the drawing and, deciding it wasn't all that bad, rolled it up for safekeeping. The three men stood side by side as the Indians made their way across the clearing, their feet flopping against the flanks of the horse. Never once did the Indians look back.

"You gave them that horse without making them finish their work?" Augustus asked Dr. Lear when he turned to go back to the excavation.

"We don't need that horse and they would have taken it anyway," Patrick Lear replied. "Besides, we both have bigger battles to fight in the world than squabbling over a spent horse. They may not like us, but at least there are two Indians in the world who will not think a white man cheated them or changed his mind about what he was willing to give."

Dr. Lear looked over the dig site.

"Where's Peterson? Let's get this finished so we can get out of here ourselves. I'm afraid there are other Indians out there with whom we may not have such positive encounters."

I followed Patrick Lear inside the cavern, where the dirt and debris had been carved away to reveal a string of vertebrae still articulated as if frozen in time. The dim yellow light of the lanterns illuminated four cervical and twelve dorsal vertebrae, giving way to what appeared to be a partial ilium and a broken piece of pubis. Bits of caudal vertebrae were strewn throughout the side of the mountain like pebbles trapped in sand.

Dr. Lear lifted the lantern to inspect what appeared to be a scapula jutting from the wall. As he illuminated the rough piece of bone, his own body, with its military-like demeanor beneath his rumpled clothing, softened and faded into the dark. I could barely see him, but in such close environs I could smell his sweat and hear his labored breathing.

Jeb scurried back and forth with buckets filled with rubble and sand from the far side of the cavern, where Little Bear was exposing another very large bone. As Dr. Lear stepped out of the boy's way, the lantern cast a pool of light across bits of bone scattered on the ground. I picked up a small symmetrical piece and rolled it over and over in my palm.

"I have taken extensive measurements along this wall, Peterson, but if you don't mind, I'd prefer to show them to you outside. I find it difficult to breathe in here."

I followed him back into the morning. Patrick Lear squinted in the light, a line of sweat following the jagged trail along the side of his cheek. He pushed at his hairline with the back of his hand and walked into the shade of the mound, where Augustus sat with his umbrella, easel, and eyeglass, taking in the view.

The morning was calm and flies swarmed. Again Dr. Lear pushed at his hair, and opened a small leather-bound field journal in his lap. His sketches were thick and clumsy and not rendered to scale, but the bones had been painstakingly measured by length, width, and, when known, circumference, so that I could use them as a reference for my work. Even the height and graduated width of the spinal canal had been measured on those vertebrae where it had been exposed.

"How much more do you think you will need before we can go, Peterson? I'd like to send your documentation to the Captain as soon as possible."

Before I could respond to him, Augustus called from his outpost atop the mound. "We've got some big animals moving along that horizon," he said. "I've never seen so many buffalo."

We turned to see a herd of buffalo moving en masse across the landscape. As they ran, the animals disappeared and then appeared like phantoms from behind a curtain of dust, surging forward, those in the lead pushed on by the rush of animals from behind. When the lead animals reached the end of the plateau, they could not stop or change their direction but rather plunged head over heels down a steep incline. We could not hear their cries, but the sound seemed to reach us through our eyes as they fell, one upon the other upon the other again, into the narrow ravine.

"Those buffalo are crazed," Augustus said. "There must be something out there." He scanned the landscape to the south of the herd. "And there they are," he added.

On the far horizon, men on horseback moved across the plateau, the distant report of their guns crackling across the distance. In the dust and movement of animals and men it was difficult to see how many buffalo had fallen, but as the herd started to move away from the ravine and charge in our direction, the hunters stopped to pick up their kill.

"I don't like the looks of that." Augustus leaned forward with his glass as if trying to get a better view. "If they're taking down that many animals, there must be a large number of Indians nearby."

He handed the glass to Patrick Lear, who scanned the horizon. The air seemed to shift from the direction of the fallen buffalo, and one of our horses whinnied from the brush. Dr. Lear put down the glass and turned to me.

"You were going to tell me, Peterson, how much more time you will need to help me prepare my report."

I needed a few moments to make some preliminary drawings, so that I could compare my sketches with his, but I assured him that I could document the site from the measurements he had already taken.

"Excellent," he replied. "Let's finish up here and get back to James' land. We'll secure the area around the cave and cover up the skull. The Captain can send out a crew to get it later. And Starwood, you would be doing us both a favor if you moved down the embankment a bit. Not only will you give the rest of us away, some Cheyenne might like to test his manhood by counting coup on you by pulling you off that chair. Or, if he's not feeling all that brave, he might prefer to shoot you instead."

I worked inside the cavern, making quick notes and documenting the vertebrae and bone fragments exposed along the wall. Little Bear helped Patrick Lear haul rocks and cut down bushes to disguise the location of the skull, while Jeb harnessed the other team of horses and started loading the wagon to get it ready to go. From time to time, Jeb would push his way past me in the dark to gather picks and buckets and shovels, but he left me with the lanterns and a small stool so that I could reach the highest bones.

Dr. Lear was right. It was stifling in the cave, and the damp air was close, making it difficult to breathe. It seemed like months ago that James Huntington had told stories about Egypt and how tomb robbers had worked underground with candles and rough maps, stealing gold from the dead. I was not stealing, but I felt as though I were working in a tomb nonetheless.

Augustus crawled back in through the small opening and stooped next to me, carrying a lantern for one last view.

"Lear says it's time for us to go," he said. He stood next to me and held the lantern close to the wall. "Looks as if you have uncovered what you came to Montana to find, Cousin. The question now is, can you transform those chicken scratches in your book into the future you were hoping for?" He reached out and touched two of the vertebrae and then lifted the lantern toward me. "Assuming, that is, you are still dreaming of a profession?"

His question surprised me, and what surprised me more was that I had to stop and consider. I was no longer certain what it was I wanted, but now that the bones had been exposed by Dr. Lear and his men, I knew they had to be allowed to see the light of day.

Augustus scanned the glistening rock with his lantern one final time. Once again he had lost his eagle feather and I could not help myself from pointing this out to him. He removed his hat and looked at the empty hatband and shrugged.

"I may have diminished powers, my darling, but I still think I have what it takes. She likes me, Cousin, and I am going to stay."

He returned his hat to his head. "I told Lear I would retrieve you, so we'd better get ready to go."

He offered me his hand and directed me out from the confines of the cave. Jeb hurried past to retrieve the last of the lanterns and tools, while Augustus clambered out with my stool and his lantern in hand.

When Augustus passed Jeb, the boy called out something about taking one last look at the monsters of the deep, but as the boy disappeared into the excavation, a deep rumbling emanated from inside the cave. Augustus turned and called back to Jeb to leave the tools and get out. Again the earth shuddered, sending a thick cloud of dust from the cave's opening.

"Jeb," Augustus shouted, "get out of there!"

Augustus crawled back into the cavern, just as another cloud of dust spewed from the earth. Realizing what was happening, Little Bear rushed up with shovels and picks. He cried to Patrick Lear for help.

The earth shuddered again and then seemed to settle. Dust spewed from the opening of the cave, and rubble from overhead tumbled down around them, blocking their path.

Little Bear tore at the rock until he had created a space large enough for a man to reenter. Finding it open below the initial blockage, he dropped back into the excavation, while Patrick Lear and I used shovels and our hands to clear fallen debris.

"Augustus?" Little Bear called from inside the mountain. "Tell me where you are."

"I have him back here," Augustus shouted back. "I'm trying to make a little more space, and then I'll hand him out to you."

"Get yourself out, too," Little Bear yelled. "I don't think this opening can hold."

"Let me get the boy out first," Augustus called. "One of those big thigh bones has fallen loose, and his leg is trapped underneath it. But I've almost got it free."

Patrick Lear, not satisfied to wait on the outside looking in, dug at the side of the mountain, sending dirt flying over his head and behind his back. He shoveled away the last pile of rubble in time to see a small white hand emerge from the darkness. Little Bear handed up the boy and climbed out after him. Jeb was coughing and at first blinded by the sunlight, but otherwise appeared to be fine. Patrick Lear carried the boy gently in his arms and placed him in the bed of the wagon.

I rushed over to greet him, but then I realized Augustus wasn't there.

"Augustus," I cried. "Where's Augustus?"

"He's right behind me," Little Bear replied. "One of those bones was in his way, but he's fine." He stroked Jeb's hair. "Now let's get this little one a drink."

He opened his canteen and handed it to Jeb, just as the earth let out another gasp. Then it shuddered as if the entire mountain had collapsed from within. Patrick Lear turned as more rock and debris tumbled from overhead.

"Starwood," he cried.

Dr. Lear's military-like discipline, which had always seemed so at odds with the wildness of our surroundings, had prepared him for just such an emergency. After depleting his energy digging Little Bear and Jeb free, he plowed into the side of the mountain with the focus and energy of a man reborn. Little Bear joined him, and the two men worked side by side, attacking the mountain as if they were at war. When Jeb realized what was happening, he hobbled back from the wagon and he, too, started pushing and pulling rocks out of harm's way. Again the mountain shuddered, and from deep inside the earth came the report of crushing rock and bones.

Little Bear fell to his knees and stared at the impenetrable mountain rising before him, but Patrick Lear ignored the sound as if it were nothing more than the distant rumble of guns. He focused his attention on the next pile of dirt which had to be removed, tearing through the rubble and shouting at Little Bear to keep the passage free. Little Bear stood again and, with Jeb behind him, cleared the rock and debris that Dr. Lear appeared to be removing by the single force of his will alone. Within minutes that seemed like days, Dr. Lear had opened a new passage into the excavation and was calling into the dark mountain.

"Starwood," Patrick Lear called. "We're coming to get you. Let us know where you are."

When there was no response, Dr. Lear and Little Bear dug deeper into the side of the mountain, sending more dirt and rock flying. Jeb and I worked in their wake, doing the best that we could to keep the path behind them clear.

"Starwood," Dr. Lear called again, but still there was no reply.

"Light," Little Bear called out. "We need light."

Jeb ran for the lanterns. He lit one and handed it in to Little Bear. The second one he lit and kept ready by the side of the hill.

"There," we could hear Little Bear calling. "Over there."

More dirt spewed from the mouth of the cavern, followed by the distinct sound of Augustus' moan. Tears welled in my eyes, but I could do nothing to prevent them.

"You can't cry now," Jeb said, hauling out yet another bucket of dirt. "Please, Miss Peterson. I hurt real bad, so please, you can't cry now."

I grabbed an empty bucket and helped Jeb remove more dirt from the excavation. The two men shouted at each other from inside the earth as they tried to uncover Augustus and pull him free. "Move that beam." "No, that one there." "I've got him." "Careful." "Where's that light?" "Little Bear, I need your help here. I'm over here." "Careful." "Oh, God." "Oh, God."

Patrick Lear crawled out from the collapsed opening and turned to help lift Augustus up and out of the small hole. Little Bear scrambled back out after him, and the two men carried Augustus to the wagon and stretched him out in the bed. Augustus moaned as he tried to turn his head away from the bright summer light. He could not move, so Jeb and I stood in the path of the sunlight, casting an uneven shadow across Augustus' face.

Little Bear removed the dirt and debris from Augustus'

mouth and eyes, one of which was already swollen shut. The other was open but filling with blood. Little Bear did the best that he could to clean Augustus' face, which was bruised and scraped in one place all the way to the bone, and to make the large man comfortable in the small space in the bed of the wagon.

Behind us a large boulder rolled down the side of the mountain and smashed open against a tree. And then, as if relieved of all its treasures, the mountain shuddered and collapsed with a final sigh.

Augustus looked out at me from a distance. "Cousin," he whispered, barely able to open his mouth. I leaned in closer so that I might hear him. "You are all covered with dirt. Promise me you'll take a proper bath."

22. Photograph of Tombstone, Let Your Indulgence Set Me Free

We buried Augustus on the bluff overlooking the river on James Huntington's land. I asked Maggie if she would prefer to have him buried on her land, but she refused, saying he would only get in her way.

We stood huddled on the upper embankment, James Huntington, Patrick Lear, Ian Hacker, Chen, Jack, Maggie, and Jeb. Little Bear stood off to one side, wearing his finest Indian beadwork and leggings. He had hacked off his hair in mourning, but I believe he was also preparing himself for his reentry into the rest of the world. The Welsh workmen stood with us, their hats in their hands, their dark faces scrubbed. The frame of the house they had labored on over the summer was nearing completion, even though the woman it was being raised for was already on a steamboat headed east, where Mr. Huntington would reunite with her in the fall.

Since Augustus had never been even remotely religious, we did not send to Fort Benton for a preacher but I asked if someone might say a few words over his grave instead. Dr. Lear clung to his copy of the Bible but when he finally did step forward he could not bring himself to read from it. He stared instead without comment at the small offering of Little Bear's sacred tobacco placed atop the casket and shook his head as if not quite believing what he saw.

"We have all experienced too much death and dying in our lives," he said at last. "Even this," he added, indicating the Bible in his hand, "cannot console us or help us understand."

Dr. Lear lowered his head as if in prayer. When still he did not speak, James Huntington stepped forward and placed his arm around his friend's shoulder. Patrick Lear looked up just as three crows, or perhaps they were ravens, flew noisily overhead.

"I realize that Augustus Starwood did not believe any of this is divinely guided," Dr. Lear said, "or that we benefit from a life after death, but I, for one, believe he will live on. That is perhaps my greatest weakness, but it provides me with a consolation of sorts." He shrugged as if to himself.

Mr. Huntington gave his friend an almost imperceptible embrace and turned his attention to me.

"I, too, believe Augustus Starwood will live on," Mr. Huntington said, "and that someday people will see our world as he saw it. Full of very bad lands, as he was fond of calling them, but also punctuated by mountains of gold and rivers ripe with the future. And people. He will live through the people he loved and painted and touched in his effusive way. I know I, for one, will never be the same."

As Mr. Huntington spoke, a bright yellow butterfly with black wingtips alighted on his arm. He cupped it in his hand and held it over Augustus' grave.

"Never trust a man who spreads and pins butterflies. Isn't that what Augustus once told you, Miss Peterson?"

He smiled as he unfurled his fingers. The butterfly righted itself in his palm and, after airing its wings, took flight and headed downriver just as six more crows made their way across the sky.

Maggie put her arm around Jeb, who leaned in against his mother. It was unclear who was consoling whom. Jeb's face and arm were bruised, and he had a few bad scrapes on his forehead and along one cheek, but he was alive and had seen his monsters from the deep. Maggie made no attempt to hide the fact that she was crying. For Augustus and, I believe, for her son.

I tried to thank them all for their kindness, for accepting and accommodating the two of us without question, but when I went to mouth the words, I discovered I did not have the heart to speak. I could see Augustus' tepee standing by the river and his birds still fluttering in their cage. Three crows called out as they flew across the clearing, followed by three more and then six, then ten, and then one more flying on its own. More than fifty crows blackened the sky overhead, their voices calling, calling, and then they, too, were gone, headed home.

I opened Augustus' copy of The Collected Works of Shakespeare and started to read.

> "Now my charms are all o'erthrown,
> And what strength I have's mine own,
> Which is most faint: now, 'tis true,
> I must be here confined by you . . ."

When I found I could not continue, Mr. Huntington skipped ahead as if this were what we had been talking about all along.

"'Let your indulgence set me free,'" he said.

"'Let your indulgence set me free,'" I replied.

I placed the book atop the casket next to the tobacco and stood back, not certain what else I should do.

Chen stepped forward to make an offering of his own. He held a handful of gold dust over the grave and spilled it from his hand, just as a soft, fragrant breeze lifted up from the river. It swirled the dust like a wave, before it settled particle by particle, dust to dust, upon the casket, a million distant stars shimmering in the hot summer air.

"Gussie," Ian Hacker cried. "Oh, Gussie."

Eleanor Peterson
Great Falls, Mont.
August 30, 1919

Mr. John Wilson
Smithsonian Institution
Washington

Dear Mr. Wilson,

I'm sorry I do not have more to add for your records. To the best of my knowledge Augustus' sister wired James Huntington, asking if he would store the paintings and other effects until she could make suitable arrangements. Mr. Huntington, who was a collector and had a good understanding of these things, assured her that the work could be worth a considerable amount of money should she ever decide to sell, but I don't know what happened to the collection after that.

Ian Hacker and Chen left the morning after the funeral, sailing down the Missouri on their way to the Black Hills in search of gold. Maggie returned to settle on her land and made a life for herself cooking for the men in town. I later read a notice in the Academy's proceedings that Jeb had joined a paleontological expedition financed by Professor Cope. He discovered teeth and a few skull fragments of a new species of Laelaps, which the Professor described for publication and named in honor of the young man. I never did learn what happened to Little Bear and his bear.

Jack and I boarded the last steamboat of the season, catching it at Cow Island, since the Missouri was too low for the ship to make it any farther upstream. On the trip downriver we passed a number of Indian encampments, including a group of Yankton Sioux near Wolf Point and a tribe of over a thousand Hunkpapas moving north. They did not look dangerous, but they did not appear frightened, either. They were simply on the move, clouds of dust rising from their feet and the hooves of their ponies, oblivious to General Miles and whatever else awaited them ahead. Jack completed his doctorate in medicine, but he did it at

Harvard, not at Yale. I think he worked after that, at least for a while, on a reservation.

I traveled to Yale College that fall to return the Captain's journal, since Patrick Lear said he would return the other illustrations and the maps. The Captain was most gracious and accommodating, and took a quick look at the work I had done. He seemed impressed by the documentation and informed me that, although it did not contribute to his work on the evolution of birds, he was still planning to write a scientific paper on the Bison alticornis, as he referred to it, and would use my field illustrations as a reference. Then, after expressing his condolences over the loss of my cousin, he asked if I was still living in Philadelphia. When I informed him I hadn't yet taken new rooms, since I was not certain what arrangements might be made for me, he said it didn't matter and that he would be in touch. I never heard from him again. I can't even tell you for certain whether or not he sent another party to Montana, although years later I saw an illustration that looked surprisingly like the beast Dr. Lear had uncovered. Of course, both the illustration and the discovery bore the Captain's name.

As for Patrick Lear, I met him by chance as I walked across the Yale College grounds. The air was cool and the trees bristled red and gold. Dr. Lear was hurrying across the quad, bundled in a heavy woolen jacket and a red scarf tied at his throat. I recognized his stiff, uncompromising demeanor at once.

"Peterson," he said, as if expecting me. "It's good to see you. I'm headed for Wyoming and would have been disappointed if we had not met before I left. I have something I want to show you."

We walked through the damp grass to a stone building on the far end of the square, down a narrow stairway, and through a heavy door smelling of fresh paint. We entered a dark storeroom, where crates were stacked from the ceiling to the floor. The boxes were labeled in heavy letters: "Cretaceous chalk, Smoky Hill River," "Ft. Wallace," "Tertiary, Green R. Basin," and "Uintah Mtns."

Dr. Lear untied his scarf, folded it upon a table, and then lifted his hand to one of the boxes just as he had done when we had stood underground with the bones.

"He has built this public monument in his uncle's name, where he displays a few insignificant bones, none of them articulated," he said, "but this is where the real treasures are stored. In crates in the basement, where only he can have access to them."

"Still underground, like secrets of the earth," I said.

Dr. Lear nodded, but it was to himself. "When he first hired me, he told me to forget everything I had been taught. I assumed he meant my religious upbringing, but I soon discovered that he meant my university education. Anatomy. Natural history. All of it. I was to study only birds, particularly his Odontornithes, and learn to see them in his way. I have never met a man so narrow, so full of contempt for anyone's knowledge or experiences other than that which could be harnessed to bolster his own."

Two young men walked through the storeroom, each carrying a tray of fossilized vertebrae. Seeing Patrick Lear, they lowered their voices, and exited through the opposite door. Their feet crunched leaves as they climbed the outside stairs.

"You can see what the problem is here," Dr. Lear said when the young men's voices trailed off outside. He picked up his scarf and smoothed the soft wool in his hand. Then he looked at me and smiled, an expression that seemed out of place on his face.

"So I'm moving to Princeton. They are mounting their own expeditions and have asked me to lead one. They'll pay me sixty dollars a month and all of my expenses, but only if I agree to publish my results. Can you imagine?" he asked. "They want to publicly acknowledge my work."

He slipped his scarf back around his neck and reached again toward one of the boxes. His face was relaxed, and for a moment I believe he had forgotten I was even there. "You know he calls himself the Captain," he said at last, "but he never even served in the war. He was offered a commission as a major, but he declined it. His uncle sent him to Europe to tour museums instead."

Dr. Lear led the way back up the stairway. When we reached the grassy square, he turned to face me one last time. "What about you, Peterson?" he asked. "There's a battle raging over all these discoveries, and someone who can document them for immediate publication is bound to be in great demand."

After my conversation with the Captain, I had to admit that I wasn't sure. I only knew for certain that I had no interest in serving in any man's army, or being swept up in any more of their wars.

"Oh, Peterson," Dr. Lear said before leaving. "Thought you might want to know that James has moved to New York City. He's working for the new American Museum there. He's passionate about his collecting, so now he'll have a building as large as this college in which to house it all."

I tried to ask about Mr. Huntington's fiancée, but Dr. Lear had already turned to go and was walking with a single purpose across the square toward Chapel Street. It was the last time I would ever see him, although I would later see his name, as O'Leary, associated with several new discoveries made on behalf of Princeton College.

That winter I visited the American Museum to return Mr. Huntington's book about the Amazon, but he was in South America when I called. I tried to locate his wife, but no one at the museum seemed to know of her, nor could anyone tell me where I might find the Huntington home. In fact, no one seemed to know anything about Mr. Huntington, since apparently he traveled, collecting for the museum, most of the time.

Early the following summer, after closing out Augustus' rooms and my own, I returned to Montana. I am not sure what I was looking for or what I was hoping to find, but I convinced myself that I needed to revisit Augustus' grave and to tend it now that it had settled and the weather had once again improved.

The captain of the steamboat allowed me to disembark at the trading post, where I hired a draft horse and stored my bag. The slow-gaited animal took its time moving along the road that Mr. Hacker and I had once traveled, which gave me time to appreciate how much of the country was the same, and yet how much of it had also changed. Clouds still mounded along the horizon and birds circled overhead, but the buffalo were disappearing and most of the Indians were gone, already confined to reservations and government agencies by that time. Those few Indians who made a futile attempt to escape to Canada would be captured within the year.

It was a relief, then, to discover that James Huntington's home site was much the way I remembered it, with the stone and wood structure unfinished but intact, and the line of transplanted trees marking the site's borders leafed out as their roots dug deep into the earth to make their own way.

I stood on the porch of Mr. Huntington's library and peered in through the glass. The room and bookshelves had been emptied, but the woodstove in which he had expressed such pride was still standing, even though there was nothing left for it to keep warm. I did not attempt to enter, but rather sat on the log bench, watching birds skim the river while my horse pulled at a few tufts of grass sprouting in the dirt.

It was getting late and the clouds were threatening rain, so I found a shovel in the storeroom and walked over to Augustus' grave, planning to clear it the best that I could of debris. I was surprised but then pleased at what I found. The grave and surrounding area had been cleared and a wild rose planted by the marker, the one Mr. Huntington had arranged to be carved. The rose seemed to be thriving and was in flower at the time.

I decided then to stay in Montana and, just as Mr. Huntington had once predicted, I am happy here. I have a small house with a library, which is more than adequate to meet my needs. Since I still have the copy of Mr. Huntington's book, I read about the Amazon from time to time, although I am obliged to agree with the author that the contemplation of nature alone is not sufficient to fill the human heart and mind.

I have three of Augustus' landscapes, so I can look upon the Missouri River any time of day, and two of his portraits, the one of me on the river and one of James Huntington, sitting with a book on his lap, his feet propped on the rough railing that wrapped around his porch. In the painting, the river stretches for miles behind him, still as alive in the sunlight of a Montana summer as Mr. Huntington appears to me even now. I also kept the wayward ammonite, three crystals, and a heart-shaped rock. These I store on the window ledge so that they, too, can live in the light.

I wish I could tell you more about the collection, but that is all that I know.

My very best regards,
Eleanor Peterson

Acknowledgments

Although a leading paleontologist did venture into the Montana badlands right after the Battle of the Little Bighorn, *Pictures from an Expedition* is entirely a work of fiction, as are the individual characters and all of the events described therein.

I would like to thank Amy Chew, Lois Roe, and Vince Santucci for the time they spent reviewing an early draft, and particularly Paul Slovak for pushing me to dig deeper throughout the process of writing the book. Needless to say, the mistakes I've made since they offered their excellent insights and advice are mine alone.

I would also like to thank the archivists at the American Museum of Natural History for their generosity in accommodating my schedule while in New York City; historian David Walter for providing a guidebook to the Montana Territory in 1876; Matt and Tammy Smith and Sue Frary for allowing me to work with their extensive collection of "dragon bones" and to contribute in my small way to the Smiths' reconstruction of the *Quetzalcoatlus*; Walt Kirn for accompanying me into the badlands; and Mary Kirkaldy, Mickey Rowe, and Sam McLeod for encouraging specialists and amateurs alike to explore the world of dinosaurs and vertebrate paleontology.

Finally, I would like to thank Richard Wheeler and Sue Hart for their friendship and commitment to the stories of Montana, my brother, Steve Smith, and my daughter, Hannah.